THE

By
GEORGIANA
CAVENDISH,
DUCHESS OF
DEVONSHIRE

COMPLETE

"Ye Sylphs and Sylphids, to your chief give ear,
Fays, Fairies, Genii, Elves, and Demons, hear!
Ye know the spheres, and various tasks assign'd
By laws eternal to th'aërial kind:
Some in the fields of purest æther play,
And bask, and whiten, in the blaze of day;
Some guide the course of wand'ring orbs on high,
Or roll the planets thro' the boundless sky:
Our humbler province is to tend the Fair,
Not a less pleasing, *nor* less glorious care."

POPE's Rape of the Lock.
Contents

VOLUME I

LETTER I.

TO LORD BIDDULPH.

It is a certain sign of a man's cause being bad, when he is obliged to quote precedents in the follies of others, to excuse his own. You see I give up my cause at once. I am convinced I have done a silly thing, and yet I can produce thousands who daily do the same with, perhaps, not so good a motive as myself. In short, not to puzzle you too much, which I know is extremely irksome to a man who loves to have every thing as clear as a proposition in Euclid; your friend (now don't laugh) is married. "Married!" Aye, why not? don't every body marry? those who have estates, to have heirs of their own; and those who have *nothing*, to get *something*; so, according to my system, every body marries. Then why that stare of astonishment? that look of unbelief? Yes, thou infidel, I am married, and to such a woman! though, notwithstanding her beauty and other accomplishments, I shall be half afraid to present her in the world, she's such a rustic! one of your sylvan deities. But I was mad for her. "So you have been for half the women in town." Very true, my Lord, so I have, till I either gained them, or saw others whose image obliterated theirs. You well know, love with me has ever been a laughing God, "Rosy lips and cherub smiles," none of its black despairing looks have I experienced.

What will the world say? How will some exult that I am at last taken in! What, the gay seducive Stanley shackled!

But, I apprehend, your Lordship will wish to be informed how the "smiling mischief" seized me. Well, you shall have the full and true particulars of the matter how, the time when, and place where. I must, however, look back. Perhaps I have been too precipitate—I might possibly have gained the charming maid at a less expense than "adamantine everlasting chains."—But the bare idea of losing her made every former resolution of never being enslaved appear as nothing.—Her looks "would warm the cool bosom of age," and tempt an Anchorite to sin.

I could have informed you in a much better method, and have led you on through a flowery path; but as all my elaborate sketches must have ended in this disastrous truth, *I am married*, I thought it quite as well to let you into that important secret at once. As I have divided my discourse under three heads, I will, according to some able preachers, *begin with the first*.

I left you as you may remember (though perhaps the burgundy might have washed away your powers of recollection) pretty early one morning at the Thatched-house, to proceed as far as Wales to visit Lord G———. I did not find so much sport as I expected in his Lordship's grounds; and within doors, two old-fashioned maiden sisters did not promise such as is suited to my taste, and therefore pretended letters from town, which required my attendance, and in consequence made my *conge* and departed. On my journey—as I had no immediate business any where, save that which has ever been my sole employ, amusement— I resolved to make little deviations from the right road, and like a *sentimental traveller* pick up what I could find in my way conducive to the chief end of my life. I stopped at a pleasant village some distance from Abergavenny, where I rested some time, making little excursive progressions round the country. Rambling over the *cloud-capt* mountains one morning—a morning big with the fate of moor-game and your friend—from the ridge of a precipice I beheld, to me, the most delicious game in the hospitable globe, a brace of females, unattended, and, by the stile of their dress, though far removed from the vulgar, yet such as did not bespeak them of *our* world.—I drew out my glass to take a nearer ken, when such beauties shot from one in particular, that fired my soul, and ran thrilling through every vein. That instant they turned from me, and seemed to be bending their foot-steps far away. Mad with the wish of a nearer view, and fearful of losing sight of them, I hastily strove to descend. My eyes still fixed on my lovely object, I paid no regard to my situation, and, while my thoughts and every faculty were absorbed in this pleasing idea, scrambled over rocks and precipices fearless of consequences; which however might have concluded rather unfortunately, and spoiled me for adventure; for, without the least warning, which is often the case, a piece of earth gave way, and down my worship rolled to the bottom. The height from whence I had fallen, and the rough encounters I had met with, stunned me for some time, but when I came to my recollection, I was charmed to see my beautiful girls running towards me. They had seen my fall, and, from my lying still, concluded I was killed; they expressed great joy on hearing me speak, and most obligingly endeavored to assist me in rising, but their united efforts were in vain; my leg was broken. This was a great shock to us all. In the sweetest accents they condoled me on my misfortune, and offered every assistance and consolation in their power. To a genius so enterprizing as myself, any accident which furthered my wishes of making an acquaintance with the object I had been pursuing, appeared trivial, when the advantages presented themselves to my view. I sat therefore *like Patience on a monument*, and bore my misfortune with a stoical philosophy. I wanted much to discover who they were, as their appearance was rather equivocal, and might have pronounced them belonging to any station in life. Their dress was exactly the same: white jackets and petticoats, with light green ribbands, &c. I asked some questions, which I hoped would lead to the point I wished to be informed in: their answers were polite, but not satisfactory; though I cannot say they were wholly evasive, as they seemed artlessly innocent; or, if at all reserved, it was the reserve which native modesty teaches. One of them said, I was in great need of instant assistance; and she had interest enough to procure some from an house not very distant from us: on which, they were both going. I entreated the younger one to stay, as I should be the most wretched of all mortals if left to myself. "We go," said she, "in order to relieve that wretchedness." I fixed my eyes on her with the most tender languor I could assume; and, sighing, told her, "it was in her power alone to give me ease, since she was the cause of my pain: her charms had dazzled my eyes, and occasioned that false step which had brought me sooner than I expected at her feet." She smiled, and answered, "then it was doubly incumbent on her to be as quick as possible in procuring me every accommodation necessary." At that instant they spied a herdsman, not far off. They called aloud, and talking with him some little time, without saying a word further to me, tripped away like two fairies. I asked the peasant who those lovely girls were. He not answering, I repeated my question louder, thinking him deaf; but, staring at me with a stupid astonishment, he jabbered out some barbarous sounds, which I immediately discovered to be a Welsh language I knew no more than the Hottentotts. I had flattered myself with being, by this fellow's assistance, able to discover the real situation of these sweet girls: indeed I hoped to have found them within my reach; for, though I was at that moment as much in love as a man with a broken leg and bruised body could be supposed, yet I had then not the least thoughts of matrimony, I give you my honour. Thus disappointed in my views, I rested as contented as I could—hoping better fortune by and bye.

In a little time a person, who had the appearance of a gentleman, approached, with three other servants, who carried a gate, on which was laid a feather-bed. He addressed me with the utmost politeness, and assisted to place me on this litter, and begged to have the honour of attending me to his house. I returned his civilities with the same politeness, and was carried to a very good-looking house on the side of a wood, and placed on a bed in a room handsomely furnished. A surgeon came a few hours after. The fracture was reduced; and as I was ordered to be kept extremely quiet, every one left the room, except my kind host, who sat silently by the bed-side. This was certainly genuine hospitality, for I was wholly unknown, as you may suppose: however, my figure, being that of a gentleman, and my distressed situation, were sufficient recommendations.

After lying some time in a silent state, I ventured to breathe out my grateful acknowledgements; but Mr. Grenville stopped me short, nor would suffer me to say one word that might tend to agitate my spirits. I told him, I thought it absolutely necessary to inform him who I was, as the event of my accident was uncertain. I therefore gave a concise account of myself. He desired to know if I had any friend to whom I would wish to communicate my situation. I begged him to send to the village I had left that morning for my servant, as I should be glad of his attendance. Being an adroit fellow, I judged he might be of service to me in gaining some intelligence about the damsels in question: but I was very near never wanting him again; for, a fever coming on, I was for some days hovering over the grave. A good constitution at last got the better, and I had nothing to combat but my broken limb, which was in a fair way. I had a most excellent nurse, a house-keeper in the family. My own servant likewise waited on me. Mr. Grenville spent a part of every day with me; and his agreeable conversation, though rather too grave for a fellow of my fire, afforded me great comfort during my confinement: yet still something was wanting, till I could hear news of my charming wood-nymphs.

One morning I strove to make my old nurse talk, and endeavoured to draw her out; she seemed a little shy. I asked her a number of questions about my generous entertainer; she rung a peal in his praise. I then asked if there were any pretty girls in the neighbourhood, as I was a great admirer of beauty. She laughed, and told me not to let my thoughts wander that way yet a while; I was yet too weak. "Not to talk of beauty, my old girl," said I. "Aye, aye," she answered, "but you look as if talking would not content you." I then told her, I had seen the loveliest girl in the world among the Welsh mountains, not far from hence, who I found was acquainted with this family, and I would reward her handsomely if she could procure me an interview with her, when she should judge I was able to talk of love in a proper style. I then described the girls I had seen, and freely confessed the impression one of them had made on me. "As sure as you are alive," said the old cat, "it was my daughter you saw." "Your daughter!" I exclaimed, "is it possible for your daughter to be such an angel?" "Good lack! why not? What, because I am poor, and a servant, my daughter is not to be flesh and blood."

"By heaven! but she is," said I, "and such flesh and blood, that I would give a thousand pounds to take her to town with me. What say you, mother; will you let me see her?" "I cannot tell," said she, shaking her head: "To be sure my girl is handsome, and might make her fortune in town; for she's as virtuous as she's poor." "I promise you," said I, "if she is not foolish enough to be too scrupulous about one, I will take care to remove the other. But, when shall I see her?" "Lord! you must not be in such a hurry: all in good time." With this assurance, and these hopes, I was constrained to remain satisfied for some time: though the old wench every now and then would flatter my passions by extolling the charms of her daughter; and above all, commending her sweet compliant disposition; a circumstance I thought in my favour, as it would render my conquest less arduous. I occasionally asked her of the family whom she served. She seemed rather reserved on this subject, though copious enough on any other. She informed me, however, that Mr. Grenville had two daughters; but no more to be compared with her's, than she was; and that, as soon as I was able to quit my bed-chamber, they would be introduced to me.

As my strength increased, my talkative nurse grew more eloquent in the praises of her child; and by those praises inflamed my passion to the highest pitch. I thought every day an age till I again beheld her; resolving to begin my attack as soon as possible, and indulging the idea, that my task would, through the intervention of the mother, be carried on with great facility. Thus I wiled away the time when I was left to myself. Yet, notwithstanding I recovered most amazingly fast considering my accident, I thought the confinement plaguy tedious, and was heartily glad when my surgeon gave me permission to be conveyed into a dressing-room. On the second day of my emigration from my bed-chamber, Mr. Grenville informed me he would bring me acquainted with the rest of his family. I assured him I should receive such an indulgence as a mark of his unexampled politeness and humanity, and should endeavor to be grateful for such favour. I now attained the height of my wishes; and at the same time sustained a sensible and mortifying disappointment: for, in the afternoon, Mr. Grenville entered the room, and in either hand one of the lovely girls I had seen, and who were the primary cause of my accident. I attained the summit of my wishes in again beholding my charmer; but when she was introduced under the character of daughter to my host, my fond hopes were instantly crushed. How could I be such a villain as to attempt the seduction of the daughter of a man to whom I was bound by so many ties? This reflection damped the joy which flushed in my face when I first saw her. I paid my compliments to the fair sisters with an embarrassment in my air not usual to a man of the world; but which, however, was not perceptible to my innocent companions. They talked over my adventure, and congratulated my recovery with so much good-nature as endeared them both to me, at the same time that I inwardly cursed the charms that enslaved me. Upon the whole, I do not know whether pain or pleasure was predominant through the course of the day; but I found I loved her more and more every moment. Uncertain what my resolves or intentions were, I took my leave of them, and returned to my room with matter for reflection sufficient to keep me waking the best part of the night. My old tabby did not administer a sleeping potion to me, by the conversation I had with her afterwards on the subject in debate.

"Well, Sir," she asked, "how do you like my master's daughters?" "Not so well as I should your daughter, I can tell you. What the devil did you mean by your cursed long harangues about her beauty, when you knew all the while she was not attainable?" "Why not? she is disengaged; is of a family and rank in life to do any man credit; and you are enamoured of her." "True; but I have no inclination to marry."

"And you cannot hope to succeed on any other terms, even if you could form the plan of dishonouring the daughter of a man of some consequence in the world, and one who has shewn you such kindness!"

"Your sagacity happens to be right in your conjecture."

"But you would have had no scruples of conscience in your design on *my* daughter."

"Not much, I confess; money well applied would have silenced the world, and I should have left it to her and your prudence to have done the rest."

"And do you suppose, Sir," said she, "that the honour of my daughter is not as valuable to me, because I am placed so much below you, as that of the daughter of the first man in the world? Had this been my child, and, by the various artifices you might have put in practice, you had triumphed over her virtue, do you suppose, I say, a little paltry dross would have been a recompence? No, sir, know me better than to believe any worldly advantages would have silenced my wrongs. My child, thank heaven, is virtuous, and far removed from the danger of meeting with such as I am sorry to find you are; one, who would basely rob the poor of the only privilege they possess, that of being innocent, while you cowardly shrink at the idea of attacking a woman, who, in the eye of a venal world, has a sufficient fortune to varnish over the loss of reputation. I confess I knew not the depravity of your heart, till the other day, I by accident heard part of a conversation between you and your servant; before that, I freely own, though I thought you not so strict in your morals as I hoped, yet I flattered myself your principles were not corrupted, but imputed the warmth of your expressions to youth, and a life unclouded by misfortune. I further own, I was delighted with the impression which my young lady had made on you. I fancied your passion disinterested, because you knew not her situation in life; but now I know you too well to suffer her to entertain a partiality for one whose sentiments are unworthy a man of honour, and who can never esteem virtue though in her loveliest form."

"Upon my soul! mother," cried I, (affecting an air of gaiety in my manner, which was foreign to my heart, for I was cursedly chagrined), "you have really a fine talent for preaching; why what a delectable sermon have you delivered against *simple fornication*. But come, come, we must not be enemies. I assure you, with the utmost sincerity, I am not the sad dog you think me. I honour and revere virtue even in you, who, you must be sensible, are rather too advanced in life for a Venus, though I doubt not in your youth you made many a Welsh heart dance without a harp. Come, I see you are not so angry as you were. Have a little compassion on a poor young fellow, who cannot, if he wishes it, run away from your frowns. I am tied by the leg, you know, my old girl. But to tell you the serious truth, the

4

cause of the air of dissatisfaction which I wore, was, my apprehension of not having merit to gain the only woman that ever made any impression on my heart; and likewise my fears of your not being my friend, from the ludicrous manner in which I had before treated this affair."—I added some more prevailing arguments, and solemnly attested heaven to witness my innocence of actual seduction, though I had, I confessed with blushes, indulged in a few fashionable pleasures, which, though they might be stiled crimes among the Welsh-mountains, were nothing in our world. In short, I omitted nothing (as you will suppose by the lyes I already told of my *innocence of actual seduction*, and such stuff—) that I thought conducive to the conciliating her good opinion, or at least a better than she seemed to have at present.

When I argued the matter over in my own mind, I knew not on what to determine. Reflection never agreed with me: I hate it confoundedly—It brings with it a consumed long string of past transactions, that *bore* me to death, and is worse than a fit of the hypochondriac. I endeavored to lose my disagreeable companion in the *arms* of sleep; but the devil a bit: the idea of the raptures I should taste in those of my lovely Julia's, drove the drowsy God from my eye-lids—yet my pleasurable sensations were damped by the enormous purchase I must in all probability pay for such a delightful privilege: after examining the business every way, I concluded it as I do most things which require mature deliberation, left it to work its way in the best manner it could, and making chance, the first link in the chain of causes, ruler of my fate.

I now saw my Julia daily, and the encrease of passion was the consequence of every interview. You have often told me I was a fellow of no speculation or thought: I presume to say, that in the point in question, though you may conceive me running hand over head to destruction, I have shewn a great deal of fore-thought; and that the step I have taken is an infallible proof of it. Charming as both you and I think the lady Betty's and lady Bridget's, and faith have found them too, I believe neither you nor I ever intended to take any one of them *for better, for worse;* yet we have never made any resolution against entering into the pale of matrimony. Now though I like a little *badinage,* and sometimes something more, with a married woman—I would much rather that my wife, like Cæsar's, should not be suspected: where then is it so likely to meet with a woman of real virtue as in the lap of innocence? The women of our world marry, that they may have the greater privilege for leading dissipated lives. Knowing them so well as I do, I could have no chance of happiness with one of their class—and yet one must one time or other "settle soberly and raise a brood."—And why not now, while every artery beats rapidly, and nature is alive?

However, it does not signify bringing this argument, or that, to justify my procedure; I could not act otherwise than I have done. I was mad, absolutely dying for her. By heaven! I never saw so many beauties under one form. There is not a limb or feature which I have not adored in as many different women; here, they are all assembled with the greatest harmony: and yet she wants the polish of the world: a *je ne sçai quoi,* a *tout ensemble,* which nothing but mixing with people of fashion can give: but, as she is extremely docile, I have hopes that she will not disgrace the name of Stanley.

Shall I whisper you a secret—but publish it not in the streets of Askalon—I could almost wish my whole life had passed in the same innocent tranquil manner it has now for several weeks. No tumultuous thoughts, which, as they are too often excited by licentious excess, must be lost and drowned in wine. No cursed qualms of conscience, which will appall the most hardy of us, when nature sickens after the fatigue of a debauch. Here all is peaceful, because all is innocent: and yet what voluptuary can figure a higher joy than I at present experience in the possession of the most lovely of her sex, who thinks it her duty to contribute to my pleasure, and whose every thought I can read in her expressive countenance? Oh! that I may ever see her with the same eyes I do at this moment! Why cannot I renounce a world, the ways of which I have seen and despise from my soul? What attachments have I to it, guilty ones excepted? Ought I to continue them, when I have sworn—Oh! Christ! what is come to me now? can a virtuous connexion with the sex work miracles? but you cannot inform me—having never made such: and who the devil can, till they marry—and then it is too late: the die is cast.

I hope you will thank me for making you my confidant—and, what is more, writing you so enormous a long letter. Most likely I shall enhance your obligation by continuing my correspondence, as I do not know when I shall quit, what appears to me, my earthly paradise. Whether you will congratulate me from your heart I know not, because you may possibly imagine, from some virtuous emanations which have burst forth in the course of this epistle, that you shall lose your old companion. No, no, not quite so bad neither—though I am plaguy squeamish at present, a little town air will set all to rights again, and I shall no doubt fall into my old track with redoubled alacrity from this recess. So don't despair, my old friend: you will always find me,

Your lordship's devoted,
W. STANLEY.

LETTER II.

TO THE SAME.

What a restless discontented animal is man! Even in Paradise unblest. Do you know I am, though surrounded with felicity, languishing for *sin and sea-coal* in your regions. I shall be vapoured to death if I stay here much longer. Here is nothing to exercise the bright genius with which I am endued: all one calm sunshine;

"And   days   of   peace   do   still   succeed
To nights of calm repose."

How unfit to charm a soul like mine! I, who love every thing that the moderns call pleasure. I must be amongst you, and that presently. My Julia, I am certain, will make no resistance to my will. Faith! she is the wife for me. Mild, passive, duteous, and innocent: I may lead my life just as I please; and she, dear creature! will have no idea but that I am a very good husband!

"And   when   I   am   weary   of   wandering   all   day,
To thee, my delight, in the evening I, come."

I did intend, when first I began my correspondence with your lordship, to have informed you of the whole process of this affair; but, upon my soul, you must excuse me. From being idle, I am become perfectly indolent;—besides, it is unfashionable to talk so much of one's wife. I shall only say, I endeavoured, by all those little attentions which are so easily assumed by us, to gain her affections,—and at the same time, to make sure work, declared myself in form to her father.

One day, when I could hobble about, I took occasion to say to Mr. Grenville, that I was meditating a return for his civilities, which was no other than running away with his daughter Julia: that, in the whole course of my life, I had never seen a woman whom I thought so capable of making me happy; and that, were my proposals acceptable to him and her, it would be my highest felicity to render her situation such. I saw the old man was inwardly pleased.—In very polite terms he assured me, he should have no objection to such an alliance, if Julia's heart made none; that although, for very particular reasons, he had quarreled with the world, he did not wish to seclude his children from partaking of its pleasures. He owned, he thought Julia seemed to have an inclination to see more of it than he had had an opportunity of shewing her; and that, as he had for ever renounced it, there was no protector, after a father, so proper as a husband. He then paid me some compliments, which perhaps, had his acquaintance been of as long standing as yours and mine, he might have thought rather above my desert: but he knows no more of me than he has heard from me,—and the devil is in it, if a man won't speak well of himself when he has an opportunity.

It was some time before I could bring myself to the pious resolution of marrying.—I was extremely desirous of practising a few manœuvres first, just to try the strength of the citadel;—but madam house-keeper would have blown me up. "You are in love with my master's daughter," said she, one day, to me; "if you make honourable proposals, I have not a doubt but they will be accepted;—if I find you endeavouring to gain her heart in a clandestine manner,—remember you are in my power. My faithful services in this family have given me some influence, and I will certainly use it for their advantage. The best and loveliest of her sex shall not be left a prey to the artful insinuating practices of a man too well versed in the science of deceit. Marry her; she will do you honour in this world, and by her virtues ensure your happiness in the next."

I took the old matron's advice, as it so perfectly accorded with my own wishes. The gentle Julia made no objection.—Vanity apart, I certainly have some attractions; especially in the eyes of an innocent young creature, who yet never saw a reasonable being besides her father; and who had likewise a secret inclination to know a little how things go in the world. I shall very soon gratify her wish, by taking her to London.—I am sick to death of the constant *routine* of circumstances here—*the same to-day, to-morrow, and forever.* Your mere good kind of people are really very insipid sort of folks; and as such totally unsuited to my taste. I shall therefore leave them to their pious meditations in a short time, and whirl my little Julia into the giddy circle, where alone true joy is to be met with.

I shall not invite her sister to accompany her; as I have an invincible dislike to the idea of marrying a whole family. Besides, sisters sometimes are more quick-sighted than wives: and I begin to think (though from whence she has gained her knowledge I know not, I hope honestly!) that Louisa is mistress of more penetration than my *rib*.—She is more serious, consequently more observing and attentive.

Sylph is fixed on.—Our *suite* will be a Welsh *fille de chambre*, yclep'd Winifred, and an old male domestick, who at present acts in capacity of groom to me, and who I foresee will soon be the butt of my whole house;—as he is chiefly composed of Welsh materials, I conclude we shall have fine work with him among our *beaux d'esprits* of the motley tribe.—I shall leave Taffy to work his way as he can. Let every one fight their own battles I say.—I hate to interfere in any kind of business. I burn with impatience to greet you and the rest of your confederates. Assure them of my best wishes.—I was going to say services,—but alas! I am not my own master! I am married. After that, may I venture to conclude myself your's?

W. STANLEY.

LETTER III.

TO Miss GRENVILLE.

How strange does it seem, my dearest Louisa, to address you at this distance! What is it that has supported me through this long journey, and given me strength to combat with all the softer feelings; to quit a respectable parent and a beloved sister; to leave such dear and tender relations, and accompany a man to whom four months since I was wholly a stranger! I am a wretched reasoner at best.—I am therefore at a loss to unravel this mystery. It is true, it became my duty to follow my husband; but that a duty so newly entered into should supersede all others is certainly strange. You will say, you wonder these thoughts did not arise sooner;—they did, my dear; but the continual agitation of my spirits since I married, prevented my paying any attention to them. Perhaps, those who have been accustomed to the bustles of the world would laugh at my talking of the agitation of spirits in the course of an affair which was carried on with the most methodical exactness; but then it is their being accustomed to bustles, which could insure their composure on such an important occasion. I am young and inexperienced—and what is worst of all, a perfect stranger to the disposition of Sir William. He may be a very good sort of man; yet he may have some faults, which are at present unknown to me.—I am resolved, however, to be as indulgent to them as possible, should I discover any.—And as for my own, I will strive to conceal them, under an implicit obedience to his will and pleasure.

As to giving you an account of this hurrying place, it is totally out of my power. I made Sir William laugh very heartily several times at my ignorance. We came into town at a place called Piccadilly, where there was such a croud of carriages of all sorts, that I was perfectly astonished, and absolutely frightened. I begged Sir William would order the drivers to stop till they were gone by.—This intreaty threw him almost into a convulsion of laughter at my simplicity; but I was still more amazed, when he told me, they would continue driving with the same vehemence all night. For my part, I could not hear my own voice for the continual rattle of coaches, &c.—I still could not help thinking it must be some particular rejoicing day, from the immense concourse of people I saw rushing from all quarters;—and yet Sir William assured me the town was very empty. "Mercy defend us!" cried Winifred, when I informed her what her master had said, "what a place must it be when it is full, for the people have not room to walk as it is!" I cautioned Win, to discover her ignorance as little as possible;—but I doubt both mistress and maid will be subjects of mirth for some time to come.

I have not yet seen any thing, as there is a ceremony to be observed among people of rank in this place. No married lady can appear in public till she has been properly introduced to their majesties. Alas! what will become of me upon an occasion so singular!—Sir William has been so obliging as to bespeak the protection of a lady, who is perfect mistress of the *etiquettes* of courts. She will pay me a visit previous to my introduction; and under her tuition, I am told, I have nothing to fear. All my hopes are, that I may acquit myself so as to gain the approbation of my husband. Husband! what a sound has that, when pronounced by a girl barely seventeen,—and one whose knowledge of the world is merely speculative;—one, who, born and bred in obscurity, is equally unacquainted with men and manners.—I have often revolved in my mind what could be the inducement of my father's total seclusion from the world; for what little hints I (and you, whose penetration is deeper than mine) could gather, have only served to convince us, he must have been extremely ill treated by it, to have been constrained to make a vow never again to enter into it,—and in my mind the very forming of a vow looks as if he had loved it to excess, and therefore made his retreat from it more solemn than a bare resolution, lest he might, from a change of circumstances or sentiments, again be seduced by its attractions, and by which he had suffered so much.

Do you know, I have formed the wish of knowing some of those incidents in his history which have governed his actions? will you, my dear Louisa, hint this to him? He may, by such a communication, be very serviceable to me, who am such a novice.

I foresee I shall stand in need of instructors; otherwise I shall make but an indifferent figure in the drama. Every thing, and every body, makes an appearance so widely opposite to my former notions, that I find myself every moment at a loss, and know not to whom to apply for information. I am apprehensive I shall tire Sir William to death with my interrogatories; besides, he gave me much such a hint as I gave Win, not to betray my ignorance to every person I met with; and yet, without asking questions, I shall never attain the knowledge of some things which to me appear extremely singular. The ideas I possessed while among the mountains seem intirely useless to me here. Nay, I begin to think, I might as well have learnt nothing; and that the time and expence which were bestowed on my education were all lost, since I even do not know how to walk a minuet properly. Would you believe it? Sir William has engaged a dancing-master to put me into a genteel and polite method of acquitting myself with propriety on the important circumstance of moving about a room gracefully. Shall I own I felt myself mortified when he made the proposition? I could even have shed tears at the humiliating figure I made in my own eyes; however, I had resolution to overcome such an appearance of weakness, and turned it off with a smile, saying, "I thought I had not stood in need of any accomplishments, since I had had sufficient to gain his affections." I believe he saw I was hurt, and therefore took some pains to re-assure me. He told me, "that though my person was faultless, yet, from my seclusion from it, I wanted an air of the world. He himself saw nothing but perfection in me; but he wished those, who were not blinded by passion, should think me not only the most beautiful, but likewise the most polished woman at court." Is there not a little vanity in this, Louisa? But Sir William is, I find, a man of the world; and it is my duty to comply with every thing he judges proper, to make me what he chuses.

Monsieur Fierville pays me great compliments. "Who is he?" you will ask. Why my dancing-master, my dear. I am likewise to take some lessons on the harpsichord, as Sir William finds great fault with my fingering, and thinks I want taste in singing. I always looked on taste as genuine and inherent to ourselves; but here, taste is to be acquired; and what is infinitely more astonishing still, it is variable. So, though I may dance and sing in taste now, a few months hence I may have another method to learn, which will be the taste then. It is a fine time for teachers, when scholars are never taught. We used to think, to be made perfect mistress of any thing was sufficient; but in this world it is very different; you have a fresh lesson to learn every winter. As a proof, they had last winter one of the first singers in the world at the opera-house; this winter they had one who surpassed her. This assertion you and I should think nonsense, since, according to our ideas, nothing can exceed perfection: the next who comes over will be superior to all others that ever arrived. The reason is, every one has a different mode of singing; a taste of their own, which by arbitrary custom is for that cause to be the taste of the whole town. These things appear incomprehensible to me; but I suppose use will reconcile me to them, as it does others, by whom they must once have been thought strange.

I think I can discover Sir William Stanley has great pride, that is, he is a slave to fashion. He is ambitious of being a leading man. His house, his equipage, and wife—in short, every thing which belongs to him must be admired; and I can see, he is not a little flattered when they meet with approbation, although from persons of whose taste and knowledge of life he has not the most exalted idea.

It would look very ungrateful in me, if I was to make any complaints against my situation; and yet would it not be more so to my father and you, if I was not to say, I was happier whilst with you? I certainly was. I will do Sir William the justice to say, he contributed to make my last two months residence very pleasant. He was the first lover I ever had, at least the first that ever told me he loved. The distinction he paid me certainly made some impression on my heart. Every female has a little vanity; but I must enlarge my stock before I can have a proper confidence in myself in this place.

My singing-master has just been announced. He is a very great man in his way, so I must not make him wait; besides, my letter is already a pretty reasonable length. Adieu, my dearest sister! say every thing duteous and affectionate for me to my father; and tell yourself that I am ever your's,

JULIA STANLEY.

LETTER IV.

TO Colonel MONTAGUE.

Dear JACK,

I was yesterday introduced to the loveliest woman in the universe; Stanley's wife. Yes, that happy dog is still the favourite of Fortune. How does he triumph over me on every occasion! If he had a soul of worth, what a treasure would he possess in such an angel! but he will soon grow tired even of her. What immense pains did he take to supplant me in the affections of Lucy Gardner, though he has since sworn to you and many others he proposed no other advantage to himself than rivaling me, and conquering her prejudices in my favour. He thinks I have forgot all this, because I did not call him to an account for his ungenerous conduct, and because I still style him my friend; but let him have a care; my revenge only slept till a proper opportunity called it forth. As to retaliating, by endeavouring to obtain any of his mistresses, that was too trivial a satisfaction for me, as he is too phlegmatic to be hurt by such an attempt. I flatter myself, I shall find an opening by and by, to convince him I have neither forgotten the injury, or am of a temper to let slip an occasion of piercing his heart by a method effectual and secure. Men, who delight to disturb the felicity of others, are most tenacious of their own. And Stanley, who has allowed himself such latitude of intrigue in other men's families, will very sensibly feel any stain on his. But of this in future; let me return to Lady Stanley. She is not a perfect beauty: which, if you are of my taste, you will think rather an advantage than not; as there is generally a formality in great regularity of features, and most times an insipidity. In her there are neither. She is in one word *animated nature*. Her height is proper, and excellently well proportioned; I might say, exquisitely formed. Her figure is such, as at once creates esteem, and gives birth to the tenderest desires. Stanley seemed to take pleasure in my commendations. "I wanted you to see her, my Lord," said he: "you are a man of taste. May I introduce Julia, without blushing through apprehension of her disgracing me? You know my sentiments. I must be applauded by the world; lovely as I yet think her, she would be the object of my hate, and I should despise myself, if she is not admired by the whole court; it is the only apology I can make to myself for marrying at all." What a brute of a fellow it is! I suppose he must be cuckolded by half the town, to be convinced his wife has charms.

Lady Stanley is extremely observant of her husband at present, because he is the only man who has paid her attention; but when she finds she is the only woman who is distinguished by his indifference, which will soon be the case, she will likewise see, and be grateful for, the assiduities paid her by other men. One of the first of those I intend to be. I shall not let you into the plan of operations at present; besides, it is impossible, till I know more of my ground, to mark out any scheme. Chance often performs that for us, which the most judicious reflection cannot bring about; and I have the whole campaign before me.

I think myself pretty well acquainted with the failings and weak parts in Stanley; and you may assure yourself I shall avail myself of them. I do not want penetration; and doubt not, from the free access which I have gained in the family, but I shall soon be master of the ruling passion of her ladyship. She is, as yet, a total stranger to the world; her character is not yet established; she cannot know herself. She only knows she is handsome; that secret, I presume, Nature has informed her of. Her husband has confirmed it, and she liked him because she found in him a coincidence of opinion. But all that rapturous nonsense will, and must soon, have an end. As to the beauties of mind, he has no more idea of them, than we have of a sixth sense; what he knows not, he cannot admire. She will soon find herself neglected; but at the same time she will find the loss of a husband's praises amply supplied by the *devoirs* of a hundred, all equal, and many superior to him. At first, she may be uneasy; but repeated flattery will soon know console herself; and the man who can touch her heart, needs fear nothing. Every thing else, as Lord Chesterfield justly observes, will then follow of course. By which assertion, whatever the world may think, he certainly pays a great compliment to the fair sex. Men may be rendered vicious by a thousand methods; but there is only one way to subdue women.

Whom do you think he has introduced as *chaperons* to his wife? Lady Besford, and Lady Anne Parker. Do not you admire his choice? Oh! they will be charming associates for her! But I have nothing to say against it, as I think their counsels will further my schemes. Lady Besford might not be so much amiss; but Lady Anne! think of her, with whom he is belied if he has not had an affair. What madness! It is like him, however. Let him then take the consequences of his folly; and such clever fellows as you and I the advantage of them. Adieu, dear Jack! I shall see you, I hope, as soon as you come to town. I shall want you in a scheme I have in my head, but which I do not think proper to trust to paper. Your's,

BIDDULPH.

LETTER V.

TO Lady STANLEY.

I have lost you, my Julia; and who shall supply your loss? How much am I alone! and yet, if you are happy, I must and will be satisfied. I should, however, be infinitely more so, if you had any companion to guide your footsteps through the devious path of life: I wish you some experienced director. Have you not yet made an acquaintance which may be useful to you? Though you are prevented appearing in public, yet I think it should have been Sir William's first care to provide you with some agreeable sensible female friend one who may love you as well as your Louisa, and may, by having lived in the world, have it more in her power to be of service to you.

My father misses you as much as I do: I will not repeat all he says, lest you should think he repents of his complying with Sir William's importunity. Write to us very often, and tell us you are happy; that will be the only consolation we can receive in your absence. Oh, this vow! It binds my father to this spot. Not that I wish to enter into the world. I doubt faithlessness and insincerity are very prevalent there, since they could find their way among our mountains. But let me not overcloud your sunshine. I was, you know, always of a serious turn. May no accident make you so, since your natural disposition is chearfulness itself!

I read your letter to my father; he seemed pleased at your wish of being acquainted with the incidents of his life: he will enter on the task very soon. There is nothing, he says, which can, from the nature of things, be a guide to you in your passage through the world, any farther than not placing too much confidence in the prospect of felicity, with which you see yourself surrounded; but always to keep in mind, we are but in a state of probation here, and consequently but for a short time: that, as our happiness is liable to change, we ought not to prize the possession so much as to render ourselves miserable when that change comes; neither, when we are oppressed with the rod of affliction, should we sink into despair, as we are certain our woe, like ourselves, is mortal. Receive the blessing of our only parent, joined with the affectionate love of a tender sister. Adieu!

LOUISA GRENVILLE

LETTER VI.

To JAMES SPENCER, Esq.

It is high time, my dear Spencer, to account to you for the whimsical journey, as you called it, which your friend undertook so suddenly. I meant not to keep that, or even my motives for it, a secret from you. The esteem you have ever shewn me merited my most unlimited confidence.

You said, you thought I must have some other view than merely to visit the ruins of a paternal estate, lost to me by the extravagant folly of my poor father. You said true; I had indeed some other view; but alas! how blasted is that view! Long had my heart cherished the fondest attachment for the loveliest and best of human beings, who inhabited the mountains, which once my father owned. My fortune was too circumscribed to disclose my flame; but I secretly indulged it, from the remote hope of having it one day in my power to receive her hand without blushing at my inferiority in point of wealth. These thoughts, these wishes, have supported me through an absence of two years from my native land, and all that made my native land dear to me.

Her loved idea heightened every joy I received, and softened every care. I knew I possessed her esteem; but I never, from the first of my acquaintance, gave the least hint of what I felt for, or hoped from, her. I should have thought myself base in the highest degree, to have made an interest in her bosom, which I had nothing to support on my side but the sanguine wishes of youth, that some turn of Fortune's wheel might be in my favour. You know how amply, as well as unexpectedly, I am now provided for by our dear Frederic's death. How severely have I felt and mourned his loss! But he is happier than in any situation which our friendship for him could have found.

I could run any lengths in praising one so dear to me; but he was equally so to you, and you are fully acquainted with my sentiments on this head; besides, I have something more to the purpose at present to communicate to you.

All the satisfaction I ever expected from the acquisition of fortune was, to share it with my love. Nothing but that hope and prospect could have enabled me to sustain the death of my friend. In the bosom of my Julia I fondly hoped to experience those calm delights which his loss deprived me of for some time. Alas! that long-indulged hope is sunk in despair! Oh! my Spencer! she's lost, lost to me for ever! Yet what right had I to think she would not be seen, and, being seen, admired, loved, and courted? But, from the singularity of her father's disposition, who had vowed never to mix in the world;—a disappointment of the tenderest kind which her elder sister had met with, and the almost monastic seclusion from society in which she lived, joined to her extreme youth, being but seventeen the day I left you in London: all these circumstances, I say, concurred once to authorize my fond hopes,—and these hopes have nursed my despair. Oh! I knew not how much I loved her, till I saw her snatched from me for ever. A few months sooner, and I might have pleaded some merit with the lovely maid from my long and unremitted attachment. My passion was interwoven with my existence,—with that it grew, and with that only will expire.

"My   dear-lov'd   Julia!   from   my   youth   began
The   tender   flame,   and   ripen'd   in   the   man;

My   dear-lov'd   Julia!   to   my   latest   age,
No other vows shall e'er my heart engage."

Full of the fond ideas which seemed a part of myself, I flew down to Woodley-vale, to reap the long-expected harvest of my hopes.—Good God! what was the fatal news I learnt on my arrival! Alas! she knew not of my love and constancy;—she had a few weeks before given her hand, and no doubt her heart, to Sir William Stanley, with whom an accident had brought her acquainted. I will not enlarge upon what were my feelings on this occasion.—Words would be too faint a vehicle to express the anguish of my soul. You, who know the tenderness of my disposition, must judge for me.

11

Yesterday I saw the dear angel, from the inn from whence I am writing; she and her happy husband stopped here for fresh horses. I had a full view of her beauteous face. Ah! how much has two years improved each charm in her lovely person! lovely and charming, but not for me. I kept myself concealed from her—I could hardly support the sight of her at a distance; my emotions were more violent than you can conceive. Her dress became her the best in the world; a riding habit of stone-coloured cloth, lined with rose-colour, and frogs of the same—the collar of her shirt was open at the neck, and discovered her lovely ivory throat. Her hair was in a little disorder, which, with her hat, served to contribute to, and heighten, the almost irresistible charms of her features. There was a pensiveness in her manner, which rendered her figure more interesting and touching than usual. I thought I discovered the traces of a tear on her cheek. She had just parted with her father and sister; and, had she shewn less concern, I should not have been so satisfied with her. I gazed till my eye-balls ached; but, when the chaise drove from the door—oh! what then became of me! "She's gone! she's gone!" I exclaimed aloud, wringing my hands, "and never knew how much I loved her!" I was almost in a state of madness for some hours—at last, my storm of grief and despair a little subsided, and I, by degrees, became calm and more resigned to my ill fate. I took the resolution, which I shall put in execution as soon as possible, to leave England. I will retire to the remaining part of my Frederic's family—and, in their friendship, seek to forget the pangs which an habitual tenderness has brought upon me.

You, who are at ease, may have it in your power to convey some small satisfaction to my wounded breast. But why do I say *small satisfaction*? To me it will be the highest to hear that my Julia is happy. Do you then, my dear Spencer, enquire, among your acquaintance, the character of this Sir William Stanley. His figure is genteel, nay, rather handsome; yet he does not look the man I could wish for her. I did not discover that look of tenderness, that soft impassioned glance, which virtuous love excites; but you will not expect a favourable picture from a rival's pen.

I mentioned a disappointment which the sister of my Julia had sustained: it was just before I left England. While on a visit at Abergavenny, she became acquainted with a young gentleman of fortune, who, after taking some pains to render himself agreeable, had the satisfaction of gaining the affections of one of the most amiable girls in the world. She is all that a woman can be, except being my Julia. Louisa was at that time extremely attached to a lady in the same house with her, who was by no means a favourite with her lover. They used frequently to have little arguments concerning her. He would not allow her any merit. Louisa fancied she saw her own image reflected in the bosom of her friend. She is warm in her attachments. Her zeal for her friend at last awakened a curiosity in her lover, to view her with more scrutiny. He had been accustomed to pay an implicit obedience to Louisa's opinion; he fancied he was still acquiescing only in that opinion when he began to discover she was handsome, and to find some farther beauties which Louisa had not painted in so favourable a light as he now saw them. In short, what at first was only a compliment to his mistress, now seemed the due of the other. He thought Louisa had hardly done her justice; and in seeking to repair that fault, he injured the woman who doated on him. Love, which in some cases is blind, is in others extremely quick-sighted. Louisa saw a change in his behaviour—a studied civility—an apprehension of not appearing sufficiently assiduous—frequent expressions of fearing to offend—and all those mean arts and subterfuges which a man uses, who wants to put in a woman's power to break with him, that he may basely shelter himself behind, what he styles, her cruelty. Wounded to the soul with the duplicity of his conduct, she, one day, insisted on knowing the motives which induced him to act in so disingenuous a manner by her. At first his answers were evasive; but she peremptorily urged an explicit satisfaction. She told him, the most unfavourable certainty would be happiness to what she now felt, and that *certainty* she now called on him in justice to grant her. He then began by palliating the fatal inconstancy of his affections, by the encomiums which she had bestowed on her friend; that his love for her had induced him to love those dear to her; and some unhappy circumstances had arisen, which had bound him to her friend, beyond his power or inclination to break through. This disappointment, in so early a part of Louisa's life, has given a tenderness to her whole frame, which is of advantage to most women, and her in particular. She has, I question not, long since beheld this unworthy wretch in the light he truly deserved; yet, no doubt, it was not till she had suffered many pangs. The heart will not recover its usual tone in a short time, that has long been racked with the agonies of love; and even when we fancy ourselves quite recovered, there is an aching void, which still reminds us of former anguish.

I shall not be in town these ten days at least, as I find I can be serviceable to a poor man in this neighbourhood, whom I believe to be an object worthy attention. Write me, therefore, what intelligence you can obtain; and scruple not to communicate the result of your inquiry to me speedily. Her happiness is the wish next my heart. Oh! may it be as exalted and as permanent as I wish it! I will not say any thing to you; you well know how dear you are to the bosom of your

HENRY WOODLEY.

LETTER VII.

TO HENRY WOODLEY, Esq.

No, my dear Harry, I can never consent to your burying yourself abroad; but I will not say all I could on that subject till we meet. I think, I shall then be able to offer you some very powerful reasons, that you will esteem sufficient to induce you to remain in your native land.—I have a scheme in my head, but which I shall not communicate at present.

Sir William Stanley is quite a man of fashion.—Do you know enough of the world to understand all that title comprehends? If you do, you will sincerely regret your Julia is married to *a man of fashion*. His passions are the rule and guide of his actions. To what mischiefs is a young creature exposed in this town, circumstanced as Lady Stanley is—without a friend or relation with her to point out the artful and designing wretch, who means to make a prey of her innocence and inexperience of life!

The most unsafe and critical situation for a woman, is to be young, handsome, and married to a man of fashion; these are thought to be lawful prey to the specious of our sex. As a man of fashion, Sir William Stanley would blush to be found too attentive to his wife;—he will leave her to seek what companions chance may throw in her way, while he is associating with rakes of quality, and glorying in those scenes in which to be discovered he should really blush. I am told he is fond of deep play—attaches himself to women of bad character, and seeks to establish an opinion, that he is quite the *ton* in every thing. I tremble for your Julia.—Her beauty, if she had no other merit, making her fashionable, will induce some of those wretches, who are ever upon the watch to ensnare the innocent, to practice their diabolical artifices to poison her mind. She will soon see herself neglected by her husband,—and that will be the signal for them to begin their attack.—She is totally unhackneyed in the ways of men, and consequently can form no idea of the extreme depravity of their hearts. May the innate virtue of her mind be her guide and support!—but to escape with honour and reputation will be a difficult task. I must see you, Harry. I have something in my mind. I have seen more of the world than you have.—For a whole year I was witness of the disorder of this great town, and, with blushes I write, have too frequently joined in some of its extravagances and follies; but, thank heaven! my eyes were opened before my morals became corrupt, or my fortune and constitution impaired.—Your virtue and my Frederic's confirmed me in the road I was then desirous of pursuing,—and I am now convinced I shall never deviate from the path of rectitude.

I expect you in town with all the impatience of a friend zealous for your happiness and advantage: but I wish not to interfere with any charitable or virtuous employment.—When you have finished your affairs, remember your faithful

J. SPENCER.

LETTER VIII.

TO Miss GRENVILLE.

Surrounded with mantua-makers, milliners, and hair-dressers, I blush to say I have hardly time to bestow on my dear Louisa. What a continual bustle do I live in, without having literally any thing to do! All these wonderful preparations are making for my appearance at court; and, in consequence of that, my visiting all the places of public amusement. I foresee my head will be turned with this whirl of folly, I am inclined to call it, in contradiction to the opinion of mankind.—If the people I am among are of any character at all, I may comprise it in few words: to me they seem to be running about all the morning, and throwing away time, in concerting measures to throw away more in the evening. Then, as to dress, to give an idea of that, I must reverse the line of an old song.

"What was our *shame*, is now our *pride*."

I have had a thousand patterns of silks brought me to make choice, and such colours as yet never appeared in a rainbow. A very elegant man, one of Sir William's friends I thought, was introduced to me the other morning.—I was preparing to receive him as a visitor; when taking out his pocket-book, he begged I would do him the honour to inspect some of the most fashionable patterns, and of the newest taste. He gave me a list of their names as he laid them on the cuff of his coat. This you perhaps will think unnecessary; and that, as colours affect the visual orb the same in different people, I might have been capable of distinguishing blue from red, and so on; but the case is quite otherwise; there are no such colours now. "This your ladyship will find extremely becoming,—it is *la cheveaux de la Regne;*—but the *colour de puce* is esteemed before it, and mixed with *d'Artois*, forms the most elegant assemblage in the world; the *Pont sang* is immensely rich; but to suit your ladyship's complexion, I would rather recommend the *feuile mort*, or *la noysette*." Fifty others, equally unintelligible, he ran off with the utmost facility. I thought, however, so important a point should be determined by wiser heads than mine;—therefore requested him to leave them with me, as I expelled some ladies on whose taste I had great reliance. As I cannot be supposed from the nature of things to judge for myself with any propriety, I shall leave the choice of my cloaths to Lady Besford and Lady Anne Parker, two ladies who have visited me, and are to be my protectors in public.

I was extremely shocked, when I sent for a mantua-maker, to find a man was to perform that office. I even refused a long time to admit him near me—and thinking myself perfectly safe that I should have him on my side, appealed to Sir William. He laughed at my ridiculous scruples, as he called them, and farther told me, "custom justified every thing; nothing was indecent or otherwise, but as it was the *ton*." I was silent, but neither satisfied or pleased,—and submitted, I believe, with but an ill grace.

Lady Besford was so extremely polite to interest herself in every thing concerning my making a fashionable appearance, and procured for me a French frizeur of the last importation, who dressed hair to a miracle, *au dernier gout*. I believe, Louisa, I must send you a dictionary of polite phrases, or you will be much at a loss, notwithstanding you have a pretty competent knowledge of the French tongue. I blush twenty times a day at my own stupidity,—and then Sir William tells me, "it is so immensely *bore* to blush;" which makes me blush ten times more, because I don't understand what he means by that expression, and I am afraid to discover my ignorance; and he has not patience to explain every ambiguous word he uses, but cries, shrugging up his shoulders, *ah! quel savage!* and then composes his ruffled spirits by humming an Italian air.

Well, but I must tell you what my dress was, in which I was presented. My gown was a silver tissue, trimmed with silver net, and tied up with roses, as large as life, I was going to say. Indeed it was very beautiful, and so it ought, for it came to a most enormous sum. My jewels are *magnifique*, and in immense quantities. Do you know, I could not find out half their purposes, or what I should do with them; for such things I never saw. What should poor Win and I have done by ourselves?—Lady Besford talked of sending her woman to assist me in dressing.—I told her I had a servant, to whom I had been accustomed for a long time.— "Ah! for heaven's sake, my dear creature!" exclaimed my husband, "don't mention the *tramontane*. She might do tolerably well for the Welsh mountains, but she will cut a most *outré* figure in the *beau monde*. I beg you will accept of Lady Besford's polite offer, till you can provide yourself with a *fille de chambre*, that knows on which side her right hand hangs." Alas! poor Winifred Jones! Her mistress, I doubt, has but few advantages over her. Lady Besford was lavish in the encomiums of her woman, who had had the honour of being dresser to one of the actresses many years.

Yesterday morning the grand task of my decoration was to commence. Ah! good Lord! I can hardly recollect particulars.—I am morally convinced my father would have been looking for his Julia, had he seen me;—and would have spent much time before he discovered me in the midst of feathers, flowers, and a thousand gew-gaws beside, too many to enumerate. I will, if I can, describe my head for your edification, as it appeared to me when Monsieur permitted me to view myself in the glass. I was absolutely ready to run from it with fright, like poor Acteon when he had suffered the displeasure of Diana; and, like him, was in danger of running my new-acquired ornaments against every thing in my way.

Monsieur alighted from his chariot about eleven o'clock, and was immediately announced by Griffith, who, poor soul! stared as if he thought him one of the finest men in the world. He was attended by a servant, who brought in two very large caravan boxes, and a number of other things. Monsieur then prepared to begin his operations.—Sir William was at that time in my dressing-room. He begged, for God's sake! "that Monsieur would be so kind as to exert his abilities, as every thing depended on the just impression my figure made."—Monsieur bowed and shrugged, just like an overgrown monkey. In a moment I was overwhelmed with a cloud of powder. "What are you doing? I do not mean to be powdered," I said. "Not powdered!" repeated Sir William; "why you would not be so barbarous as to appear without—it positively is not decent."

"I thought," answered I, "you used to admire the colour of my hair—how often have you praised its glossy hue! and called me your *nut-brown maid!*"

"Pho! pho!" said he, blushing, perhaps lest he should be suspected of tenderness, as that is very vulgar, "I can bear to see a woman without powder in summer; but now the case is otherwise. Monsieur knows what he is about. Don't interrupt or dictate to him. I am going to dress. Adieu, *ma charmante!*"

With a determination of being passive, I sat down under his hands—often, I confess, wondering what kind of being I should be in my metamorphosis,—and rather impatient of the length of time, to say nothing of the pain I felt under the pulling and frizing, and rubbing in the exquisitely-scented *pomade de Venus*. At length the words, "*vous êtes finis, madame, au dernier gout,*" were pronounced; and I rose with precaution, lest I should discompose my new built fabrick, and to give a glance at myself in the glass;—but where, or in what language, shall I ever find words to express my astonishment at the figure which presented itself to my eyes! what with curls, flowers, ribbands, feathers, lace, jewels, fruit, and ten thousand other things, my head was at least from one side to the other full half an ell wide, and from the lowest curl that lay on my shoulder, up to the top, I am sure I am within compass, if I say three quarters of a yard high; besides six enormous large feathers, black, white, and pink, that reminded me of the plumes which nodded on the immense casque in the castle of Otranto. "Good God!" I exclaimed, "I can never bear this." The man assured me I was dressed quite in taste. "Let me be dressed as I will," I answered, "I must and will be altered. I would not thus expose myself, for the universe." Saying which, I began pulling down some of the prodigious and monstrous fabrick.—The *dresser of the actresses* exclaimed loudly, and the frizeur remonstrated. However, I was inflexible: but, to stop the volubility of the Frenchman's tongue, I inquired how much I was indebted to him for making me a monster. A mere trifle! Half a guinea the dressing, and for the feathers, pins, wool, false curls, *chignion, toque, pomades,* flowers, wax-fruit, ribband, &c. &c. &c. he believes about four guineas would be the difference. I was almost petrified with astonishment. When I recovered the power of utterance, I told him, "I thought at least he should have informed me what he was about before he ran me to so much expense; three-fourths of the things were useless, as I would not by any means appear in them." "It was the same to him," he said, "they were now my property. He had run the risk of disobliging the Duchess of D——, by giving me the preference of the finest bundles of radishes that had yet come over; but this it was to degrade himself by dressing commoners. Lady Besford had intreated this favour from him; but he must say, he had never been so ill-treated since his arrival in this kingdom." In short, he flew out of the room in a great rage, leaving me in the utmost disorder. I begged Mrs. Freeman (so her ladyship's woman is called) to assist me a little in undoing what the impertinent Frenchman had taken such immense pains to effect. I had sacrificed half a bushel of trumpery, when Lady Besford was ushered into my dressing-room. "Lord bless me! my dear Lady Stanley, what still *dishabillé*? I thought you had been ready, and waiting for me." I began, by way of apology, to inform her ladyship of Monsieur's insolence. She looked serious, and said, "I am sorry you offended him; I fear he will represent you at her grace's *ruelle*, and you will be the jest of the whole court. Indeed, this is a sad affair. He is the first man in his walk of life." "And if he was the last," I rejoined, "it would be the better; however, I beg your ladyship's pardon for not being ready. I shall not detain you many minutes."

My dear Louisa, you will laugh when I tell you, that poor Winifred, who was reduced to be my gentlewoman's gentlewoman, broke two laces in endeavouring to draw my new French stays close. You know I am naturally small at bottom. But now you might literally span me. You never saw such a doll. Then, they are so intolerably wide across the breast, that my arms are absolutely sore with them; and my sides so pinched!—But it is the *ton*; and pride feels no pain. It is with these sentiments the ladies of the present age heal their wounds; to be admired, is a sufficient balsam.

Sir William had met with the affronted Frenchman, and, like Lady Besford, was full of apprehensions lest he should expose me; for my part, I was glad to be from under his hands at any rate; and feared nothing when he was gone; only still vexed at the strange figure I made. My husband freely condemned my behaviour as extremely absurd; and, on my saying I would have something to cover, or at least shade, my neck, for that I thought it hardly decent to have that intirely bare, while one's head was loaded with superfluities; he exclaimed to Lady Besford, clapping his hands together, "Oh! God! this ridiculous girl will be an eternal disgrace to me!" I thought this speech very cutting. I could not restrain a tear from starting. "I hope not, Sir William," said I; "but, lest I should, I will stay at home till I have properly learnt to submit to insult and absurdity without emotion." My manner made him ashamed; he took my hand, and, kissing it, begged my pardon, and added, "My dear creature, I want you to be admired by the whole world; and, in compliance with the taste of the world, we must submit to some things, which, from their novelty, we may think absurd; but use will reconcile them to you." Lady Besford encouraged me; and I was prevailed on to go, though very much out of spirits. I must break off here, for the present. This letter has been the work of some days already. Adieu!

IN CONTINUATION

My apprehensions increased each moment that brought us near St. James's: but there was nothing for it; so I endeavoured all in my power to argue myself into a serenity of mind, and succeeded beyond my hopes. The amiable condescension of their Majesties, however, contributed more than any thing to compose my spirits, or, what I believe to be nearer the true state of the case, I was absorbed in respect for them, and totally forgot myself. They were so obliging as to pay Sir William some compliments; and the King said, if all my countrywomen were like me, he should be afraid to trust his son thither. I observed Sir William with the utmost attention; I saw his eyes on me the whole time; but, my Louisa, I cannot flatter myself so far as to say they were the looks of love; they seemed to me rather the eyes of scrutiny, which were on the watch, yet afraid they should see something unpleasing. I longed to be at home, to know from him how I had acquitted myself. To my question, he answered, by pressing me to his bosom, crying, "Like an angel, by heaven! Upon my soul, Julia, I never was so charmed with you in my life." "And upon my honour," I returned, "I could not discover the least symptom of tenderness in your regards. I dreaded all the while that you was thinking I should disgrace you."

"You was never more mistaken. I never had more reason to be proud of any part of my family. The circle rang with your praises. But you must not expect tenderness in public, my love; if you meet with it in private, you will have no cause of complaint."

This will give you but a strange idea of the world I am in, Louisa. I do not above half like it, and think a ramble, arm in arm with you upon our native mountains, worth it all. However, my lot is drawn; and, perhaps, as times and husbands go, *I have no cause of complaint.*

Your's most sincerely,
JULIA STANLEY.

LETTER IX.

TO Lady STANLEY.
My Dearest Child,

The task you set your father is a heavy one; but I chearfully comply with any request of my Julia's. However, before I enter upon it, let me say a little to you: Are you happy, my child? Do you find the world such as you thought it while it was unknown to you? Do the pleasures you enjoy present you with an equivalent for your renunciation of a fond father, and tender sister? Is their affection amply repaid by the love of your husband? All these, and a thousand other equally important questions, I long to put to my beloved. I wish to know the true state of your heart. I then should be able to judge whether I ought to mourn or rejoice in this separation from you. Believe me, Julia, I am not so selfish to wish you here, merely to augment my narrow circle of felicity, if you can convince me you are happier where you are. But can all the bustle, the confusion you describe, be productive of happiness to a young girl, born and educated in the lap of peaceful retirement? The novelty may strike your mind; and, for a while, you may think yourself happy, because you are amused, and have not time to define what your reflections are: but in the sober hour, when stillness reigns, and the soul unbends itself from the fatigues of the day; what judgment then does cool reason form? Are you satisfied? Are your slumbers peaceful and calm? Do you never sigh after the shades of Woodley, and your rural friends? Answer these questions fairly and candidly, my Julia—prove to me you are happy, and your heart as good and innocent as ever; and I shall descend to the silent tomb with peaceful smiles.

Perhaps the resolution I formed of retiring from a world in which I had met with disgust, was too hastily concluded on. Be that as it may—it was sacred, and as such I have, and will, keep it. I lost my confidence in mankind; and I could find no one whose virtues could redeem it. Many years have elapsed since; and the manners and customs change so frequently, that I should be a total stranger among the inhabitants of this present age.

You have heard me say I was married before I had the happiness of being united to *your* amiable mother. I shall begin my narrative from the commencement of that union; only premising, that I was the son of the younger branch of a noble family, whose name I bear. I inherited the blood, but very little more, of my ancestors. However, a taste for pleasure, and an indulgence of some of the then fashionable follies, which in all ages and all times are too prevalent, conspired to make my little fortune still more contracted. Thus situated, I became acquainted with a young lady of large fortune. My figure and address won her heart; her person was agreeable and although I might not be what the world calls in love, I certainly was attached to her. Knowing the inferiority of my fortune, I could not presume to offer her my hand, even after I was convinced she wished I should; but some circumstances arising, which brought us more intimately acquainted, at length conquered my scruples; and, without consulting any other guide than our passions, we married. My finances were now extremely straitened; for although my wife was heiress of upwards of thirty thousand pounds, yet, till she came of age, I could reap no advantage of it; and to that period she wanted near four years. We were both fond of pleasure, and foolishly lived as if we were in actual possession of double that income. I found myself deeply involved; but the time drew near that was to set all to rights; and I had prevailed on my wife to consent to a retrenchment. We had formed a plan of retiring for some time in the country, to look after her estate; and, by way of taking a polite leave of our friends (or rather acquaintance; for, when they were put to the test, I found them undeserving of that appellation); by way, I say, of quitting the town with *éclat*, my wife proposed giving an elegant entertainment on her birth-day, which was on the twenty-fourth of December. Christmas-day fell that year upon a Monday: unwilling to protract this day of joy till the Tuesday, my wife desired to anticipate her natal festival, and accordingly Saturday was appointed. She had set her heart on dancing in the evening, and was extremely mortified on finding an extreme pain in her ancle, which she attributed to a strain. It was so violent during dinner-time, that she was constrained to leave the table. A lady, who retired with her, told her, the surest remedy for a strain, was to plunge the leg in cold water, and would procure instant relief. Impatient of the disappointment and anguish, she too fatally consented. I knew nothing of what was doing in my wife's dressing-room, till my attention was roused by repeated cries. Terribly alarmed—I flew thither, and found her in the agonies of death. Good God! what was my distraction at that moment! I then recollected what she had often told me, of all her family being subject to the gout at a very early age. Every medical assistance was procured—with all speed. The

17

physician, however, gave but small hopes, unless the disorder could be removed from her head and stomach, which it had attacked with the greatest violence. How was all our mirth in one sad moment overthrown! The day, which had risen with smiles, now promised to set in tears. In the few lucid intervals which my unhappy wife could be said to have, she instantly prayed to live till she could secure her fortune to my life; which could be done no other way than making her will; since, having had no children, the estate, should she die before she came of age—or even then, without a bequest—would devolve upon a cousin, with whose family we had preserved no intimacy, owing to the illiberal reflections part of them had cast on my wife, for marrying a man without an answerable fortune. My being allied to a noble family was no recommendation to those who had acquired their wealth by trade, and were possessed of the most sordid principles. I would not listen to the persuasion of my friends, who urged me to get writings executed, to which my wife might set her hand: such measures appeared to me both selfish and cruel; or, rather, my mind was too much absorbed in my present affliction, to pay any attention to my future security.

In her greatest agonies and most severe paroxysms, she knew and acknowledged her obligations to me, for the unremitted kindness I had shewn her during our union. "Oh! my God!" she would exclaim, "Oh! my God! let me but live to reward him! I ask not length of years—though in the bloom of life, I submit with chearful resignation to thy will. My God! I ask not length of days; I only petition for a few short hours of sense and recollection, that I may, by the disposition of my affairs, remove all other distress from the bosom of my beloved husband, save what he will feel on this separation."

Dear soul! she prayed in vain. Nay, I doubt her apprehension and terrors, lest she should die, encreased the agonies of her body and mind.

Unknown to me, a gentleman, by the request of my dying wife, drew up a deed; the paper lay on the bed: she meant to sign it as soon as the clock struck twelve. Till within a few minutes of that time, she continued tolerably calm, and her head perfectly clear; she flattered herself, and endeavoured to convince us, she would recover—but, alas! this was only a little gleam of hope, to sink us deeper in despair. Her pain returned with redoubled violence from this short recess; and her senses never again resumed their seat. She suffered the most excruciating agonies till two in the morning—then winged her flight to heaven—leaving me the most forlorn and disconsolate of men.

I continued in a state of stupefaction for several days, till my friends rouzed me, by asking what course I meant to pursue. I had the whole world before me, and saw myself, as it were, totally detached from any part of it. My own relations I had disobliged, by marrying the daughter of a tradesman. They were, no doubt, glad of an excuse, to rid themselves of an indigent person, who might reflect dishonour on their nobility—of them I had no hopes. I had as little probability of success in my application to the friends of my late wife; yet I thought, in justice, they should not refuse to make me some allowances for the expenses our manner of living had brought on me—as they well knew they were occasioned by my compliance with her taste—at least so far as to discharge some of my debts.

I waited on Mr. Maynard, the father of the lady who now possessed the estate, to lay before him the situation of my affairs. He would hardly hear me out with patience. He upbraided me with stealing an heiress; and with meanly taking every method of obliging a dying woman to injure her relations. In short, his behaviour was rude, unmanly, and indecent. I scorned to hold converse with so sordid a wretch, and was leaving his house with the utmost displeasure, when his daughter slipped out of the room. She begged me, with many tears, not to impute "her father's incivility to her—wished the time was come when she should be her own mistress; but hoped she should be able to bring her father to some terms of accommodation; and assured me, she would use all her influence with him to induce him to do me justice."

Her influence over the mind of such a man as her father had like to have little weight—as it proved. She used all her eloquence in my favour, which only served to instigate him against me. He sent a very rude and abrupt message to me, to deliver up several articles of household furniture, and other things, which had belonged to my wife; which, however, I refused to do, unless I was honoured with the order of Miss Maynard. Her father could not prevail on her to make the requisition; and, enraged at my insolence, and her obstinacy, as he politely styled our behaviour, he swore he would be revenged. In order to make his words good, he went severally to each of the trades-people to whom I was indebted, and, collecting the sums, prevailed on them to make over the debts to him; thereby becoming the sole creditor; and how merciful I should find him, I leave you to judge, from the motive by which he acted.

In a few days there was an execution in my house, and I was conveyed to the King's-Bench. At first I took the resolution of continuing there contentedly, till either my cruel creditor should relent, or that an act of grace should take place. A prison, however, is dreadful to a free mind; and I solicited those, who had, in the days of my prosperity, professed a friendship for me: some few afforded me a temporary relief, but dealt with a scanty hand; others disclaimed me—none would bail me, or undertake my cause: many, who had contributed to my extravagance, now condemned me for launching into expences beyond my income; and those, who refused their assistance, thought they had a right to censure my conduct. Thus did I find myself deserted and neglected by the whole world; and was early taught, how little dependence we ought to place on the goods of it.

When I had been an inmate of the house of bondage some few weeks, I received a note from Miss Maynard. She deplored, in the most pathetic terms, "the steps her father had taken, which she had never discovered till that morning; and intreated my acceptance of a trifle, to render my confinement less intolerable; and if I could devise any methods, wherein she could be serviceable, she should think herself most happy." There was such a delicacy and nobleness of soul ran through the whole of this little *billet*, as, at the same time that it shewed the writer in the most amiable light, gave birth to the liveliest gratitude in my bosom. I had, till this moment, considered her only as the daughter of Mr. Maynard; as one, whose mind was informed by the same principles as his own. I now beheld her in another view; I looked on her only in her relation to my late wife, whose virtues she inherited with her fortune. I felt a veneration for the generosity of a young girl, who, from the narrow sentiments of her father, could not be mistress of any large sum; and yet she had, in the politest manner (making it a favour done to herself), obliged me to accept of a twenty-pound-note. I had a thousand conflicts with myself, whether I should keep or return it; nothing but my fear of giving her pain could have decided it. I recollected the tears she shed the last time I saw her: on reading over her note again, I discovered the paper blistered in several places; to all this, let me add, her image seemed to stand confessed before me. Her person, which I had hardly ever thought about, now was present to my imagination. It lost nothing by never having been the subject of my attention before. I sat ruminating on the picture I had been drawing in my mind, till, becoming perfectly enthusiastic in my ideas, I started up, and, clasping my hands together,—"Why," exclaimed I aloud, "why have I not twenty thousand pounds to bestow on this adorable creature!" The sound of my voice brought me to myself, and I instantly recollected I ought to make some acknowledgment to my fair benefactress. I found the task a difficult one. After writing and rejecting several, I at last was resolved to send the first I had attempted, knowing that, though less studied, it certainly was the genuine effusions of my heart. After saying all my gratitude dictated, I told her, "that, next to her society, I should prize her correspondence above every thing in this world; but that I begged she would not let compassion for an unfortunate man lead her into any inconveniencies, but be guided entirely by her own discretion. I would, in the mean time, intreat her to send me a few books—the subject I left to her, they being her taste would be their strongest recommendation." Perhaps I said more than I ought to have done, although at that time I thought I fell infinitely short of what I might have said; and yet, I take God to witness, I did not mean to engage her affection; and no thing was less from my intention than basely to practice on her passions.

In one of her letters, she asked me, if my debts were discharged, what would be my dependence or scheme of life: I freely answered, my dependence would be either to get a small place, or else serve my king in the war now nearly breaking out, which rather suited the activity of my disposition. She has since told me, she shed floods of tears over that expression—*the activity of my disposition*; she drew in her imagination the most affecting picture of a man, in the bloom and vigour of life, excluded from the common benefits of his fellow-creatures, by the merciless rapacity of an inhuman creditor. The effect this melancholy representation had on her mind, while pity endeared the object of it to her, made her take the resolution of again addressing her father in my behalf. He accused her of ingratitude, in thus repaying his care for her welfare. Hurt by the many harsh things he said, she told him, "the possession of ten times the estate could convey no pleasure to her bosom, while it was tortured with the idea, that he, who had the best right to it, was secluded from every comfort of life; and that, whenever it should be in her power, she would not fail to make every reparation she could, for the violence offered to an innocent, injured, man." This brought down her father's heaviest displeasure. He reviled her in the grossest terms; asserted, "she had been fascinated by me, as her ridiculous cousin had been before; but that he would take care his family should not run the risk of being again beggared by such a spendthrift; and that he should use such precautions, as to frustrate any scheme I might form of seducing her from her duty." She sought to exculpate me from the charges her father had brought against me; but he paid no regard to her asseverations, and remained deaf and inexorable to all her intreaties. When I learnt this, I wrote to Miss Maynard, intreating her, for her own sake, to resign an unhappy man to his evil destiny. I begged her to believe, I had sufficient resolution to support confinement, or any other ill; but that it was an aggravation to my sufferings (which to sustain was very difficult) to find her zeal for me had drawn on her the ill-usage of her father. I further requested, she would never again mention me to him; and if possible, never think of me if those thoughts were productive of the least disquiet to her. I likewise mentioned my hearing an act of grace would soon release me from my bonds; and then I was determined to offer myself a volunteer in the service, where, perhaps, I might find a cannon-ball my best friend.

A life, so different to what I had been used, brought on a disorder, which the agitation of my spirits increased so much as to reduce me almost to the gates of death. An old female servant of Miss Maynard's paid me a visit, bringing me some little nutritive delicacies, which her kind mistress thought would be serviceable to me. Shocked at the deplorable spectacle I made, for I began to neglect my appearance; which a man is too apt to do when not at peace with himself: shocked, I say, she represented me in such a light to her lady, as filled her gentle soul with the utmost terror for my safety. Guided alone by the partiality she honoured me with, she formed the resolution of coming to see me. She however gave me half an hour's notice of her intention. I employed the intermediate time in putting myself into a condition of receiving her with more decency. The little exertion I made had nearly exhausted my remaining strength, and I was more dead than alive, when the trembling, pale, and tottering guest made her approach in the house of woe. We could neither of us speak for some time. The benevolence of her heart had supported her during her journey thither; but now the native modesty of her sex seemed to point out the impropriety of visiting a man, unsolicited, in prison. Weak as I was, I saw the necessity of encouraging the drooping spirits of my fair visitor. I paid her my grateful acknowledgments for her inestimable goodness. She begged me to be silent on that head, as it brought reflections she could ill support. In obedience to her, I gave the conversation another turn; but still I could not help reverting to the old subject. She then stopped me, by asking, "what was there so extraordinary in her conduct? and whether, in her situation, would not I have done as much for her?" "Oh! yes!" I cried, with eagerness, "that I should, and ten times more." I instantly felt the impropriety of my speech. "Then I have been strangely deficient," said she, looking at me with a gentle smile. "I ask a thousand pardons," said I, "for the abruptness of my expression. I meant to evince my value for you, and my sense of what I thought you deserved. You must excuse my method, I have been long unused to the association of human beings, at least such as resemble you. You have already conferred more favours than I could merit at your hands." Miss Maynard seemed disconcerted—she looked grave. "It is a sign you think so," said she, in a tone of voice that shewed she was piqued, "as you have taken such pains to explain away an involuntary compliment.—But I have already exceeded the bounds I prescribed to myself in this visit—it is time to leave you."

I felt abashed, and found myself incapable of saying any thing to clear myself from the imputation of insensibility or ingratitude, without betraying the tenderness which I really possessed for her, yet which I thought, circumstanced as I was, would be ungenerous to the last degree to discover, as it would be tacitly laying claim to her's. The common rules of politeness, however, called on me to say something.—I respectfully took her hand, which trembled as much as mine. "Dear Miss Maynard," said I, "how shall I thank you for the pleasure your company has conveyed to my bosom?" Even then thinking I had said too much, especially as I by an involuntary impulse found my fingers compress her's, I added, "I plainly see the impropriety of asking you to renew your goodness—I must not be selfish, or urge you to take any step for which you may hereafter condemn yourself."

"I find, Sir," she replied, "your prudence is greater than mine. I need never apprehend danger from such a monitor."

"Don't mistake me," said I, with a sigh I could not repress. "I doubt I have," returned she, "but I will endeavour to develop your character. Perhaps, if I do not find myself quite perfect, I may run the risk of taking another lesson, unless you should tell me it is imprudent." So saying, she left me. There was rather an affectation of gaiety in her last speech, which would have offended me, had I not seen it was only put on to conceal her real feelings from a man, who seemed coldly insensible of her invaluable perfections both of mind and body.—Yet how was I to act? I loved her with the utmost purity, and yet fervour. My heart chid me for throwing cold water on the tenderness of this amiable girl;—but my reason told me, I should be a villain to strive to gain her affections in such a situation as I was. Had I been lord of the universe, I would have shared it with my Maria. You will ask, how I could so easily forget the lowness of my fortune in my connexion with her cousin? I answer, the case was widely different—I then made a figure in life equal to my birth, though my circumstances were contracted.—Now, I was poor and in prison:—then, I listened only to my passions—now, reason and prudence had some sway with me. My love for my late wife was the love of a boy;—my attachment to Maria the sentiments of a man, and a man visited by, and a prey to, misfortune. On reflection, I found I loved her to the greatest height. After passing a sleepless night of anguish, I came to the resolution of exculpating myself from the charge of insensibility, though at the expence of losing sight of her I loved for ever. I wrote her a letter, wherein, I freely confessed the danger I apprehended from the renewal of her visit.—I opened my whole soul before her, but at the same time told her, "I laid no claim to any more from her than compassion; shewed her the rack of constraint I put on myself, to conceal the emotions of my heart, lest the generosity of her's might involve her in a too strong partiality for so abject a wretch. I hoped she would do me the justice to believe, that as no man ever loved more, so no one on earth could have her interest more at heart than myself, since to those sentiments I sacrificed every thing dear to me." Good God! what tears did this letter cost me! I sometimes condemned myself, and thought it false generosity.—Why should I, said I to myself, why should I thus cast happiness away from two, who seem formed to constitute all the world to each other?—How rigorous are thy mandates, O Virtue! how severe thy decree! and oh! how much do I feel in obeying thee! No sooner was the letter gone, than I repented the step I had pursued.—I called myself ungrateful to the bounty of heaven; who thus, as it were, had inspired the most lovely of women with an inclination to relieve my distress; and had likewise put the means in her hands.—These cogitations contributed neither to establish my health, or compose my spirits. I had no return to my letter; indeed I had not urged one. Several days I passed in a state of mind which can be only known to those who have experienced the same. At last a pacquet was brought me. It contained an ensign's commission in a regiment going to Germany; and a paper sealed up, on which was written, "It is the request of M.M. that Mr. Grenville does not open *this* till he has crossed the seas."

There was another paper folded in the form of a letter, but not sealed; *that* I hastily opened, and found it contained only a few words, and a bank bill of an hundred pounds. The contents were as follow:

"True love knows not the nice distinctions you have made,—at least, if I may be allowed to judge from my own feelings, I think it does not. I may, however, be mistaken, but the error is too pleasing to be relinquished; and I would much rather indulge it, than listen at present to the cold prudential arguments which a too refined and ill-placed generosity points out. When you arrive at the place of your destination, you may gain a farther knowledge of a heart, capable at the same time of the tenderest partiality, and a firm resolution of conquering it."

Every word of this billet was a dagger to my soul. I then ceased not to accuse myself of ingratitude to the loveliest of women, as guilty of false pride instead of generosity. If she placed her happiness in my society, why should I deprive her of it? As she said my sentiments were too refined, I asked myself, if it would not have been my supreme delight to have raised her from the dregs of the people to share the most exalted situation with me? Why should I then think less highly of her attachment, of which I had received such proofs, than I was convinced mine was capable of? For the future, I was determined to sacrifice these nice punctilios, which were ever opposing my felicity, and that of an amiable woman, who clearly and repeatedly told me, by her looks, actions, and a thousand little nameless attentions I could not mistake, that her whole happiness depended on me. I thought nothing could convince her more thoroughly of my wish of being obliged to her, than the acceptance of her bounty: I made no longer any hesitation about it. That very day I was released from my long confinement by the grace-act, to the utter mortification of my old prosecutor. I drove immediately to some lodgings I had provided in the Strand; from whence I instantly dispatched a billet-doux to Maria, in which I said these words:

"The first moment of liberty I devote to the lovely Maria, who has my heart a slave. I am a convert to your assertion, that love makes not distinctions. Otherwise, could I support the reflection, that all I am worth in the world I owe to you? But to you the world owes all the charms it has in my eyes. We will not, however, talk of debtor and creditor, but permit me to make up in adoration what I want in wealth. Fortune attends the brave.—I will therefore flatter myself with returning loaden with the spoils of the enemy, and in such a situation, that you may openly indulge the partiality which makes the happiness of my life, without being put to the blush by sordid relations.

I shall obey your mandates the more chearfully, as I think I am perfectly acquainted with every perfection of your heart; judge then how I must value it. Before I quit England, I shall petition for the honour of kissing your hand;—but how shall I bid you adieu!"

The time now drew nigh when I was to take leave of my native land—and what was dearer to me, my Maria.—I was too affected to utter a word;—her soul had more heroic greatness.—"Go," said she, "pursue the paths of glory; have confidence in Providence, and never distrust me. I have already experienced some hazards on your account; but perhaps my father may be easier in his mind, when he is assured you have left England."

I pressed her to explain herself. She did so, by informing me, "her father suspected her attachment, and, to prevent any ill consequence arising, had proposed a gentleman to her for a husband, whom she had rejected with firmness. No artifice, or ill usage," continued she, "shall make any change in my resolution;—but I shall say no more, the pacquet will more thoroughly convince you of what I am capable."

"Good God!" said I, in an agony, "why should your tenderness be incompatible with your duty?"

"I do not think it," she answered;—"it is my duty to do justice; and I do no more, by seeking to restore to you your own."

We settled the mode of our future correspondence; and I tore myself from the only one I loved on earth. When I joined the regiment, I availed myself of the privilege given me to inspect the papers. Oh! how was my love, esteem, and admiration, increased! The contents were written at a time, when she thought me insensible, or at least too scrupulous. She made a solemn vow never to marry; but as soon as she came of age, to divide the estate with me, making over the remainder to any children I might have; but the whole was couched in terms of such delicate tenderness, as drew floods of tears from my eyes, and riveted my soul more firmly to her. I instantly wrote to her, and concealed not a thought or sentiment of my heart—*that* alone dictated every line. In the letter she returned, she sent me her picture in a locket, and on the reverse a device with her hair; this was an inestimable present to me.—It was my sole employ, while off duty, to gaze on the lovely resemblance of the fairest of women.

For some months our correspondence was uninterrupted.—However, six weeks had now passed since I expected a letter.

Love is industrious in tormenting itself. I formed ten thousand dreadful images in my own mind, and sunk into despair from each. I wrote letter after letter, but had still no return.

I had no other correspondent in England.—Distraction seized me. "She's dead!" cried I to myself, "she's dead! I have nothing to do but to follow her." At last I wrote to a gentleman who lived in the neighbourhood of Mr. Maynard, conjuring him, in the most affecting terms, to inform me of what I yet dreaded to be told.—I waited with a dying impatience till the mails arrived.—A letter was brought me from this gentleman.—He said, Mr. Maynard's family had left L. some time;—they proposed going abroad; but he believed they had retired to some part of Essex;—there had a report prevailed of Miss Maynard's being married; but if true, it was since they had left L. This news was not very likely to clear or calm my doubts. What could I think?—My reflections only served to awaken my grief. I continued two years making every inquiry, but never received the least satisfactory account.

A prey to the most heartfelt affliction, life became insupportable to me.—Was she married, I revolved in my mind all the hardships she must have endured before she would be prevailed on to falsify her vows to me, which were registered in heaven.—Had death ended her distress, I was convinced it had been hastened by the severity of an unnatural father.—Whichsoever way I turned my thoughts, the most excruciating reflections presented themselves, and in each I saw her sufferings alone.

In this frame of mind, I rejoiced to hear we were soon to have a battle, which would in all probability be decisive. I was now raised to the rank of captain-lieutenant. A battalion of our regiment was appointed to a most dangerous post. It was to gain a pass through a narrow defile, and to convey some of our heavy artillery to cover a party of soldiers, who were the flower of the troops, to endeavour to flank the enemy. I was mortified to find I was not named for this service. I spoke of it to the captain, who honoured me with his friendship.—"It was my care for you, Grenville," said he, "which prevented your name being inrolled. I wish, for the sakes of so many brave fellows, this manoeuvre could have been avoided. It will be next to a miracle if we succeed; but success must be won with the lives of many; the first squadron must look on themselves as a sacrifice." "Permit me then," said I, "to head that squadron; I will do my duty to support my charge; but if I fall, I shall bless the blow which rids me of an existence intolerable to me."

"You are a young man, Grenville," replied the captain, "you may experience a change in life, which will repay you for the adversities you at present complain of. I would have you courageous, and defy dangers, but not madly rush on them; that is to be despairing, not brave; and consequently displeasing to the Deity, who appoints us our task, and rewards us according to our acquittal of our duty. The severest winter is followed oftentimes by the most blooming spring:" "It is true," said I:

"But   when   will   spring   visit   the   mouldering   urn? Ah! when will it dawn on the gloom of the grave?"

"Will you, however, allow me to offer an exchange with the commanding officer?" My captain consented; and the lieutenant was very glad to exchange his post, for one of equal honour, but greater security. I was sitting in my tent the evening of the important day, ruminating on the past events of my life; and then naturally fell into reflections of what, in all probability, would be the consequence of the morrow's attack. We looked on ourselves as devoted men; and though, I dare say, not one in the whole corps was tired of his life, yet they all expressed the utmost eagerness to be employed. Death was the ultimate wish of my soul. "I shall, before to-morrow's sun goes down," said I, addressing myself to the resemblance of my Maria; "I shall, most lovely of women, be re-united to thee; or, if yet thy sufferings have not ended thy precious life, I shall yet know where thou art, and be permitted, perhaps, to hover over thee, to guide thy footsteps, and conduct thee to those realms of light, whose joys will be incomplete without thee." With these rhapsodies I was amusing my mind, when a serjeant entered, and acquainted me, there was, without, a young man enquiring for me, who said, he must be admitted, having letters of the greatest importance from England. My heart beat high against my breast, my respiration grew thick and difficult, and I could hardly articulate these words,—"For God's sake, let me see him! Support me, Oh, God! what is it I am going to hear?"

A cold sweat bedewed my face, and an universal tremor possessed my whole frame.

A young gentleman, wrapped up in a Hussar cloak, made his appearance. "Is this Lieutenant Grenville?" I bowed. "I am told, Sir," said I, in a tremulous voice, "you have letters from England; relieve my doubts I beseech you."—"Here, Sir, is one," said the youth, extending his hand, which trembled exceedingly.—I hastily snatched it, ready to devour the contents;—what was my agitation, when I read these words!

"If, after a silence of two long years, your Maria is still dear to you, you will rejoice to hear she still lives for you alone. If her presence is wished for by you, you will rejoice on finding her at no great distance from you. But, if you love with the tenderness she does, how great, how extatic, will be your felicity, to raise your eyes, and fix them on her's!"

The paper dropped from my enervate hand, while I raised my eyes, and beheld, Oh! my God! under the disguise of a young officer, my beloved, my faithful, long-lost Maria!

"Great God!" cried I, in a transport of joy, clasping my hands together, "have then my prayers been heard! do I again behold her!" But my situation recurring to my imagination; the dangers which I had unnecessarily engaged myself in for the morrow; her disguise; the unprotected state in which I should leave her, in a camp, where too much licentiousness reigned; all these ideas took instant possession of my mind, and damped the rising joy her loved presence had at first excited. The agonizing pangs which seized me are past description. "Oh! my God!" I exclaimed in the bitterness of soul, "why did we thus meet! Better,—Oh! how much better would it have been, that my eyes had closed in death, than, to see all they adored thus exposed to the horrid misery and carnage of destructive war." The conflict became too powerful; and in all the energy of woe I threw myself on the ground. Poor Maria flung herself on a seat, and covered her face in her great coat.—Audible sobs burst from her bosom—I saw the convulsive heavings, and the sight was as daggers to me.—I crawled on my knees to her, and, bending over her,—"Oh! my Maria!" said I, "these pangs I feel for you; speak to me, my only love; if possible, ease my sufferings by thy heavenly welcome voice."—She uttered not a word; I sought to find her hand; she pushed me gently from her, then rising,—"Come, thou companion of my tedious and painful travel, come, my faithful Hannah," said she, to one I had not before taken notice of, who stood in the entrance of the tent, "let us be gone, here we are unwelcome visitors. Is it thus," continued she, lifting up her hands to heaven, "is it thus I am received? Adieu! Grenville! My love has still pursued you with unremitting constancy: but it shall be your torment no longer. I will no longer tax your compassion for a fond wretch, who perhaps deserves the scorn she meets." She was leaving the tent. I was immoveably rooted to the ground while she spake.— I caught her by the coat. "Oh! leave me not, dearest of women, leave me not! You know not the love and distress which tear this wretched bosom by turns. Injure me not, by doubting the first,—and if you knew the latter, you would find me an object intitled to your utmost pity. Oh! that my heart was laid open to your view! then would you see it had wasted with anguish on the supposition of your death. Yes, Maria, I thought you dead. I had a too exalted idea of your worth to assign any other cause; I never called you cruel, or doubted your faith. Your memory lived in my fond breast, such as my tenderness painted you. But you can think meanly of me, and put the most ungenerous construction on the severest affliction that ever tore the heart of man."

"Oh! my Grenville," said she, raising me, "how have I been ungenerous? Is the renunciation of my country, relations, and even sex, a proof of want of generosity? Will you never know, or, knowing, understand me? I believe you have suffered, greatly suffered; your pallid countenance too plainly evinces it; but we shall now, with the blessing of heaven, soon see an end to them.—A few months will make me mistress of my fortune. In the mean time, I will live with my faithful Hannah retired; only now and then let me have the consolation of seeing you, and hearing from your lips a confirmation that I have not forfeited your affection."

I said all that my heart dictated, to reassure my lovely heroic Maria, and calm her griefs. I made her take some refreshment; and, as the night was now far spent, and we yet had much to say, we agreed to pass it in the tent. My dear Maria began to make me a little detail of all that had passed. She painted out the persecutions of her father in the liveliest colours; the many artifices he used to weaken her attachment to me; the feigning me inconstant; and, when he found her opinion of my faith too firmly rooted, he procured a certificate of my death. As she was then released from her engagement, he more strongly urged her to marry; but she as resolutely refused. On his being one day more than commonly

24

urgent, she knelt down, and said, in the most solemn manner; "Thou knowest, O God! had it pleased thee to have continued him I doated on in this life, that I was bound, by the most powerful asseverations, to be his, and only his:—hear me now, O God! while I swear still to be wedded to his memory. In thy eye, I was his wife; I attest thee to witness, that I will never be any other. In his grave shall all my tenderness be buried, and with him shall it rise to heaven." Her father became outrageous; and swore, if she would not give him a son, he would give her a mother; and, in consequence married the housekeeper—a woman sordid as himself, and whose principles and sentiments were as low as her birth.

The faithful Hannah had been discharged some time before, on finding out she aided our correspondence. My letters had been for a long time intercepted. Maria, one day, without the least notice, was taken out of her chamber, and conveyed to a small house in the hundreds of Essex, to some relations of her new mother's, in hopes, as she found, that grief, and the unhealthiness of the place, might make an end of her before she came of age. After a series of ill-usage and misfortunes, she at length was so fortunate as to make her escape. She wrote to Hannah, who came instantly to her; from her she learnt I was still living. She then formed the resolution of coming over to Germany, dreading again falling into the hands of her cruel parent. The plan was soon fixed on, and put in execution. To avoid the dangers of travelling, they agreed to put on men's cloaths; and Maria, to ensure her safety, dressed herself like an English officer charged with dispatches to the British army.

While she was proceeding in her narrative, I heard the drum beat to arms. I started, and turned pale. Maria hastily demanded the cause of this alteration! I informed her, "We were going to prepare for battle. And what, oh! what is to become of you? Oh! Maria! the service I am going on is hazardous to the last degree. I shall fall a sacrifice; but what will become of you?"

"Die with you," said she, firmly, rising, and drawing her sword. "When I raise my arm," continued she, "who will know it is a woman's. Nature has stamped me with that sex, but my soul shrinks not at danger. In what am I different from the Romans, or even from some of the ancient Britons? They could lose their lives for less cause than what I see before me. As I am firmly resolved not to outlive you—so I am equally determined to share your fate. You are certainly desirous my sex should remain concealed. I wish the same—and, believe me, no womanish weakness on my part shall betray it. Tell your commander, I am a volunteer under your direction. And, assure yourself, you will find me possessed of sufficient courage to bear any and every thing, for your sake."

I forbore not to paint out the horrors of war in the most dreadful colours. "I shudder at them," said she, "but am not intimidated." In short, all my arguments were in vain. She vowed she would follow me: "Either you love me, Grenville, or you love me not—if the first, you cannot refuse me the privilege of dying with you—if the last sad fate should be mine, the sooner I lose my life the better." While I was yet using dissuasives, the Captain entered my tent. "Come, Grenville," said he, "make preparations, my good lad. There will be hot work to-day for us all. I would have chosen a less dangerous situation for you: but this was your own desire. However, I hope heaven will spare you."

"I could have almost wished I had not been so precipitate, as here is a young volunteer who will accompany me."

"So young, and so courageous!" said the captain, advancing towards my Maria. "I am sure, by your looks, you have never seen service."

"But I have gone through great dangers, Sir," she answered, blushing—"and, with so brave an officer as Lieutenant Grenville, I shall not be fearful of meeting even death."

"Well said, my little hero," rejoined he, "only, that as a volunteer you have a right to chuse your commander, I should be happy to have the bringing you into the field myself. Let us, however, as this may be the last time we meet on earth, drink one glass to our success. Grenville, you can furnish us." We soon then bid each other a solemn adieu!

I prevailed on Maria and poor Hannah (who was almost dead with her fears) to lie down on my pallet-bed, if possible, to procure a little rest. I retired to the outside of the tent, and, kneeling down, put up the most fervent prayers to heaven that the heart of man could frame. I then threw myself on some baggage, and slept with some composure till the second drum beat.

Hannah hung round her mistress; but such was her respect and deference, that she opened not her lips. We began our march, my brave heroine close at my side, with all the stillness possible. We gained a narrow part of the wood, where we wanted to make good our pass; but here, either by the treachery of our own people, or the vigilance of our enemy, our scheme was intirely defeated. We marched on without opposition, and, flushed with the appearance of success, we went boldly on, till, too far advanced to make a retreat, we found ourselves surrounded by a party of the enemy's troops. We did all in our power to recover our advantage, and lost several men in our defence. Numbers, however, at last prevailed; and those who were not left dead on the field were made prisoners, among whom were my Maria and myself. I was wounded in the side and in the right arm. She providentially escaped unhurt. We were conveyed to the camp of the enemy, where I was received with the respect that one brave man shews another. I was put into the hospital, where my faithful Maria attended me with the utmost diligence and tenderness.

When the event of this day's disaster was carried to the British camp, it struck a damp on all. But poor Hannah, in a phrenzy of distress, ran about, wringing her hands, proclaiming her sex, and that of the supposed volunteer, and intreating the captain to use his interest to procure our release. She gave him a brief detail of our adventures—and concluded by extolling the character of her beloved mistress. The captain, who had at that time a great regard for me, was touched at the distressful story; and made a report to the commander in chief, who, after getting the better of the enemy in an engagement, proposed an exchange of prisoners, which being agreed to, and I being able to bear the removal, we were once more at liberty.

I was conveyed to a small town near our encampment, where my dear Maria and old Hannah laid aside their great Hussar cloaks, which they would never be prevailed on to put off, and resumed their petticoats. This adventure caused much conversation in the camp; and all the officers were desirous of beholding so martial a female. But, notwithstanding the extraordinary step she had been induced to take, Miss Maynard possessed all the valued delicacy of her sex in a very eminent degree; and therefore kept very recluse, devoting herself entirely to her attendance on me.

Fearful that her reputation might suffer, now her sex was known, I urged her to complete my happiness, by consenting to our marriage. She, at first, made some difficulties, which I presently obviated; and the chaplain of the regiment performed the ceremony, my Captain acting as father, and, as he said, bestowing on me the greatest blessing a man could deserve.

I was now the happiest of all earthly creatures, nor did I feel the least allay, but in sometimes, on returning from duty in the field, finding my Maria uncommonly grave. On enquiry she used to attribute it to my absence; and indeed her melancholy would wear off, and she would resume all her wonted chearfulness.

About three months after our marriage, my dear wife was seized with the small-pox, which then raged in the town. I was almost distracted with my apprehensions. Her life was in imminent danger. I delivered myself up to the most gloomy presages. "How am I marked out for misfortune!" said I, "am I destined to lose both my wives on the eve of their coming of age?" Her disorder was attended with some of the most alarming symptoms. At length, it pleased heaven to hear my prayers, and a favourable crisis presented itself. With joy I made a sacrifice of her beauty, happy in still possessing the mental perfections of this most excellent of women. The fear of losing her had endeared her so much the more to me, that every mark of her distemper, reminding me of my danger, served to render her more valuable in my eyes. My caresses and tenderness were redoubled; and the loss of charms, which could not make her more engaging to her husband, gave my Maria no concern.

Our fears, however, were again alarmed on Hannah's account. That good and faithful domestic caught the infection. Her fears, and attention on her beloved mistress, had injured her constitution before this baleful distemper seized her. She fell a sacrifice to it. Maria wept over the remains of one who had rendered herself worthy of the utmost consideration. It was a long time before she could recover her spirits. When the remembrance of her loss had a little worn off, we passed our time very agreeably; and I, one day, remarking the smiles I always found on my Maria's face, pressed to know the melancholy which had formerly given me so much uneasiness. "I may now," said she, "resolve your question, without any hazard; the cause is now entirely removed. You know there was a time when I was thought handsome; I never wished to appear so in any other eyes than your's; unfortunately, another thought so, and took such measures to make me sensible of the impression my beauty had made, as rendered me truly miserable. Since I am as dear to you as ever, I am happy in having lost charms that were fated to inspire an impious passion in one, who, but for me, might have still continued your friend."

I asked no more, I was convinced she meant the captain, who had sought to do me some ill offices; but which I did not resent, as I purposed quitting the army at the end of the campaign. By her desire, I took no notice of his perfidy, only by avoiding every opportunity of being in his company.

One day, about a fortnight after Maria came of age, I was looking over some English news-papers, which a brother officer had lent me to read, in which I saw this extraordinary paragraph:

"Last week was interred the body of Miss Maria Maynard, daughter of James Maynard, Esq; of L. in Bedfordshire, aged twenty years, ten months, and a fortnight. Had she lived till she attained the full age of twenty-one, she would have been possessed of an estate worth upwards of forty thousand pounds, which now comes to her father, the above-mentioned James Maynard, Esq.

By a whimsical and remarkable desire of the deceased, a large quantity of quick-lime was put into the coffin."

This piece of intelligence filled us with astonishment, as we could not conceive what end it was likely to answer: but, on my looking up to Maria, by way of gathering some light from her opinion, and seeing not only the whole form of her face, but the intire cast of her countenance changed; it immediately struck into my mind, that it would be a difficult matter to prove her identity—especially as by the death of Hannah we had lost our only witness. This may appear a very trivial circumstance to most people; but, when we consider what kind of man we had to deal with, it will wear a more serious aspect. It was plain he would go very great lengths to secure the estate, since he had taken such extraordinary measures to obtain it: he had likewise another motive; for by this second marriage he had a son. It is well known that the property of quick-lime, is to destroy the features in a very short space; by which means, should we insist on the body's being taken up, no doubt he had used the precaution of getting a supposititious one; and, in all probability, the corrosive quality of the lime would have left it very difficult to ascertain the likeness after such methods being used to destroy it. We had certainly some reason for our apprehensions that the father would disown his child, when it was so much his interest to support his own assertion of her death, and when he had gone so far as actually to make a sham-funeral; and, above all, when no one who had been formerly acquainted with could possibly know her again, so totally was she altered both in voice and features. However, the only step we could take, was to set off for England with all expedition—which accordingly we did.

I wrote Mr. Maynard a letter, in which I inclosed one from his daughter. He did not deign to return any answer. I then consulted some able lawyers; they made not the least doubt of my recovering my wife's fortune as soon as I proved her identity. That I could have told them; but the difficulty arose how I should do it. None of the officers were in England, who had seen her both before and after the small-pox, and whose evidence might have been useful.

Talking over the affair to an old gentleman, who had been acquainted with my first wife's father—and who likewise knew Maria: "I have not a doubt," said he, "but this lady is the daughter of old Maynard, because you both tell me so—otherwise I could never have believed it. But I do not well know what all this dispute is about: I always understood you was to inherit your estate from your first wife. She lived till she came of age; did she not?"

"According to law," said I, "she certainly did; she died that very day, but she could not make a will."

"I am strangely misinformed," replied he, "if you had not a right to it from that moment.—But what say the writings?"

"Those I never saw," returned I. "As I married without the consent of my wife's relations, I had no claim to demand the sight of them; and, as she died before she could call them her's, I had no opportunity."

"Then you have been wronged, take my word for it. I assert, that her fortune was her's on the day of marriage, unconditionally. I advise you to go to law with the old rogue (I beg your pardon, Madam, for calling your father so); go to law with him for the recovery of your first wife's estate; and let him thank heaven his daughter is so well provided for."

This was happy news for us. I changed my plan, and brought an action against him for detaining my property. In short, after many hearings and appeals, I had the satisfaction of casting him. But I became father to your sister and yourself before the cause was determined. We were driven to the utmost straits while it was in agitation. At last, however, right prevailed; and I was put in possession of an estate I had unjustly been kept out of many years.

Now I thought myself perfectly happy. "Fortune," said I, "is at length tired of persecuting me; and I have before me the most felicitous prospect." Alas! how short-sighted is man! In the midst of my promised scene of permanent delight, the most dreadful of misfortunes overtook me. My loved Maria fell into the most violent disorder, after having been delivered of a dead child.—Good God! what was my situation, to be reduced to pray for the death of her who made up my whole scheme of happiness! "Dear, dear Maria! thy image still lives in my remembrance; *that,*

—Seeks thee still in many a former scene;
Seeks thy fair form, thy lovely beaming eyes,
Thy pleasing converse, by gay lively sense
Inspir'd: whose moral wisdom mildly shone,
Without the toil of art; and virtue glow'd
In all her smiles, without forbidding pride."

Oh! my Julia, such was thy mother! my heart has never tasted happiness since her lamented death. Yet I cease not to thank heaven for the blessings it has given me in thee and my Louisa. May I see you both happy in a world that to me has lost its charms!

The death of my Maria seemed to detach me from all society. I had met with too many bad people in it to have any regard for it; and now the only chain that held me was broken. I retired hither and, in my first paroxysms of grief, vowed never to quit this recluse spot; where, for the first years of your infancy, I brooded my misfortunes, till I became habituated and enured to melancholy. I was always happy when either you or your sister had an opportunity of seeing a little of the world. Perhaps my vow was a rash one, but it is sacred.

As your inclination was not of a retired turn, I consented to a marriage, which, I hope, will be conducive to your felicity. Heaven grant it may! Oh! most gracious Providence, let me not be so curst as to see my children unhappy! I feel I could not support such an afflicting stroke. But I will not anticipate an evil I continually pray to heaven to avert.

Adieu, my child! May you meet with no accident or misfortune to make you out of love with the world!

Thy tender and affectionate father,
E. GRENVILLE.

LETTER X.

TO Miss GRENVILLE.

I have just perused my father's long packet: I shall not however comment upon it, till I have opened my whole mind to you in a more particular manner than I yet have done.

The first part of my father's letter has given me much concern, by awakening some doubts, which I knew not subsisted in my bosom. He asks such questions relative to my real state of happiness, as distress me to answer. I have examined my most inward thoughts. Shall I tell you, my Louisa, the examination does not satisfy me? I believe in this life, and particularly in this town, we must not search too deeply—to be happy, we must take both persons and things as we in general find them, without scrutinizing too closely. The researches are not attended with that pleasure we would wish to find.

The mind may be amused, or, more properly speaking, employed, so as not to give it leisure to think; and, I fancy, the people in this part of the world esteem reflection an evil, and therefore keep continually hurrying from place to place, to leave no room or time for it. For my own part, I sometimes feel some little compunction of mind from the dissipated life I lead; and wish I had been cast in a less tumultuous scene. I even sometimes venture to propose to Sir William a scheme of spending a little more time at home—telling him, it will be more for our advantage with respect to our health, as the repeated hurries in which we are engaged must, in future, be hurtful to us. He laughs at my sober plan. "Nothing," he says, "is so serviceable to the body, as unbending the mind—as to the rest, my notions are owing to the prejudices of education; but that in time he hopes my rusticity will yield to the *ton*. For God's sake," he continues, "make yourself ready—you know you are to be at the opera—" or somewhere or other. So away goes reflection; and we are whirled away in the stream of dissipation, with the rest of the world. This seems a very sufficient reason for every thing we do, *The rest of the world does so*: that's quite enough.

But does it convey to the heart that inward secret pleasure which increases on reflection? Too sure it does not. However, it has been my invariable plan, from which I have not nor do intend to recede, to be governed in these matters by the will of my husband: he is some years older than me, and has had great experience in life. It shall be my care to preserve my health and morals;—in the rest, *he* must be my guide.

My mind is not at the same time quite at ease. I foresee I shall have some things to communicate to you which I shall be unwilling should meet my father's eye. Perhaps the world is altered since he resided in it; and from the novelty to him, the present modes may not meet his approbation. I would wish carefully to conceal every thing from him which might give him pain, and which it is not in his power to remedy. To you, my Louisa, I shall ever use the most unbounded confidence. I may sometimes tell you I am dissatisfied; but when I do so, it will not be so much out of a desire of complaint, as to induce you to give me your advice. Ah! you would be ten times fitter to live in the world than I. Your solidity and excellent judgment would point out the proper path, and how far you might stray in it unhurt; while my vivacity impels me to follow the gay multitude; and when I look back, I am astonished to behold the progress I have made. But I will accustom myself to relate every circumstance to you: though they may in themselves be trivial, yet I know your affection to me will find them interesting. Your good sense will point out to you what part of our correspondence will be fit for my father's ear.

I mentioned to you two ladies, to whose protection and countenance I had been introduced by Sir William. I do not like either of them, and wish it had suited him to have procured me intimates more adapted to my sentiments. And now we are upon this subject, I must say, I should have been better pleased with my husband, if he had proposed your coming to town with me. He may have a high opinion of my integrity and discretion; but he ought in my mind to have reflected how very young I was; and, he scruples not frequently to say, how totally unlearned in polite life.—Should I not then have had a real protector and friend? I do not mention my early years by way of begging an excuse for any impropriety of conduct; far from it: there is no age in which we do not know right from wrong; nor is extreme youth an extenuation of guilt: but there is a time of life which wants attention, and should not be left too much to its own guidance.

With the best propensities in the world, we may be led, either by the force of example, or real want of judgment, too far in the flowery path of pleasure. Every scene I engage in has the charm of novelty to recommend it. I see all to whom I am introduced do the same; besides, I am following the taste of Sir William; but I am (if I may be allowed to say so) too artless. Perhaps what I think is his inclination, may be only to make trial of my natural disposition. Though he may choose to live in the highest *ton*, he may secretly wish his wife a more retired turn. How then shall I act? I do every thing with a chearful countenance; but that proceeds from my desire of pleasing him. I accommodate myself to what I think his taste; but, owing to my ignorance of mankind, I may be defeating my own purpose. I once slightly hinted as much to Lady Besford. She burst out into a fit of laughter at my duteous principles. I supposed I was wrong, by exciting her mirth: this is not the method of reforming me from my errors; but thus I am in general treated. It reminds me of a character in the Spectator, who, being very beautiful, was kept in perfect ignorance of every thing, and who, when she made any enquiry in order to gain knowledge, was always put by, with, "You are too handsome to trouble yourself about such things." This, according to the present fashion, may be polite; but I am sure it is neither friendly nor satisfactory.

Her ladyship, the other day, shewed me a very beautiful young woman, Lady T. "She is going to be separated from her husband," said she. On my expressing my surprize,— "Pshaw! there is nothing surprizing in those things," she added: "it is customary in this world to break through stone-walls to get together this year; and break a commandment the next to get asunder. But with regard to her ladyship, I do not know that she has been imprudent; the cause of their disagreement proceeds from a propensity she has for gaming; and my lord is resolved not to be any longer answerable for her debts, having more of that sort on his own hands than he can well discharge." Thus she favours me with sketches of the people of fashion. Alas! Louisa, are these people to make companions of?—They may, for want of better, be acquaintance, but never can be friends.

By her account, there is not a happy couple that frequents St. James's.—Happiness in her estimate is not an article in the married state. "Are you not happy?" I asked one day. "Happy! why yes, probably I am; but you do not suppose my happiness proceeds from my being married, any further than that state allowing greater latitude and freedom than the single. I enjoy title, rank, and liberty, by bearing Lord Besford's name. We do not disagree, because we very seldom meet. He pursues his pleasures one way, I seek mine another; and our dispositions being very opposite, they are sure never to interfere with each other. I am, I give you my word, a very unexceptionable wife, and can say, what few women of quality would be able to do that spoke truth, that I never indulged myself in the least liberty with other men, till I had secured my lord a lawful heir." I felt all horror and astonishment.—She saw the emotion she excited. "Come, don't be prudish," said she: "my conduct in the eye of the world is irreproachable. My lord kept a mistress from the first moment of his marriage. What law allows those privileges to a man, and excludes a woman from enjoying the same? Marriage now is a necessary kind of barter, and an alliance of families;—the heart is not consulted;—or, if that should sometimes bring a pair together,—judgment being left far behind, love seldom lasts long. In former times, a poor foolish woman might languish out her life in sighs and tears, for the infidelity of her husband. Thank heaven! they are now wiser; but then they should be prudent. I extremely condemn those, who are enslaved by their passions, and bring a public disgrace on their families by suffering themselves to be detected; such are justly our scorn and ridicule; and you may observe they are not taken notice of by any body. There is a decency to be observed in our amours; and I shall be very ready to offer you my advice, as you are young and inexperienced. One thing let me tell you; never admit your *Cicisbeo* to an unlimited familiarity; they are first suspected. Never take notice of your favourite before other people; there are a thousand ways to make yourself amends in secret for that little, but necessary, sacrifice in public."

"Nothing," said I, "but the conviction that you are only bantering me, should have induced me to listen to you so long; but be assured, madam, such discourses are extremely disagreeable to me."

"You are a child," said she, "in these matters; I am not therefore angry or surprized; but, when you find all the world like myself, you will cease your astonishment."

"Would to heaven," cried I, "I had never come into such a depraved world! How much better had it been to have continued in ignorance and innocence in the peaceful retirement in which I was bred! However, I hope, with the seeds of virtue which I imbibed in my infancy, I shall be able to go through life with honour to my family, and integrity to myself. I mean never to engage in any kind of amour, so shall never stand in need of your ladyship's advice, which, I must say, I cannot think Sir William would thank you for, or can have the least idea you would offer."

"She assured me, Sir William knew too much of the world to expect, or even wish, his wife to be different from most women who composed it; but that she had nothing further to say.—I might some time hence want a *confidante*, and I should not be unfortunate if I met with no worse than her, who had ever conducted herself with prudence and discretion."

I then said, "I had married Sir William because I preferred him,—and that my sentiments would not alter."

"If you can answer for your future sentiments," replied Lady Besford, "you have a greater knowledge, or at least a greater confidence, in yourself than most people have.—As to your preference of Sir William, I own I am inclined to laugh at your so prettily deceiving yourself.—Pray how many men had you seen, and been addressed by, before your acquaintance with Sir William? Very few, I fancy, that were likely to make an impression on your heart, or that could be put into a competition with him, without an affront from the comparison. So, because you thought Sir William Stanley a handsome man, and genteeler in his dress than the boors you had been accustomed to see—add to which his being passionately enamoured of you—you directly conclude, you have given him the preference to all other men, and that your heart is devoted to him alone: you may think so; nay, I dare say, you do think so; but, believe me, a time may come when you will think otherwise. You may possibly likewise imagine, as Sir William was so much in love, that you will be for ever possessed of his heart:—it is almost a pity to overturn so pretty a system; but, take my word for it, Lady Stanley, Sir William will soon teach you another lesson; he will soon convince you, the matrimonial shackles are not binding enough to abridge him of the fashionable enjoyments of life; and that, when he married, he did not mean to seclude himself from those pleasures, which, as a man of the world, he is intitled to partake of, because love was the principal ingredient and main spring of your engagement. That love may not last for ever. He is of a gay disposition, and his taste must be fed with variety."

"I cannot imagine," I rejoined, interrupting her ladyship, "I cannot imagine what end it is to answer, that you seem desirous of planting discord between my husband and me.—I do not suppose you have any views on him; as, according to your principles, his being married would be no obstacle to that view.—Whatever may be the failings of Sir William, as his wife, it is my duty not to resent them, and my interest not to see them. I shall not thank your ladyship for opening my eyes, or seeking to develope my sentiments respecting the preference I have shewed him; any more than he is obliged to you, for seeking to corrupt the morals of a woman whom he has made the guardian of his honour. I hope to preserve that and my own untainted, even in this nursery of vice and folly. I fancy Sir William little thought what instructions you would give, when he begged your protection. I am, however, indebted to you for putting me on my guard; and, be assured, I shall be careful to act with all the discretion and prudence you yourself would wish me." Some company coming in, put an end to our conversation. I need not tell you, I shall be very shy of her ladyship in future. Good God! are all the world, as she calls the circle of her acquaintance, like herself? If so, how dreadful to be cast in such a lot! But I will still hope, detraction is among the catalogue of her failings, and that she views the world with jaundiced eyes.

As to the male acquaintance of Sir William, I cannot say they are higher in my estimation than the other sex. Is it because I am young and ignorant, that they, one and all, take the liberty of almost making love to me? Lord Biddulph, in particular, I dislike; and yet he is Sir William's most approved friend. Colonel Montague is another who is eternally here. The only unexceptionable one is a foreign gentleman, Baron Ton-hausen. There is a modest diffidence in his address, which interests one much in his favour. I declare, the only blush I have seen since I left Wales was on his cheek when he was introduced. I fancy he is as little acquainted with the vicious manners of the court as myself, as he seemed under some confusion on his first conversation. He is but newly known to Sir William; but, being a man of rank, and politely received in the *beau monde*, he is a welcome visitor at our house. But though he comes often, he is not obtrusive like the rest. They will never let me be at quiet—for ever proposing this or the other scheme—which, as I observed before, I comply with, more out of conformity to the will of Sir William, than to my own taste. Not that I would have you suppose I do not like any of the public places I frequent. I am charmed at the opera; and receive a very high, and, I think, rational, delight at a good play. I am far from being an enemy to pleasure—but then I would wish to have it under some degree, of subordination; let it be the amusement, not the business of life.

Lord Biddulph is what Lady Besford stiles, my *Cicisbeo*—that is, he takes upon him the task of attending me to public places, calling my chair—handing me refreshments, and such-like; but I assure you, I do not approve of him in the least: and Lady Besford may be assured, I shall, at least, follow her kind advice in this particular, not to admit him to familiarities; though his Lordship seems ready enough to avail himself of all opportunities of being infinitely more assiduous than I wish him.

Was this letter to meet the eye of my father, I doubt he would repent his ready acquiescence to my marriage. He would not think the scenes, in which I am involved, an equivalent for the calm joys I left in the mountains. And was he to know that Sir William and I have not met these three days but at meals, and then surrounded with company; he would not think the tenderness of an husband a recompence for the loss of a father's and sister's affection. I do not, however, do well to complain. I have no just reasons, and it is a weakness to be uneasy without a cause. Adieu then, my Louisa; be assured, my heart shall never know a change, either in its virtuous principles, or in its tender love to you. I might have been happy, superlatively so, with Sir William in a desert; but, in this vale of vice, it is impossible, unless one can adapt one's sentiments to the style of those one is among. I will be every thing I can, without forgetting to be what I ought, in order to merit the affection you have ever shewed to your faithful
JULIA STANLEY.

LETTER XI.

TO Lady STANLEY.

Three days, my Julia, and never met but at meals! Good God! to what can this strange behaviour be owing? You say, you tell me every circumstance. Have you had any disagreement; and is this the method your husband takes to shew his resentment? Ah! Julia, be not afraid of my shewing your letters to my father; do you think I would precipitate him with sorrow to the grave, or at least wound his reverend bosom with such anguish? No, Julia, I will burst my heart in silence, but never tell my grief. Alas! my sister, friend of my soul, why are we separated? The loss of your loved society I would sacrifice, could I but hear you were happy. But can you be so among such wretches? Yet be comforted, my Julia; have confidence in the rectitude of your own actions and thoughts; but, above all, petition heaven to support you in all trials. Be assured, while you have the protection of the Almighty, these impious vile wretches will not, cannot, prevail against you. Your virtue will shine out more conspicuously, while surrounded with their vices.

That horrid Lady Besford! I am sure you feel all the detestation you ought for such a character. As you become acquainted with other people, (and they cannot be all so bad)— you may take an opportunity of shaking her off. Dear creature! how art thou beset! Surely, Sir William is very thoughtless: with his experience, he ought to have known how improper such a woman was for the protector of his wife. And why must this Lord—what's his odious name?—why is he to be your *escorte?* Is it not the husband's province to guard and defend his wife? What a world are you cast in!

I find poor Win has written to her aunt Bailey, and complains heavily of her situation. She says, Griffith is still more discontented than herself; since he is the jest of all the other servants. They both wish themselves at home again. She likewise tells Mrs. Bailey, that she is not fit to dress you according to the fashion, and gives a whimsical account of the many different things you put on and pull off when you are, what she calls, high-dressed. If she is of no use to you, I wish you would send her back before her morals are corrupted. Consider, she has not had the advantage of education, as you have had; and, being without those resources within, may the more easily fall a prey to some insidious betrayer; for, no doubt, in such a place,
"Clowns   as   well   can   act   the   rake,
As those in higher sphere."

Let her return, then, if she is willing, as innocent and artless as she left us. Oh! that I could enlarge that wish! I should have been glad you had had Mrs. Bailey with you; she might have been of some service to you. Her long residence in *our* family would have given her some weight in *your's*, which I doubt is sadly managed by Win's account. The servants are disorderly and negligent. Don't you think of going into the country? Spring comes forward very fast; and next month is the fairest of the year.

Would to heaven you were here!—I long ardently for your company; and, rather than forego it, would almost consent to share it with the dissipated tribe you are obliged to associate with;—but that privilege is not allowed me. I could not leave my father. Nay, I must further say I should have too much pride to come unasked; and you know Sir William never gave me an invitation.

I shed tears over the latter part of your letter, where you say, *I could be happy, superlatively so, with Sir William in a desert; but here it is impossible.* Whatever he may think, he would be happy too; at least he appeared so while with us. Oh! that he could have been satisfied with our calm joys, which mend the heart, and left those false delusive ones, which corrupt and vitiate it!

Dearest Julia, adieu!

Believe me your faithful

LOUISA GRENVILLE.

LETTER XII.

TO Miss GRENVILLE.

Louisa! my dearest girl! who do you think I have met with?—No other than Lady Melford! I saw her this day in the drawing-room. I instantly recognized her ladyship, and, catching her eye, made my obeisance to her. She returned my salute, in a manner which seemed to say, "I don't know you; but I wish to recollect you."—As often as I looked up, I found I engaged her attention. When their majesties were withdrawn, I was sitting in one of the windows with Lady Anne Parker, and some other folks about me.—I then saw Lady Melford moving towards me. I rose, and pressed her to take my place. "You are very obliging," said she: "I will, if you please, accept part of it, as I wish informed who it is that is so polite as to pay such civility to an old woman." Lady Anne, finding we were entering on conversation, wished me a good day, and went off.

"I am perfectly well acquainted with your features," said her ladyship; "but I cannot call to my memory what is your name."

"Have you then quite forgot Julia Grenville, to whom you was so kind while she was on a visit with your grandfather at L.?"

"Julia Grenville! Aye, so it is; but, my dear, how came I to meet you in the drawing-room at St. James's, whom I thought still an inmate of the mountains? Has your father rescinded his resolution of spending his life there? and where is your sister?"

"My father," I replied, "is still in his favourite retreat; my sister resides with him.—I have been in town some time, and am at present an inhabitant of it."

"To whose protection could your father confide you, my dear?"

"To the best protector in the world, madam," I answered, smiling—"to an husband."

"A husband!" she repeated, quite astonished, "What, child, are you married? And who, my dear, is this husband that your father could part with you to?"

"That gentleman in the blue and silver velvet, across the room,—Sir William Stanley. Does your ladyship know him?"

"By name and character only," she answered. "You are very young, my dear, to be thus initiated in the world. Has Sir William any relations, female ones I mean, who are fit companions for you?—This is a dangerous place for young inexperienced girls to be left to their own guidance."

I mentioned the ladies to whom I had been introduced. "I don't know them," said Lady Melford; "no doubt they are women of character, as they are the friends of your husband. I am, however, glad to see you, and hope you are happily married. My meeting you here is owing to having attended a lady who was introduced; I came to town from D. for that purpose."

I asked her ladyship, if she would permit me to wait on her while she remained in town. She obligingly said, "she took it very kind in a young person shewing such attention to her, and should always be glad of my company."

The counsel of Lady Melford may be of service to me. I am extremely happy to have seen her. I remember with pleasure the month I passed at L. I reproach myself for not writing to Jenny Melford. I doubt she thinks me ungrateful, or that the busy scenes in which

I am immersed have obliterated all former fond remembrances. I will soon convince her, that the gay insignificant crowd cannot wear away the impression which her kindness stamped on my heart in early childhood.

Your letter is just brought to my hands. Yes, my dear Louisa, I have not a doubt but that, while I deserve it, I shall be the immediate care of heaven. Join your prayers to mine; and they will, when offered with heart-felt sincerity, be heard.

I have nothing to apprehend from Lady Besford.—Such kind of women can never seduce me. She shews herself too openly; and the discovery of her character gives me no other concern, than as it too evidently manifests in my eyes the extreme carelessness of Sir William: I own *there* I am in some degree piqued. But, if *he* is indifferent about my morals and well-doing in life, it will more absolutely become my business to take care of myself,—an arduous task for a young girl, surrounded with so many incitements to quit the strait paths, and so many examples of those that do.

As to the œconomy of my family, I fear it is but badly managed.—However, I do not know how to interfere, as we have a house-keeper, who is empowered to give all orders, &c. If Win is desirous of returning, I shall not exert my voice to oppose her inclinations, though I own I shall be very sorry to lose the only domestic in my family in whom I can place the least confidence, or who is attached to me from any other motive than interest. I will never, notwithstanding my repugnance to her leaving me, offer any objections which may influence her conduct; but I do not think with you her morals will be in any danger, as she in general keeps either in my apartments, or in the house-keeper's.

I do not know how Griffith manages; I should be concerned that he should be ill-used by the rest of the servants; his dialect, and to them singular manners, may excite their boisterous mirth; and I know, though he is a worthy creature, yet he has all the irascibility of his countrymen; and therefore they may take a pleasure in thwarting and teasing the poor Cambro-Briton; but of this I am not likely to be informed, as being so wholly out of my sphere.

I could hardly help smiling at that part of your letter, wherein you say, you think the husband the proper person to attend his wife to public places. How different are your ideas from those of the people of this town, or at least to their practice!—A woman, who would not blush at being convicted in a little affair of gallantry, would be ready to sink with confusion, should she receive these *tendres* from an husband in public, which when offered by any other man is accepted with pleasure and complacency. Sir William never goes with me to any of these fashionable movements. It is true, we often meet, but very seldom join, as we are in general in separate parties. *Whom God hath joined, let no man put asunder*, is a part of the ceremony; but here it is the business of every one to endeavour to put a man and wife asunder;—fashion not making it decent to appear together.

These *etiquettes*, though so absolutely necessary in polite life, are by no means reconcilable to reason, or to my wishes. But my voice would be too weak to be heard against the general cry; or, being heard, I should be thought too insignificant to be attended to.

"Conscience makes cowards of us all," some poet says; and your Julia says, fashion makes fools of us all; but she only whispers this to the dear bosom of her friend. Oh! my Louisa, that you were with me!—It is with this wish I end all my letters; mentally so, if I do not openly thus express myself.—Absence seems to increase my affection.—One reason is, because I cannot find any one to supply me the loss I sustain in you; out of the hundreds I visit, not one with whom I can form a friendly attachment. My attachment to Sir William, which was strong enough to tear me from your arms, is not sufficient to suppress the gushing tear, or hush the rising sigh, when I sit and reflect on what I once possessed, and what I so much want at this moment. Adieu, my dear Louisa! continue your tender attention to the best of fathers, and love me always.

JULIA STANLEY.

LETTER XIII.

TO THE SAME.

I spent a whole morning with Lady Melford, more to my satisfaction than any one I have passed since I left you. But this treat cannot be repeated; her ladyship leaves town this day. She was so good as to say, she was sorry her stay was so short, and wished to have had more time with me. I can truly join with her. Her conversation was friendly and parental. She cautioned me against falling into the levities of the sex—which unhappily, she observed, were now become so prevalent; and further told me, how cautious I ought to be of my female acquaintance, since the reputation of a young woman rises and falls in proportion to the merit of her associates. I judged she had Lady Besford in her mind. I answered, I thought myself unhappy in not having you with me, and likewise possessing so little penetration, that I could not discover who were, or who were not, proper companions; that, relying on the experience of Sir William, I had left the choice of them to him, trusting he would not introduce those whose characters and morals were reprehensible; but whether it proceeded from my ignorance, or from the mode of the times, I could not admire the sentiments of either of the ladies with whom I was more intimately connected, but wished to have the opinion of one whose judgment was more matured than mine.

Lady Melford replied, the circle of her acquaintance was rather confined;—and that her short residences at a time in town left her an incompetent judge: "but, my dear," she added, "the virtuous principles instilled into you by your excellent father, joined to the innate goodness of your heart, must guide you through the warfare of life. Never for one moment listen to the seductive voice of folly, whether its advocate be man or woman.—If a man is profuse in flattery, believe him an insidious betrayer, who only watches a favourable moment to ruin your peace of mind for ever. Suffer no one to lessen your husband in your esteem: no one will attempt it, but from sinister views; disappoint all such, either by grave remonstrances or lively sallies. Perhaps some will officiously bring you informations of the supposed infidelity of your husband, in hopes they may induce you to take a fashionable revenge.—Labour to convince such, how you detest all informers; speak of your confidence in him,—and that nothing shall persuade you but that he acts as he ought. But, since the heart of man naturally loves variety, and, from the depravity of the age, indulgences, which I call criminal, are allowed to them, Sir William may not pay that strict obedience to his part of the marriage contract as he ought; remember, my dear, his conduct can never exculpate any breach in your's. Gentleness and complacency on your part are the only weapons you should prove to any little irregularity on his. By such behaviour, I doubt not, you will be happy, as you will deserve to be so."

Ah! my dear Louisa, what a loss shall I have in this venerable monitress! I will treasure up her excellent advice, and hope to reap the benefit of it.

If I dislike Lady Besford, I think I have more reason to be displeased with Lady Anne Parker.—She has more artifice, and is consequently a more dangerous companion. She has more than once given hints of the freedoms which Sir William allows in himself.—The other night at the opera she pointed out one of the dancers, and assured me, "Sir William was much envied for having subdued the virtue of that girl. That," continued she, "was her *vis à vis* that you admired this morning; she lives in great taste; I suppose her allowance is superb." It is quite the *ton* to keep opera-girls, though, perhaps, the men who support them never pay them a visit.—I therefore concluded this affair was one of that sort. Such creatures can never deprive me of my husband's heart, and I should be very weak to be uneasy about such connexions.

Last night, however, a circumstance happened, which, I own, touched my heart more sensibly. Lady Anne insisted on my accompanying her to the opera. Sir William dined out; and, as our party was sudden, knew not of my intention of being there. Towards the end of the opera, I observed my husband in one of the upper-boxes, with a very elegant-looking woman, dressed in the genteelest taste, to whom he appeared very assiduous.—"There is Sir William," said I.—"Yes," said Lady Anne, "but I dare say, he did not expect to see you here."

"Possibly not," I answered. A little female curiosity urged me to ask, if she knew who that lady was? She smiled, and answered, "she believed she did." A very favourite air being then singing, I dropped the conversation, though I could not help now and then stealing a look at my husband. I was convinced he must see and know me, as my situation in the house was very conspicuous; but I thought he seemed industriously to avoid meeting my eyes.—

The opera being ended, we adjourned to the coffee-room; and, having missed Sir William a little time before, naturally expected to see him there; as it is customary for all the company to assemble there previous to their going to their carriages.

A great number of people soon joined us. Baron Ton-hausen had just handed me a glass of orgeat; and was chatting in an agreeable manner, when Lord Biddulph came up. "Lady Stanley," said he, with an air of surprize, "I thought I saw you this moment in Sir William's chariot. I little expected the happiness of meeting you here."

"You saw Sir William, my Lord, I believe," said Lady Anne; "but as to the Lady, you are mistaken—though I should have supposed you might have recognized your old friend Lucy Gardiner; they were together in one of the boxes.—Sly wretch! he thought we did not see him."

"Oh! you ladies have such penetrating eyes," replied his Lordship, "that we poor men—and especially the married ones, ought to be careful how we conduct ourselves. But, my dear Lady Stanley, how have you been entertained? Was not Rauzzini exquisite?"

"Can you ask how her Ladyship has been amused, when you have just informed her, her *Caro Sposo* was seen with a favourite Sultana?"

"Pshaw!" said his Lordship, "there is nothing in that—*tout la mode de François*. The conduct of an husband can not discompose a Lady of sense. What says the lovely Lady Stanley?"

"I answer," I replied very seriously, "Sir William has an undoubted right to act as he pleases. I never have or ever intend to prescribe rules to him; sufficient, I think, to conduct self."

"Bravo!" cried Lord Biddulph, "spoke like a heroine: and I hope my dear Lady Stanley will act as she pleases too."

"I do when I can," I answered.—Then, turning to Lady Anne, "Not to break in on your amusement," I continued, "will you give me leave to wait on you to Brook-street? you know you have promised to sup with me."

"Most chearfully," said she;—"but will you not ask the beaux to attend us?"

Lord Biddulph said, he was most unfortunately engaged to Lady D—'s route. The Baron refused, as if he wished to be intreated. Lady Anne would take no denial; and, when I assured him his company would give me pleasure, he consented.

I was handed to the coach by his Lordship, who took that opportunity of condemning Sir William's want of taste; and lavishing the utmost encomiums on your Julia—with whom they passed as nothing. If Sir William is unfaithful, Lord Biddulph is not the man to reconcile me to the sex. I feel his motives in too glaring colours. No, the soft timidity of Ton-hausen, which, while it indicates the profoundest respect, still betrays the utmost tenderness—he it is alone who could restore the character of mankind, and raise it again in my estimation. But what have I said? Dear Louisa, I blush at having discovered to you, that I am, past all doubt, the object of the Baron's tender sentiments. Ah! can I mistake those glances, which modest reserve and deference urge him to correct? Yet fear me not. I am married. My vows are registered in the book of heaven; and as, by their irreversible decree, I am bound to *honour* and *obey* my husband, so will I strive to *love* him, and him alone; though I have long since ceased to be the object of his? Of what consequence, however, is that? I am indissolubly united to him; he was the man of my choice—to say he was the first man I almost ever saw—and to plead my youth and inexperience—oh! what does that avail? Nor does his neglect justify the least on my part.

"For man the lawless libertine may rove."

But this is a strange digression. The Baron accompanied us to supper. During our repast, Lady Anne made a thousand sallies to divert us. My mind, however, seemed that night infected by the demon of despair. I could not be chearful—and yet, I am sure, I was not jealous of this Lucy Gardiner. Melancholy was contagious: Ton-hausen caught it—I observed him sometimes heave a suppressed sigh. Lady Anne was determined to dissipate the gloom which inveloped us, and began drawing, with her satirical pen, the characters of her acquaintance.

"Baron," said she, "did you not observe Lord P—, with his round unthinking face—how assiduous he was to Miss W——, complimenting her on the brilliancy of her complexion, though he knows she wore more *rouge* than almost any woman of quality—extolling her *forest of hair*, when most likely he saw it this morning brought in a band-box—and celebrating the pearly whiteness of her teeth, when he was present at their transplanting? But he is not a slave to propriety, or even common sense. No, dear creature, he has a soul above it. But did you not take notice of Lady L——, how she ogled Capt. F. when her booby Lord turned his head aside? What a ridiculous fop is that! The most glaring proofs will not convince him of his wife's infidelity. 'Captain F.' said he to me yesterday at court; 'Captain F. I assure you, Lady Anne, is a great favourite with me.' 'It is a family partiality,' said I; 'Lady L. seems to have no aversion to him.' 'Ah, there you mistake, fair Lady. I want my Lady to have the same affection for him I have. He has done all he can to please her, and yet she does not seem satisfied with him.' 'Unconscionable!' cried I, 'why then she is never to be satisfied.' 'Why so I say; but it proceeds from the violence of her attachment to me. Oh! Lady Anne, she is the most virtuous and discreetest Lady. I should be the happiest man in the world, if she would but shew a little more consideration to my friend.' I think it a pity he does not know his happiness, as I have not the least doubt of F. and her Ladyship having a pretty good understanding together." Thus was the thoughtless creature running on unheeded by either of us, when her harangue was interrupted by an alarming accident happening to me. I had sat some time, leaning my head on my hand; though, God knows! paying very little attention to Lady Anne's sketches, when some of the superfluous ornaments of my head-dress, coming rather too near the candle, caught fire, and the whole farrago of ribbands, lace, and gew-gaws, were instantly in flames. I shrieked out in the utmost terror, and should have been a very great sufferer—perhaps been burnt to death—had not the Baron had the presence of mind to roll my head, flames and all, up in my shawl, which fortunately hung on the back of my chair; and, by such precaution, preserved the*capitol*. How ridiculous are the fashions, which render us liable to such accidents! My fright, however, proved more than the damage sustained. When the flames were extinguished, I thought Lady Anne would have expired with mirth; owing to the disastrous figure I made with my singed feathers, &c. The whimsical distress of the heroine of the Election Ball presented itself to her imagination; and the pale face of the affrighted Baron, during the conflagration, heightened the picture. "Even such a man," she cried, "so dead in look, so woe-be-gone! Excuse me, dear Ton-hausen—The danger is over now. I must indulge my risible faculties."

"I will most readily join with your Ladyship," answered the Baron, "as my joy is in proportion to what were my apprehensions. But I must condemn a fashion which is so injurious to the safety of the ladies."

The accident, however, disconcerted me not a little, and made me quite unfit for company. They saw the chagrin painted on my features, and soon took leave of me.

I retired to my dressing-room, and sent for Win, to inspect the almost ruinated fabrick; but such is the construction now-a-days, that a head might burn for an hour without damaging the genuine part of it. A lucky circumstance! I sustained but little damage—in short, nothing which Monsieur *Corross* could not remedy in a few hours.

My company staying late, and this event besides, retarded my retiring to rest till near three in the morning. I had not left my dressing-room when Sir William entered.

"Good God! not gone to bed yet, Julia? I hope you did not sit up for me. You know that is a piece of ceremony I would chuse to dispense with; as it always carries a tacit reproach under an appearance of tender solicitude." I fancied I saw in his countenance a consciousness that he deserved reproach, and a determination to begin first to find fault. I was vexed, and answered, "You might have waited for the reproach at least, before you pre-judged my conduct. Nor can you have any apprehensions that I should make such, having never taken that liberty. Neither do you do me justice in supposing me capable of the meanness you insinuate, on finding me up at this late hour. That circumstance is owing to an accident, by which I might have been a great sufferer; and which, though you so unkindly accuse me of being improperly prying and curious, I will, if you permit me, relate to you, in order to justify myself." He certainly expected I should ask some questions which would be disagreeable to him; and therefore, finding me totally silent on that head, his features became more relaxed; he enquired, with some tenderness, what alarming accident I hinted at. I informed him of every circumstance.—My account put him into good humour; and we laughed over the droll scene very heartily. Observing, however, I was quite *en dishabille*, "My dear girl," cried he, throwing his arm round me, "I doubt you will catch cold, notwithstanding you so lately represented a burning-mountain. Come," continued he, "will you go to bed?" While he spoke, he pressed me to his bosom; and expressed in his voice and manner more warmth of affection than he had discovered since I forsook the mountains. He kissed me several times with rapture; and his eyes dwelt on me with an ardor I have long been unused to behold. The adventure at the opera returned to my imagination. These caresses, thought I, have been bestowed on one, whose prostituted charms are more admired than mine. I sighed—"Why do you sigh, Julia?" asked my husband. "I know not," I answered. "I ought not to sigh in the very moment I am receiving proofs of your affection. But I have not lately received such proofs, and therefore perhaps I sighed."

"You are a foolish girl, Julia, yet a good one too"—cried he, kissing me again: "Foolish, to fancy I do not love you; and a good girl, not to ask impertinent questions. That is, your tongue is silent, but you have wicked eyes, Julia, that seek to look into my inmost thoughts."—"Then I will shut them," said I, affecting to laugh—but added, in a more serious tone—"I will see no further than you would wish me; to please you, I will be *blind, insensible and blind.*"

"But, as you are not deaf, I will tell you what you well know—that I was at the opera—and with a lady too.—Do not, however, be jealous, my dear: the woman I was with was perfectly indifferent to me. I met her by accident—but I had a mind to see what effect such a piece of flirtation would have on you. I am not displeased with your behaviour; nor would I have you so with mine."

"I will in all my best obey you," said I.—"Then go to bed," said he—"*To bed, my love, and I will follow thee.*"

You will not scruple to pronounce this a reasonable long letter, my dear Louisa, for a modern fine lady.—Ah! shield me from that character! Would to heaven Sir William was no more of the modern fine gentleman in his heart! I could be happy with him.—Yes, Louisa— was I indeed the object of his affections, not merely so of his passions, which, I fear, I am, I could indeed be happy with him. My person still invites his caresses—but for the softer sentiments of the soul—that ineffable tenderness which depends not on the tincture of the skin—of that, alas! he has no idea. A voluptuary in love, he professes not that delicacy which refines all its joys. His is all passion; sentiment is left out of the catalogue. Adieu!

JULIA STANLEY.

LETTER XIV.

TO THE SAME.

I hope, my dearest Louisa will not be too much alarmed at a whole fortnight's silence. Ah! Louisa, the event which occasioned it may be productive of very fatal consequences to me—yet I will not despair. No, I will trust in a good God, and the virtuous education I have had. They will arm me to subdue inclinations, irreversible fate has rendered improper. But to the point.

Two or three nights after I wrote my last, I went to the play.—Lady Anne, Colonel Montague, and a Miss Finch, were the party. Unhappily, the after-piece represented was one obtruded on the public by an author obnoxious to some of them; and there were two parties formed, one to condemn, the other to support. Wholly unacquainted with a thing of this kind, I soon began to be alarmed at the clamour which rang from every part of the house. The glass chandeliers first fell a victim to a hot-headed wretch in the pit; and part of the shattered fragments was thrown into my lap. My fears increased to the highest degree—No one seemed to interest themselves about me. Colonel Montague being an admirer of Miss Finch, his attention was paid to her. The ladies were ordered out of the house. I was ready enough to obey the summons, and was rushing out, when my passage was stopped by a concourse of people in the lobby. The women screaming—men swearing—altogether—I thought I should die with terror. "Oh! let me come out, let me come out!" I cried, with uplifted hands.—No one regarded me. And I might have stood screaming in concert with the rest till this time, had not the Baron most seasonably come to my assistance. He broke through the croud with incredible force, and flew to me. "Dearest Lady Stanley," cried he, "recover your spirits—you are in no danger. I will guard you to your carriage." Others were equally anxious about their company, and every one striving to get out first increased the difficulty. Many ladies fainted in the passages, which, being close, became almost suffocating. Every moment our difficulties and my fears increased. I became almost insensible. The Baron most kindly supported me with one arm—and with the other strove to make way. The men even pushed with rudeness by me. Ton-hausen expostulated and raved by turns: at length he drew his sword, which terrified me to such a degree, that I was sinking to the earth—and really gave myself up totally to despair. The efforts he made at last gained us a passage to the great door—and, without waiting to ask any questions, he put me into a coach that happened to be near: as to my carriage, it was not to be found—or probably some others had used the same freedom with that we had now with one unknown to us.

As soon as we were seated, Ton-hausen expressed his joy in the strongest terms, that we had so happily escaped any danger. I was so weak, that he thought it necessary to support me in his arms; and though I had no cause to complain of any freedom in his manner, yet the warmth of his expression, joined to my foregoing fright, had such an effect on me, that, though I did not wholly lose my senses, I thought I was dying—I never fainted in my life before; to my ignorance, then, must be imputed my fears and foolish behaviour in consequence. "Oh! carry me somewhere," cried I, gasping; "do not let me die here! for God's sake, do not let me die in the coach!"

"My angel," said the Baron, "do not give way to such imaginary terrors. I will let down the glasses—you will be better presently." But finding my head, which I could no longer support, drop on his shoulder, and a cold damp bedew my face, he gave a loose to his tenderness, which viewed itself in his attention to my welfare. He pressed me almost frantic to his bosom, called on me in the most endearing terms. He thought me insensible. He knew not I could hear the effusions of his heart. Oh! Louisa, he could have no idea how they sunk in mine. Among the rest, these broken sentences were distinct, "Oh! my God! what will become of me! Dearest, most loved of women, how is my heart distracted! And shall I lose thee thus? Oh! how shall I support thy loss! Too late found—ever beloved of my soul! Thy Henry will die with thee!" Picture to yourself, my Louisa, what were my sensations at this time. I have no words to express them—or, if I could, they would be unfit for me to express. The sensations themselves ought not to have found a passage in my bosom. I will drive them away, Louisa, I will not give them harbour. I no longer knew what was become of me: I became dead to all appearance. The Baron, in a state of distraction, called to the coachman, to stop any where, where I could receive assistance. Fortunately we were near a chemist's. Ton-hausen carried me in his arms to a back room—and, by the application of drops, &c. I was restored to life. I found the Baron kneeling at my feet, and supporting me. It was a long time before he could make me sensible where I was. My situation in a strange place, and the singularity of our appearance, affected me extremely—I burst into tears, and entreated the Baron to get me a chair to convey me home. "A chair! Lady Stanley; will not you then permit me to attend you home? Would you place yourself under the protection of two strangers, rather than allow me that honour?"

"Ah! excuse me, Baron," I answered, "I hardly know what I said. Do as you please, only let me go home." And yet, Louisa, I felt a dread on going into the same carriage with him. I thought myself extremely absurd and foolish; yet I could not get the better of my apprehensions. How vain they were! Never could any man behave with more delicate attention, or more void of that kind of behaviour which might have justified my fears. His despair had prompted the discovery of his sentiments. He thought me incapable of hearing the secret of his soul; and it was absurd to a degree for me, by an unnecessary circumspection, to let him see I had unhappily been a participater of his secret. There was, however, an aukward consciousness in my conduct towards him, I could not divest myself of. I wished to be at home. I even expressed my impatience to be alone. He sighed, but made no remonstrances against my childish behaviour, though his pensive manner made it obvious he saw and felt it. Thank God! at last we got home. "It would be rude," said he, "after your ladyship has so frequently expressed your wish to be alone, to obtrude my company a moment longer than absolutely necessary; but, if you will allow me to remain in your drawing-room till I hear you are a little recovered, I shall esteem it a favour."

"I have not a doubt of being much better," I returned, "when I have had a little rest. I am extremely indebted to you for the care you have taken. I must repay it, by desiring you to have some consideration for yourself: rest will be salutary for both; and I hope to return you a message in the morning, that I am not at all the worse for this disagreeable adventure. Adieu, Baron, take my advice." He bowed, and cast on me such a look—He seemed to correct himself.—Oh! that look! what was not expressed in it! Away, away, all such remembrances.

The consequences, however, were not to end here. I soon found other circumstances which I had not thought on. In short my dear Louisa, I must now discover to you a secret, which I had determined to keep some time longer at least. Not even Sir William knew of it. I intended to have surprized you all; but this vile play-house affair put an end to my hopes, and very near to my life. For two days, my situation was very critical. As soon as the danger was over, I recovered apace. The Baron was at my door several times in the day, to enquire after me. And Win said, who once saw him, that he betrayed more anxiety than any one beside.

Yesterday was the first of my seeing any company. The Baron's name was the first announced. The sound threw me into a perturbation I laboured to conceal. Sir William presented him to me. I received his compliment with an aukward confusion. My embarrassment was imputed, by my husband, to the simple bashfulness of a country rustic— a bashfulness he generally renders more insupportable by the ridiculous light he chuses to make me appear in, rather than encouraging in me a better opinion of myself, which, sometimes, he does me the honour of saying, I ought to entertain. The Baron had taken my hand in the most respectful manner. I suffered him to lift it to his lips. "Is it thus," said Sir William, "you thank your deliverer? Had I been in your place, Julia, I should have received my champion with open arms—at least have allowed him a salute. But the Baron is a modest young man. Come, I will set you the example."—Saying which, he caught me in his arms, and kissed me. I was extremely chagrined, and felt my cheeks glow, not only with shame, but anger. "You are too violent, Sir William," said I very gravely. "You have excessively disconcerted me." "I will allow," said he, "I might have been too eager: now you shall experience the difference between the extatic ardor of an adoring husband, and the cool complacency of a friend. Nay, nay," continued he, seeing a dissenting look, "you must reward the Baron, or I shall think you either very prudish, or angry with me." Was there ever such inconsiderate behaviour? Ton-hausen seemed fearful of offending—yet not willing to lose so fair an opportunity. Oh! Louisa, as Sir William said, I *did* experience a difference. But Sir William is no adoring husband. The Baron's lips trembled as they touched mine; and I felt an emotion, to which I was hitherto a stranger.

I was doomed, however, to receive still more shocks. On the Baron's saying he was happy to see me so well recovered after my fright, and hoped I had found no disagreeable consequence—"No disagreeable consequence!" repeated Sir William, with the most unfeeling air; "Is the loss of a son and heir then nothing? It may be repaired," he continued, laughing, "to be sure; but I am extremely disappointed." Are you not enraged with your brother-in-law, Louisa? How indelicate! I really could no longer support these mortifications, though I knew I should mortally offend him; I could not help leaving the room in tears; nor would I return to it, till summoned by the arrival of other company. I did not recover my spirits the whole evening.

Good God! how different do men appear sometimes from themselves! I often am induced to ask myself, whether I really gave my hand to the man I now see in my husband. Ah! how is he changed! I reflect for hours together on the unaccountableness of his conduct. How he is carried away by the giddy multitude. He is swayed by every passion, and the last is the ruling one—

"Is every thing by starts, and nothing long."

A time may come, when he may see his folly; I hope, before it be too late to repair it. Why should such a man marry? Or why did fate lead him to our innocent retreat? Oh! why did I foolishly mistake a rambling disposition, and a transient liking, for a permanent attachment? But why do I run on thus? Dear Louisa, you will think me far gone in a phrenzy. But, believe me, I will ever deserve your tender affection.

JULIA STANLEY.

LETTER XV.

TO Lady STANLEY.

Good heavens! what a variety of emotions has your last letter excited in my breast! Surely, my Julia did not give it a second perusal! I can make allowance for the expressions of gratitude which you (in a manner lavish, not) bestow on the Baron. But oh! beware, my beloved sister, that your gratitude becomes not too warm; that sentiment, so laudable when properly placed, should it be an introduction to what my fears and tenderness apprehend, would change to the most impious.—You already perceive a visible difference between him and your husband—I assert, no woman ought to make a comparison,—'tis dangerous, 'tis fatal. Sir William was the man of your choice;—it is true you were young; but still you ought to respect your choice as sacred.—You are still young; and although you may have seen more of the world, I doubt your sentiments are little mended by your experience. The knowledge of the world—at least so it appears to me—is of no further use than to bring one acquainted with vice, and to be less shocked at the idea of it. Is this then a knowledge to which we should wish to attain?—Ah! believe me, it had been better for you to have blushed unseen, and lost your sweetness in the desart air, than to have, in *the busy haunts of men*, hazarded the privation of *that peace which goodness bosoms ever.* Think what I suffer; and, constrained to treasure up my anxious fears in my own bosom, I have no one to whom I can vent my griefs: and indeed to whom could I impart the terrors which fill my soul, when I reflect on the dangers by which my sister, the darling of my affections, is surrounded? Oh, Julia! you know how fatally I have experienced the interest a beloved object has in the breast of a tender woman; how ought we then to guard against the admission of a passion destructive to our repose, even in its most innocent and harmless state, while we are single!—But how much more should *you* keep a strict watch over every outlet of the heart, lest it should fall a prey to the insidious enemy;—you respect his silence;—you pity his sufferings.—Reprobate respect!—abjure pity!—they are both in your circumstances dangerous; and a well-experienced writer has observed, more women have been ruined by pity, than have fallen a sacrifice to appetite and passion. Pity is a kindred virtue, and from the innocence and complacency of her appearance, we suspect no ill; but dangers inexplicable lurk beneath the tear that trembles in her eye; and, without even knowing that we do so, we make a fatal transfer to our utter and inevitable disadvantage. From having the power of bestowing compassion, we become objects of it from others, though too frequently, instead of receiving it, we find ourselves loaded with the censure of the world. We look into our own bosoms for consolation: alas! it is flown with our innocence; and in its room we feel the sharpest stings of self-reproof. My Julia, my tears obliterate each mournful passage of my pen.

LOUISA GRENVILLE.

LETTER XVI.

TO Miss GRENVILLE.

Enough, my dearest sister, enough have you suffered through your unremitted tenderness to your Julia;—yet believe her, while she vows to the dear bosom of friendship, no action of her's shall call a blush on your cheek. Good God! what a wretch should I be, if I could abuse such sisterly love! if, after such friendly admonitions, enforced with so much moving eloquence, your Julia should degenerate from her birth, and forget those lessons of virtue early inculcated by the best of fathers! If, after all these, she should suffer herself to be immersed in the vortex of folly and vice, what would she not deserve! Oh! rest assured, my dearest dear Louisa, be satisfied, your sister cannot be so vile,—remember the same blood flows through our veins; one parent stock we sprang from; nurtured by one hand; listening at the same time to the same voice of reason; learning the same pious lesson—why then these apprehensions of my degeneracy? Trust me, Louisa, I will not deceive you; and God grant I may never deceive myself! The wisest of men has said, "the heart of man is deceitful

41

above all things." I however will strictly examine mine; I will search into it narrowly; at present the search is not painful; I have nothing to reproach myself with; I have, I hope, discharged my filial and fraternal duties; my matrimonial ones are inviolate: I have studied the temper of Sir William, in hopes I should discover a rule for my actions; but how can I form a system from one so variable as he is? Would to heaven he was more uniform! or that he would suffer himself to be guided by his own understanding, and not by the whim or caprice of others so much inferior to himself! All this I have repeated frequently to you, together with my wish to leave London, and the objects with which I am daily surrounded.—Does such a wish look as if I was improperly attached to the world, or any particular person in it? You are too severe, my love, but when I reflect that your rigidity proceeds from your unrivaled attachment, I kiss the rod of my chastisement;—I long to fold my dear lecturer in my arms, and convince her, that one, whose heart is filled with the affection that glows in mine, can find no room for any sentiment incompatible with virtue, of which she is the express image. Adieu!

JULIA STANLEY.

LETTER XVII.

To Miss GRENVILLE.

If thy Julia falls, my beloved sister, how great will be her condemnation! With such supports, and I hope I may add with an inward rectitude of mind, I think she can never deviate from the right path. You see, my Louisa, that not you alone are interested in my well-doing. I have a secret, nay I may say, celestial friend and monitor,—a friend it certainly is, though unknown;—all who give good counsel must be my true and sincere friends. From whom I have received it, I know not; but it shall be my study to merit the favour of this earthly or heavenly conductor through the intricate mazes of life. I will no longer keep you in ignorance of my meaning, but without delay will copy for you a letter I received this morning; the original I have too much veneration for to part with, even to you, who are dearer to me than almost all the world beside.——

THE LETTER.

"I cannot help anticipating the surprize your ladyship will be under, from receiving a letter from an unknown hand; nor will the signature contribute to develop the cloud behind which I chuse to conceal myself.

My motives, I hope, will extenuate the boldness of my task; and I rely likewise on the amiable qualities you so eminently possess, to pardon the temerity of any one who shall presume to criticise the conduct of one of the most lovely of God's works.

I feel for you as a man, a friend, or, to sum up all, a guardian angel. I see you on the brink of a steep precipice. I shudder at the danger which you are not sensible of. You will wonder at my motive, and the interest I take in your concerns.—It is from my knowledge of the goodness of your heart: were you less amiable than you are, you would be below my solicitude; I might be charmed with you as a woman, but I should not venerate you;—nay, should possibly—enchanted as every one must be with your personal attractions, join with those who seek to seduce you to their own purposes. The sentiments I profess for you are such as a tender father would feel—such as your own excellent father cherishes; but they are accompanied by a warmth which can only be equalled by their purity; such sentiments shall I ever experience while you continue to deserve them, and every service in my power shall be exerted in your favour. I have long wished for an opportunity of expressing to you the tender care I take in your conduct through life. I now so sensibly feel the necessity of apprizing you of the dangers which surround you, that I wave all forms, and thus abruptly introduce myself to your acquaintance—unknown, indeed, to you, but knowing you well, reading your thoughts, and seeing the secret motives of all your actions. Yes, Julia, I have watched you through life. Nay, start not, I have never seen any action of your's but what had virtue for its guide.—But to remain pure and uncontaminated in this vortex of vice, requires the utmost strength and exertion of virtue. To avoid vice, it is necessary to know its colour and complexion; and in this age, how many various shapes it assumes! my task shall be to point them out to you, to shew you the traps, the snares, and pitfalls, which the unwary too frequently sink into;—to lead you by the hand through those intricate paths beset with quicksands and numberless dangers;—to direct your eyes to such objects as you may with safety contemplate, and induce you to shut them for ever against such as may by their dire fascination intice you to evil;—to conduct you to those endless joys hereafter, which are to be the reward of the virtuous; and to have myself the ineffable delight of partaking them with you, where no rival shall interrupt my felicity.

I am a Rosicrusian by principle; I need hardly tell you, they are a sect of philosophers, who by a life of virtue and self-denial have obtained an heavenly intercourse with aërial beings;—as my internal knowledge of you (to use the expression) is in consequence of my connexion with the Sylphiad tribe, I have assumed the title of my familiar counsellor. This, however, is but as a preface to what I mean to say to you;—I have hinted, I knew you well;—when I thus expressed myself, it should be understood, I spoke in the person of the Sylph, which I shall occasionally do, as it will be writing with more perspicuity in the first instance; and, as he is employed by me, I may, without the appearance of robbery, safely appropriate to myself the knowledge he gains.

Every human being has a guardian angel; my skill has discovered your's; my power has made him obedient to my will; I have a right to avail myself of the intelligences he gains; and by him I have learnt every thing that has passed since your birth;—what your future fortune is to be, even he cannot tell; his view is circumscribed to a small point of time; he only can tell what will be the consequence of taking this or that step, but your free-agency prevents his impelling you to act otherwise than as you see fit. I move upon a more enlarged sphere; he tells me what will happen; and as I see the remote, as well as immediate consequence, I shall, from time to time, give you my advice.—Advice, however, when asked, is seldom adhered to; but when given voluntarily, the receiver has no obligation to follow it.—I shall in a moment discover how this is received by you; and your deviation from the rules I shall prescribe will be a hint for me to withdraw my counsel where it is not acceptable. All that then will remain for me, will be to deplore your too early initiation in a vicious world, where to escape unhurt or uncontaminated is next to a miracle.

I said, I should soon discover whether my advice would be taken in the friendly part it is offered: I shall perceive it the next time I have the happiness of beholding you, and I see you every day; I am never one moment absent from you in idea, and in my *mind's eye* I see you each moment; only while I conceal myself from you, can I be of service to you;—press not then to discover who I am; but be convinced—nay, I shall take every opportunity to convince you, that I am the most sincere and disinterested of your friends; I am a friend to your soul, my Julia, and I flatter myself mine is congenial with your's.

I told you, you were surrounded with dangers; the greatest perhaps comes from the quarter least suspected; and for that very reason, because, where no harm is expected, no guard is kept. Against such a man as Lord Biddulph, a watchful centinel is planted at every avenue. I caution you not against him; there you are secure; no temptation lies in that path, no precipice lurks beneath those footsteps. You never can fall, unless your heart takes part with the tempter; and I am morally certain a man of Lord Biddulph's cast can never touch your's; and yet it is of him you seem most apprehensive. Ask yourself, is it not because he has the character of a man of intrigue? Do you not feel within your own breast a repugnance to the assiduities he at all times takes pains to shew you? Without doubt, Lord Biddulph has designs upon you;—and few men approach you without. Oh! Julia, it is difficult for the most virtuous to behold you daily, and suppress those feelings your charms excite. In a breast inured to too frequent indulgence in vicious courses, your beauty will be a consuming fire, but in a soul whose delight is moral rectitude, it will be a cherishing flame, that animates, not destroys. But how few the latter! And how are you to distinguish the insidious betrayer from the open violator. To you they are equally culpable; but only one can be fatal. Ask your own heart—the criterion, by which I would have you judge—ask your own heart, which is intitled to your detestation most; the man who boldly attacks you, and by his threats plainly tells you he is a robber; or the one, who, under the semblance of imploring your charity, deprives you of your most valued property? Will it admit of a doubt? Make the application: examine yourself, and I conjure you examine your acquaintance; but be cautious whom you trust. Never make any of your male visitors the *confidant* of any thing which passes between yourself and husband. This can never be done without a manifest breach of modest decorum. Have I not said enough for the present? Yet let me add thus much, to secure to myself your confidence. I wish you to place an unlimited one in me; continue to do so, while I continue to merit it; and by this rule you shall judge of my merit—The moment you discover that I urge you to any thing improper, or take advantage of my self-assumed office, and insolently prescribe when I should only point out, or that I should seem to degrade others in your eyes, and particularly your husband, believe me to be an impostor, and treat me as such; disregard my sinister counsel, and consign me to that scorn and derision I shall so much deserve. But, while virtue inspires my pen, afford me your attention; and may that God, whom I attest to prove my truth, ever be indulgent to you, and for ever and ever protect you! So prays

Your SYLPH."

Who can it be, my Louisa, who takes this friendly interest in my welfare? It cannot be Lady Melford; the address bespeaks it to be a man; but what man is the question; one too who sees me every day: it cannot be the Baron, for he seems to say, Ton-hausen is a more dangerous person than Lord Biddulph. But why do I perplex myself with guessing? Of what consequence is it who is my friend, since I am convinced he is sincere. Yes! thou friendly monitor, I will be directed by thee! I shall now act with more confidence, as my Sylph tells me he will watch over and apprize me of every danger. I hope his task will not be a difficult one; for, though ignorant, I am not obstinate—on the contrary, even Sir William, whom I do not suspect of flattery, allows me to be extremely docile. I am, my beloved Louisa, most affectionately, your's,

JULIA STANLEY.

LETTER XVIII.

TO Lady STANLEY.

Blessed, forever blessed, be the friendly monitor! Oh! my Julia, how fortunate are you, thus to become the care of heaven, which has raised you up a guide, with all the dispositions, but with more enlarged abilities than thy poor Louisa!—And much did you stand in need of a guide, my sister: be not displeased that I write thus. But why do I deprecate your anger? you, who were ever so good, so tender, and indulgent to the apprehensions of your friends. Yet, indeed, my dear, you are reprehensible in many passages of your letters, particularly the last. You say, you cannot suspect Sir William of flattery; would you wish him to be a flatterer? Did you think him such, when he swore your charms had kindled the brightest flames in his bosom? No, Julia, you gave him credit then for all he said; but, allowing him to be changed, are you quite the same? No; with all the tenderness of my affection, I cannot but think you are altered since your departure from the vale of innocent simplicity. It is the knowledge of the world which has deprived you of those native charms, above all others. Why are you not resolute with Sir William, to leave London? Our acquiescence in matters which are hurtful both to our principles and constitution is a weakness. Obedience to the will of those who seek to seduce us from the right road is no longer a virtue; but a reprehensible participation of our leader's faults. Be assured, your husband will listen to your persuasive arguments. Exert all your eloquence: and, Heaven, I beseech thee, grant success to the undertaking of the dearest of all creatures to,

LOUISA GRENVILLE.

LETTER XIX.

To Miss GRENVILLE.

Ah! my dear Louisa, you are single, and know not the trifling influence a woman has over her husband in this part of the world. Had I the eloquence of Demosthenes or Cicero, it would fail. Sir William is wedded—I was going to say, to the pleasures of this bewitching place. I corrected myself in the instant; for, was he wedded, most probably he would be as tired of it as he is of his wife. If I was to be resolute in my determination to leave London, I must go by myself and, notwithstanding such a circumstance might accord with his wishes, I do not chuse to begin the separation. All the determination I can make is, to strive to act so as to deserve a better fate than has fallen to my lot. And, beset as I am on all sides, I shall have some little merit in so doing. But you, my love, ought not to blame me so severely as you do. Indeed, Louisa, if you knew the slights I hourly receive from my husband, and the conviction which I have of his infidelity, you would not criticize my expressions so harshly. I could add many more things, which would justify me in the eye of the world, were I less cautious than I am; but his failings would not extenuate any on my side.

Would you believe that any man, who wished to preserve the virtue of his wife, would introduce her to the acquaintance and protection of a woman with whom he had had an intrigue? What an opinion one must have in future of such a man! I am indebted for this piece of intelligence to Lord Biddulph. I am grateful for the information, though I despise the motive which induced him. Yes, Louisa! Lady Anne Parker is even more infamous than Lady Besford—Nay, Lord Biddulph offered to convince me they still had their private assignations. My pride, I own it, was more wounded than my love, from this discovery, as it served to confirm me in my idea, that Sir William never had a proper regard for me; but that he married me merely because he could obtain me on no other terms. Yet, although I was sensibly pained with this news, I endeavoured to conceal my emotions from the disagreeable prying eyes of my informer. I affected to disbelieve his assertions, and ridiculed his ill-policy in striving to found his merit on such base and detestable grounds. He had too much *effronterie* to be chagrined with my raillery. I therefore assumed a more serious air; and plainly told him, no man would dare to endeavour to convince a woman of the infidelity of her husband, but from the basest and most injurious motives; and, as such, was intitled to my utmost contempt; that, from my soul, I despised both the information and informer, and should give him proofs of it, if ever he should again have the confidence to repeat his private histories to the destruction of the peace and harmony of families. To extenuate his fault, he poured forth a most elaborate speech, abounding with flattery; and was proceeding to convince me of his adoration; but I broke off the discourse, by assuring him, "I saw through his scheme from the first; but the man, who sought to steal my heart from my husband, must pursue a very different course from that he had followed; as it was very unlikely I should withdraw my affections from one unworthy object, to place them on another infinitely worse." He attempted a justification, which I would not allow him opportunity of going on with, as I left the room abruptly. However, his Lordship opened my eyes, respecting the conduct of Lady Anne. I have mentioned, in a former letter, that she used to give hints about my husband. I am convinced it was her jealousy, which prompted her to give me, from time to time, little anecdotes of Sir William's *amours*. But ought I to pardon him for introducing me to such a woman? Oh! Louisa! am I to blame, if I no longer respect such a man?

Yesterday I had a most convincing proof, that there are a sort of people, who have all the influence over the heart of a man which a virtuous wife ought to have—but seldom has: by some accident, a hook of Sir William's waistcoat caught hold of the trimming of my sleeve. He had just received a message, and, being in a hurry to disengage himself, lifted up the flap of the waistcoat eagerly, and snatched it away; by which means, two or three papers dropped out of the pocket; he seemed not to know it, but flew out of the room, leaving them on the ground. I picked them up but, I take heaven to witness, without the least intention or thought of seeing the contents—when one being open, and seeing my name written in a female hand, and the signature of *Lucy Gardener*, my curiosity was excited to the greatest degree—yet I had a severe conflict first with myself; but *femaleism* prevailed, and I examined the contents, which were as follow, for I wrote them down:

"Is it thus, Sir William, you repay my tenderness in your favour? Go, thou basest of all wretches! am I to be made continually a sacrifice to every new face that strikes thy inconstant heart? If I was contented to share you with a wife, and calmly acquiesced, do not imagine I shall rest in peace till you have given up Lady Anne. How have you sworn you would see her no more! How have you falsified your oath! you spent several hours *tête à tête* with her yesterday. Deny it not. I could tear myself to pieces when I reflect, that I left Biddulph, who adored me, whose whole soul was devoted to me,—to be slighted thus by you.—Oh! that Lady Stanley knew of your baseness! yet she is only your wife. Her virtue may console her for the infidelity of her husband; but I have sacrificed every thing, and how am I repaid! Either be mine alone, or never again approach

LUCY GARDENER."

The other papers were of little consequence. I deliberated some time what I should do with this precious *morçeau*, at last I resolved to burn it, and give the remainder, with as much composure as possible, to Sir William's *valet*, to restore to his master. I fancied he would hardly challenge me about the *billet*, as he is the most careless man in the universe. You will perceive there is another case for Lord Biddulph seeking to depreciate my husband. He has private revenge to gratify, for the loss of his mistress. Oh! what wretches are these men! Is the whole world composed of such?—No! even in this valley of vice I see some exceptions; some, who do honour to the species to which they belong. But I must not whisper to myself their perfections; and it is less dangerous for me to dwell upon the vices of the one than the virtues of the other. Adieu!

JULIA STANLEY.

LETTER XX.

To Miss GRENVILLE.

To keep my mind constantly employed upon different objects, and prevent my thoughts attaching themselves to improper ones, I have lately attended the card-tables. From being an indifferent spectator of the various fashionable games, I became an actor in them; and at length play proved very agreeable. As I was an utter novice at games of skill, those of chance presented themselves as the best. At first I risked only trifles; but, by little and little, my party encroached upon the rules I had laid down, and I could no longer avoid playing their stake. But I have done with play for ever. It is no longer the innocent amusement I thought it; and I must find out some other method of spending my time—since this might in the end be destructive.

The other night, at a party, we made up a set at bragg, which was my favourite game. After various vicissitudes, I lost every shilling I had in my pocket; and, being a broken-merchant, sat silently by the table. Every body was profuse in the offers of accommodating me with cash; but I refused to accept their contribution. Lord Biddulph, whom you know to be justly my aversion, was very earnest; but I was equally peremptory. However, some time after, I could not resist the entreaty of Baron Ton-hausen, who, in the genteelest manner, intreated me to make use of his purse for the evening; with great difficulty he prevailed on me to borrow ten guineas—and was once more set up. Fortune now took a favourable turn, and when the party broke up, I had repaid the Baron, replaced my original stock, and brought off ninety-five guineas. Flushed with success, and more attached than ever to the game; I invited the set to meet the day after the next at my house. I even counted the hours till the time arrived. Rest departed from my eye-lids, and I felt all the eagerness of expectation.

About twelve o'clock of the day my company were to meet, I received a pacquet, which I instantly knew to be from my ever-watchful Sylph. I will give you the transcript.

TO Lady STANLEY.

"I should be unworthy the character I have assumed, if my pen was to lie dormant while I am sensible of the unhappy predilection which your ladyship has discovered for gaming. Play, under proper restrictions,—which however in this licentious town can never take place—may not be altogether prejudicial to the morals of those who engage in it for trifling sums. Your Ladyship finds it not practicable always to follow your own inclinations, even in that particular. The triumphant joy which sparkled in your eyes when success crowned your endeavours, plainly indicated you took no common satisfaction in the game. You, being a party so deeply interested, could not discover the same appearances of joy and triumph in the countenances of some of those you played with; nor, had you made the observation, could you have guessed the cause. It has been said, by those who will say any thing to carry on an argument which cannot be supported by reason, that cards prevent company falling upon topics of scandal; it is a scandal to human nature, that it should want such a resource from so hateful and detested a vice. But be it so. It can only be so while the sum played for is of too trifling a concern to excite the anxiety which avaricious minds experience; and every one is more or less avaricious who gives up his time to cards.

If your ladyship could search into the causes of the unhappiness which prevails in too many families in this metropolis, you would find the source to be gaming either on the one

46

side or the other. Whatever appears licentious or vicious in men, in your sex becomes so in a tenfold degree. The passionate exclamation—the half-uttered imprecation, and the gloomy pallidness of the losing gamester, ill accords with the female delicacy. But the evil rests not here. When a woman has been drawn-in to lose larger sums than her allowance can defray— even if she can submit to let her trades-people suffer from her extravagant folly;—it most commonly happens, that they part with their honour to discharge the account; at least, they are always suspected. Would not the consideration of being obnoxious to such suspicion be sufficient to deter any woman of virtue from running the hazard? You made a firm resolution of not borrowing from the purses of any of the gentlemen who wished to serve you; you for some time kept that resolution; but, remember, it lasted no longer than when one particular person made the offer. Was it your wish to oblige him? or did the desire of gaming operate in that instant more powerful than in any other? Whatever was your motive, the party immediately began to form hopes of you; hopes, which, being founded in your weakness, you may be certain were not to your advantage.

To make a more forcible impression on your mind, your Ladyship must allow me to lay before you a piece of private history, in which a noble family of this town was deeply involved. The circumstances are indubitable facts—their names I shall conceal under fictitious ones. A few years since, Lord and Lady D. were the happiest of pairs in each other. Love had been the sole motive of their union; and love presided over every hour of their lives. Their pleasures were mutual, and neither knew an enjoyment, in which the other did not partake. By an unhappy mischance, Lady D. had an attachment to cards—which yet, however, she only looked on as the amusement of an idle hour. Her person was beautiful, and as such made her an object of desire in the eyes of Lord L. Her virtue and affection for her husband would have been sufficient to have damped the hopes of a man less acquainted with the weakness of human nature than Lord L. Had he paid her a more than ordinary attention, he would have awakened her suspicions, and put her on her guard; he therefore pursued another method. He availed himself of her love of play—and would now and then, seemingly by accident, engage her in a party at picquet, which was her favourite game. He contrived to lose trifling sums, to increase her inclination for play. Too fatally he succeeded. Her predilection gathered strength every day. After having been very unsuccessful for some hours at picquet, Lord L. proposed a change of the game; a proposal which Lady D. could not object to, as having won so much of his money. He produced a pair of dice. Luck still ran against him. A generous motive induced Lady D. to offer him his revenge the next evening at her own house. In the morning preceding the destined evening, her lord signified his dislike of gaming with dice; and instanced some families to whom it had proved destructive. Elate, however, with good fortune—and looking on herself engaged in honour to give Lord L. a chance of recovering his losses, she listened not to the hints of her husband, nor did they recur to her thoughts till too late to be of any service to her.

The time so ardently expected by Lord L. now arrived, the devoted time which was to put the long-destined victim into the power of her insidious betrayer. Fortune, which had hitherto favoured Lady D—, now deserted her—in a short time, her adversary reimbursed himself, and won considerably besides. Adversity only rendered her more desperate. She hazarded still larger stakes; every throw, however, was against her; and no otherwise could it be, since his dice were loaded, and which he had the dexterity to change unobserved by her. He lent her money, only to win it back from her; in short, in a few hours, she found herself stripped of all the cash she had in possession, and two thousand five hundred pounds in debt. The disapprobation which her husband had expressed towards dice-playing, and her total inability to discharge this vast demand without his knowledge, contributed to make her distress very great. She freely informed Lord L. she must be his debtor for some time—as she could not think of acquainting Lord D. with her imprudence. He offered to accept of part of her jewels, till it should be convenient to her to pay the whole—or, if she liked it better, to play it off. To the first, she said, she could not consent, as her husband would miss them—and to the last she would by no means agree, since she suffered too much already in her own mind from the imprudent part she had acted, by risking so much more than she ought to have done. He then, approaching her, took her hand in his; and, assuming the utmost tenderness in his air, proceeded to inform her, it was in her power amply to repay the debt, without the knowledge of her husband—and confer the highest obligations upon himself. She earnestly begged an explanation—since there was nothing she would not submit to, rather than incur the censure of so excellent a husband. Without further preface, Lord L. threw himself on his knees before her—and said, "if her heart could not suggest the restitution, which the most ardent of lovers might expect and hope for—he must take the liberty of informing her, that bestowing on him the delightful privilege of an husband was the only means of securing her from the resentment of one." At first, she seemed thunderstruck, and unable to articulate a sentence. When she recovered the use of speech, she asked him what he had seen in her conduct, to induce him to believe she would not submit to any ill consequences which might arise from the just resentment of her husband, rather than not shew her detestation of such an infamous proposal. "Leave me," added she; "leave me," in perfect astonishment at such insolence of behaviour. He immediately rose, with a very different aspect—and holding a paper in his hand, to which she had signed her name in acknowledgment of the debt—"Then, Madam," said he, with the utmost *sang-froid*—"I shall, to-morrow morning, take the liberty of waiting on Lord D. with this." "Stay, my Lord, is it possible you can be so cruel and hard a creditor?—I consent to make over to you my annual allowance, till the whole is discharged." "No, Madam," cried he, shaking his head,—"I cannot consent to any such subterfuges, when you have it in your power to pay this moment." "Would to heaven I had!" answered she.—"Oh, that you have, most abundantly!" said he.—"Consider the hours we have been *tête à tête* together; few people will believe we have spent all the time at play. Your reputation then will suffer; and, believe me while I attest heaven to witness, either you must discharge the debt by blessing me with the possession of your charms, or Lord D. shall be made acquainted with every circumstance. Reflect," continued he, "two thousand five hundred pounds is no small sum, either for your husband to pay, or me to receive.—Come, Madam, it grows late.—In a little time, you will not have it in your power to avail yourself of the alternative. Your husband will soon return and then you may wish in vain that you had yielded to my love, rather than have subjected yourself to my resentment." She condescended to beg of him, on her knees, for a longer time for consideration; but he was inexorable, and at last she fatally consented to her own undoing. The next moment, the horror of her situation, and the sacrifice she had made, rushed on her tortured imagination. "Give me the fatal paper," cried she, wringing her hands in the utmost agony, "give me that paper, for which I have parted with my peace for ever, and leave me. Oh! never let me in future behold you.—What do I say? Ah! rather let my eyes close in everlasting darkness;—they are now unworthy to behold the face of Heaven!" "And do you really imagine, Madam, (all-beautiful as you are) the lifeless half-distracted body, you gave to my arms, a recompence for five-and-twenty hundred pounds?—Have you agreed to your bargain? Is it with tears, sighs, and reluctant struggles, you meet your husband's caresses? Be mine as you are his, and the bond is void—otherwise, I am not such a spendthrift as to throw away thousands for little less than a rape."

"Oh! thou most hateful and perfidious of all monsters! too dearly have I earned my release—Do not then, do not with-hold my right."

"Hush, Madam, hush," cried he with the most provoking coolness, "your raving will but expose you to the ridicule of your domestics. You are at present under too great an agitation of spirits to attend to the calm dictates of reason. I will wait till your ladyship is in a more even temper. When I receive your commands, I will attend them, and hope the time will soon arrive when you will be better disposed to listen to a tender lover who adores you, rather than to seek to irritate a man who has you in his power." Saying which, he broke from her, leaving her in a state of mind, of which you, Madam, I sincerely hope, will never be able to form the slightest idea. With what a weight of woe she stole up into her bed-chamber, unable to bear the eye of her domestic! How fallen in her own esteem, and still bending under the penalty of her bond, as neither prayers nor tears (and nothing else was she able to offer) could obtain the release from the inexorable and cruel Lord L.

How was her anguish increased, when she heard the sound of her Lord's footstep! How did she pray for instant death! To prevent any conversation, she feigned sleep—sleep, which now was banished from her eye-lids. Guilt had driven the idea of rest from her bosom. The morning brought no comfort on its wings—to her the light was painful. She still continued in bed. She framed the resolution of writing to the destroyer of her repose. She rose for that purpose; her letter was couched in terms that would have pierced the bosom of the most obdurate savage. All the favour she intreated was, to spare the best of husbands, and the most amiable and beloved of men, the anguish of knowing how horrid a return she had made, in one fatal moment, for the years of felicity she had tasted with him: again offered her alimony, or even her jewels, to obtain the return of her bond. She did not wish for life. Death was now her only hope;—but she could not support the idea of her husband's being acquainted with her infamy. What advantage could he (Lord L.) propose to himself from the possession of her person, since tears, sighs, and the same reluctance, would still accompany every repetition of her crime—as her heart, guilty as it now was, and unworthy as she had rendered herself of his love, was, and ever must be, her husband's only. In short, she urged every thing likely to soften him in her favour. But this fatal and circumstantial disclosure of her guilt and misfortunes was destined to be conveyed by another messenger than she designed. Lord D—, having that evening expected some one to call on him, on his return enquired, "if any one had been there." He was answered, "Only Lord L." "Did he stay?" "Yes, till after eleven."—Without thinking of any particularity in this, he went up to bed. He discovered his wife was not asleep—to pretend to be so, alarmed him. He heard her frequently sigh; and, when she thought him sunk in that peaceful slumber she had forfeited, her distress increased. His anxiety, however, at length gave way to fatigue; but with the morning his doubts and fears returned; yet, how far from guessing the true cause! He saw a letter delivered to a servant with some caution, whom he followed, and insisted on knowing for whom it was intended. The servant, ignorant of the contents, and not at all suspicious he was doing an improper thing, gave it up to his Lordship. Revenge lent him wings, and he flew to the base destroyer of his conjugal happiness.—You may suppose what followed.—In an hour Lord D. was brought home a lifeless corpse. Distraction seized the unhappy wife; and the infamous cause of this dreadful calamity fled his country. He was too hardened, however, in guilt, to feel much remorse from this catastrophe, and made no scruple of relating the circumstances of it.

To you, Madam, I surely need make no comment. Nor do I need say any more to deter you from so pernicious a practice as gaming. Suspect a Lord L. in every one who would induce you to play; and remember they are the worst seducers, and the most destructive enemies, who seek to gain your heart by ruining your principles.

Adieu, Madam! Your ever-watchful angel will still hover over you. And may that God, who formed both you and me, enable me to give you good counsel, and dispose your heart to follow it!

Your faithful SYLPH."

Lady STANLEY in Continuation

Alas, my Louisa! what would become of your Julia without this respectable monitor? Would to heaven I knew who he was! or, how I might consult him upon some particular circumstances! I examine the features of my guests in hopes to discover my secret friend; but my senses are perplexed and bewildered in the fruitless search. It is certainly a weakness; but, absolutely, my anxiety to obtain this knowledge has an effect on my health and spirits; my thoughts and whole attention rest solely on this subject. I call it a weakness, because I ought to remain satisfied with the advantages which accrue to me from this correspondence, without being inquisitively curious who it may be; yet I wish to ask some questions. I am uneasy, and perhaps in some instances my Sylph would solve my doubts; not that I think him endued with a preternatural knowledge; yet I hardly know what to think neither. However, I bless and praise the goodness of God, that has raised me up a friend in a place where I may turn my eyes around and see myself deprived of every other.

Even my protector—he who has sworn before God and man;—but you, Louisa, will reprehend my indiscreet expressions. In my own bosom, then, shall the sad repository be. Adieu!

JULIA STANLEY.

LETTER XXI.

TO Miss GRENVILLE.

49

As you have entertained an idea that Sir William could not be proof against any occasional exertion of my eloquence, I will give you a sketch of a matrimonial *tête à tête*, though it may tend to subvert your opinion of both parties.

Yesterday morning I was sitting in my dressing-room, when Sir William, who had not been at home all night, entered it: He looked as if he had not been in bed; his hair disordered; and, upon the whole, as forlorn a figure as you ever beheld, I was going to say; but you can form very little idea of these rakes of fashion after a night spent as they usually spend it. To my inquiry after his health, he made a very slight or rather peevish answer; and flung himself into a chair, with both hands in his waistcoat pockets, and his eyes fixed on the fire, before which he had placed himself. As he seemed in an ill-humour, and I was unconscious of having given him cause, I was regardless of the consequences, and pursued my employment, which was looking over and settling some accounts relative to my own expences. He continued his posture in the strictest silence for near a quarter of an hour; a silence I did not feel within myself the least inclination to break through: at last he burst forth into this pretty soliloquy.

"Damn it; sure there never was a more unfortunate dog than I am! Every thing goes against me. And then to be so situated too!" Unpromising as the opening sounded, I thought it would be better to bear a part in the conversation.—"If it is not impertinent, Sir William," said I, "may I beg to know what occasions the distress you seem to express? or at least inform me if it is in my power to be of service to you."—"No, no, you can be of no use to me—though," continued he, "you are in part the cause."—"I the cause!—for God's sake, how?" cried I, all astonishment. "Why, if your father had not taken advantage of my cursed infatuation for you, I should not have been distressed in pecuniary matters by making so large a settlement."

"A cursed infatuation! do you call it? Sure, that is a harsh expression! Oh! how wretched would my poor father feel, could he imagine the affection which he fancied his unhappy daughter had inspired you with, would be stiled by yourself, and to *her* face, *a cursed infatuation!*" Think you, Louisa, I was not pained to the soul? Too sure I was—I could not prevent tears from gushing forth. Sir William saw the effect his cruel speech had on me; he started from his seat, and took my hand in his. A little resentment, and a thousand other reasons, urged me to withdraw it from his touch.—"Give me your hand, Julia," cried he, drawing his chair close to mine, and looking at my averted face—"give me your hand, my dear, and pardon the rashness of my expressions; I did not mean to use such words;—I recall them, my love: it was ungenerous and false in me to arraign your father's conduct. I would have doubled and trebled the settlement, to have gained you; I would, by heavens! my Julia.—Do not run from me in disgust; come, come, you shall forgive me a thoughtless expression, uttered in haste, but seriously repented of."

"You cannot deny your sentiments, Sir William; nor can I easily forget them. What my settlement is, as I never wished to out-live you, so I never wished to know how ample it was. Large I might suppose it to be, from the conviction that you never pay any regard to consequences to obtain your desires, let them be what they will. I was the whim of the day; and if you have paid too dearly for the trifling gratification, I am sorry for it; heartily sorry for it, indeed, Sir William. You found me in the lap of innocence, and in the arms of an indulgent parent; happy, peaceful, and serene; would to heaven you had left me there!" I could not proceed; my tears prevented my utterance. "Pshaw!" cried Sir William, clapping his fingers together, and throwing his elbow over the chair, which turned his face nearer me, "how ridiculous this is! Why, Julia, I am deceived in you; I did not think you had so much resentment in your composition. You ought to make some allowance for the *derangement* of my affairs. My hands are tied by making a larger settlement than my present fortune would admit; and I cannot raise money on my estate, because I have no child, and it is entailed on my uncle, who is the greatest curmudgeon alive. Reflect on all these obstacles to my release from some present exigencies; and do not be so hard-hearted and inexorable to the prayers and intreaties of your husband."—During the latter part of this speech, he put his arm round my waist, and drew me almost on his knees, striving by a thousand little caresses to make me pardon and smile on him; but, Louisa, caresses, which I now know came not from the heart, lose the usual effect on me; yet I would not be, as he said, inexorable. I therefore told him, I would no longer think of any thing he would wish me to forget.—With the utmost appearance of tenderness he took my handkerchief, and dried my eyes; laying his cheek close to mine, and pressing my hands with warmth,—in short, acting over the same farce as (once) induced me to believe I had created the most permanent flame in his bosom. I could not bear the reflection that he should suffer from his former attachment to me; and I had hopes that my generosity might rouze him from his lethargy, and save him from the ruin which was likely to involve him. I told him, "I would with the greatest chearfulness relinquish any part of my settlement, if by that means he could be extricated from his present and future difficulties."—"Why, to be sure, a part of it would set me to rights as to the present; but as for the future, I cannot look into futurity, Julia."—"I wish you could, Sir William, and reflect in time."—"Reflect! Oh, that is so *outré!* I hate reflection. Reflection cost poor D—r his life the other day; he, like me, could not bear reflection."

"I tremble to hear you thus lightly speak of that horrid event. The more so, as I too much fear the same fatal predilection has occasioned your distress: but may the chearfulness with which I resign my future dependence awaken in you a sense of your present situation, and secure you from fresh difficulties!"

"Well said, my little *monitress!* why you are quite an *orator* too. But you shall find I can follow your lead, and be *just* at least, if not so generous as yourself. I would not for the world accept the whole of your jointure. I do not want it; and if I had as much as I could raise on it, perhaps I might not be much richer for it. *Riches make to themselves wings, and fly away,* Julia. There is a sentence for you. Did you think your rattle-pated husband had ever read the book of books from whence that sentence is drawn?" I really had little patience to hear him run on in this ludicrous and trifling manner. What an argument of his insensibility! To stop him, I told him, I thought we had better not lose time, but have the writings prepared, which would enable me to do my duty as an obedient wife, and enable him to pay his debts like a man of honour and integrity; and then he need not fear his treasure flying away, since it would be laid up where neither thieves could break through, or rust destroy.

The writings are preparing, to dispose of an estate which was settled on me; it brings in at present five hundred a year; which I find is but a quarter of my jointure. Ah! would to heaven he would take all, provided it would make a change in his sentiments! But that I despair of, without the interposition of a miracle. You never saw such an alteration as an hour made on him. So alert and brisk! and apishly fond! I mean affectedly so; for, Louisa, a man of Sir William's cast never could love sincerely,—never could experience that genuine sentimental passion,

"Which,   selfish   joy   disdaining,   seeks   alone
To bless the dearer object of its soul."

No, his passions are turbulent—the madness of the moment—eager to please himself—regardless of the satisfaction of the object.—And yet I thought he loved—I likewise thought I loved. Oh! Louisa! how was I deceived! But I check my pen. Pardon me, and, if possible, excuse your sister.

    JULIA STANLEY.

LETTER XXII.

TO Colonel MONTAGUE.

What are we to make of this divine and destructive beauty? this Lady Stanley? Did you not observe with what eager avidity she became a votary to the gaming-table, and bragged away with the best of us? You must: you was witness to the glow of animation that reigned despotic over every lovely feature when she had got a pair-royal of braggers in her snowy fingers. But I am confoundedly bit! She condescended to borrow of that pattern of Germanic virtue, Baron Ton-hausen. Perhaps you will say, why did not you endeavour to be the Little Premium? No, I thought I played a better game: It was better to be the second lender; besides, I only wanted to excite in her a passion for play; and, or I am much deceived, never woman entered into it with more zeal. But what a turn to our affairs! I am absolutely cast off the scent; totally ignorant of the doubles she has made. I could hardly close my eyes, from the pleasing expectations I had formed of gratifying the wishes of my heart in both those interesting passions of love and revenge. Palpitating with hopes and fears, I descended from my chariot at the appointed hour. The party were assembled, and my devoted victim looked as beautiful as an angel of light; her countenance wore a solemnity, which added to her charms by giving an irresistible and persuasive softness to her features. I scrutinized the lineaments of her lovely face; and, I assure you, she lost nothing by the strict examination. Gods! what a transporting creature she is! And what an insensible brute is Stanley! But I recall my words, as to the last:—he was distractedly in love with her before he had her; and perhaps, if she was *my* wife, I should be as indifferent about her as *he* is, or as *I* am about the numberless women of all ranks and conditions with whom I have "trifled away the dull hours."—While I was in contemplation anticipating future joys, I was struck all of a heap, as the country-girls say, by hearing Lady Stanley say,—"It is in vain—I have made a firm resolution never to play again; my resolution is the result of my own reflections on the uneasiness which those bits of painted paper have already given me. It is altogether fruitless to urge me; for from the determination I have made, I shall never recede. My former winnings are in the sweepstake-pool at the *commerce-table*, which you will extremely oblige me to sit down to; but for me, I play no more.—I shall have a pleasure in seeing you play; but I own I feel myself too much discomposed with ill fortune; and I am not unreasonable enough to be pleased with the misfortunes of others. I have armed my mind against the shafts of ridicule, that I see pointed at me; but, while I leave others the full liberty of following their own schemes of diversion, I dare say, none will refuse me the same privilege."—We all stared with astonishment; but the devil a one offered to say a word, except against sitting down to divide her property;—there we entered into a general protest; so we set down, at least I can answer for myself, to an insipid game.—Lady Stanley was marked down as a fine *pigeon* by some of our ladies, and as a delicious *morçeau* by the men. The gentle Baron seemed all aghast. I fancy he is a little disappointed in his expectations too.—Perhaps he has formed hopes that his soft sighs and respectful behaviour may have touched the lovely Julia's heart. He felt himself flattered, no doubt, at her giving him the preference in borrowing from his purse. Well then, his hopes are *derangé*, as well as mine.— But, *courage, mi Lor,* I shall play another game now; and peradventure, as safe a one, if not more so, than what I planned before.—I will not, however, anticipate a pleasure (which needs no addition should I succeed) or add to my mortification should I fail, by expatiating on it at present.

Adieu! dear Montague! Excuse my *boring* you with these trifles;—for to a man in love, every thing is trifling except the *trifle* that possesses his heart; and to one who is not under the guidance of the *soft deity, that* is the *greatest* trifle (to use a Hibernicism) of all.

I am your's most cordially,
BIDDULPH.

LETTER XXIII.

To Miss GRENVILLE.

Well, my dear Louisa, the important point I related the particulars of in my last is quite settled, and Sir William has been able to satisfy some rapacious creditors. Would to heaven I could tell you, the butcher, baker, &c. were in the list! No, my sister; the creditors are a vile set of gamblers, or, in the language of the *polite* world—*Black-legs.* Thus is the purpose of my heart entirely frustrated, and the laudably industrious tradesman defrauded of his due. But how long will they remain satisfied with being repeatedly put by with empty promises, which are never kept? Good God! how is this to end? I give myself up to the most gloomy reflections, and see no point of time when we shall be extricated from the cruel dilemmas in which Sir William's imprudence has involved us. I vainly fancied, I should gain some advantages, at least raise myself in his opinion, from my generosity; but I find, on the contrary, he only laughs at me for being such a simpleton, to suppose the sale of five hundred a-year would set him to rights. It is plain, I have got no credit by my condescension, for he has not spent one day at home since; and his temper, when I do see him, seems more uncertain than ever.—Oh! Louisa! and do all young women give up their families, their hand, and virgin-affections, to be thus recompensed? But why do I let fall these expressions? Alas! they fall with my tears; and I can no more suppress the one than the other; I ought, however, and indeed do endeavour against both. I seek to arm my soul to support the evils with which

I see myself surrounded. I beseech heaven to afford me strength, for I too plainly see I am deprived of all other resources. I forget to caution you, my dear sister, against acquainting my father, that I have given up part of my jointure; and lest, when I am unburthening the weight of my over-charged bosom to you, I should in future omit this cautionary reserve, do you, my Louisa, keep those little passages a secret within your own kind sympathizing breast; and add not to my affliction, by planting such daggers in the heart of my dear—more dear than ever—parent. You know I have pledged my honour to you, I will never, by my own conduct, accumulate the distresses this fatal union has brought on me. Though every vow on his part is broken through, yet I will remember I am *his* wife,—and, what is more, *your* sister. Would you believe it? he—Sir William I mean—is quite displeased that I have given up cards, and very politely told me, I should be looked on as a fool by all his acquaintance,— and himself not much better, for marrying such an ignorant uninstructed rustic. To this tender and husband-like speech, I returned no other answer, than that "my conscience should be the rule and guide of my actions; and *that*, I was certain, would never lead me to disgrace him." I left the room, as I found some difficulty in stifling the resentment which rose at his indignant treatment. But I shall grow callous in time; I have so far conquered my weakness, as never to let a tear drop in his presence. Those indications of self-sorrow have no effect on him, unless, indeed, he had any point to gain by it; and then he would feign a tenderness foreign to his nature, but which might induct the ignorant uninstructed fool to yield up every thing to him.

Perhaps he knows it not; but I might have instructors enough;—but he has taught me sufficient of evil—thank God! to make me despise them all. From my unhappy connexions with one, I learn to hate and detest the whole race of rakes; I might add, of both sexes. I tremble to think what I might have been, had I not been blessed with a virtuous education, and had the best of patterns in my beloved sister. Thus I was early initiated in virtue; and let me be grateful to my kind *Sylph*, whose knowledge of human nature has enabled him to be so serviceable to me. he is a sort of second conscience to me:—What would the Sylph say? I whisper to myself. Would he approve? I flatter myself, that, insignificant as I am, I am yet the care of heaven; and while I depend on that merciful Providence and its vicegerents, I shall not fall into those dreadful pits that are open on every side: but, to strengthen my reliances, let me have the prayers of my dear Louisa; for every support is necessary for her faithful Julia.

LETTER XXIV.

TO THE SAME.

I have repeatedly mentioned to my Louisa, how earnestly I wished to have more frequent communications with my Sylph. A thought struck me the other day, of the practicability of effecting such a scheme. I knew I was safe from detection, as no one on earth, yourself excepted, knew of his agency in my affairs. I therefore addressed an advertisement to my invisible friend, which I sent to the St. James's Chronicle, couched in this concise manner.

TO THE SYLPH

"Grateful for the friendly admonition, the receiver of the Sylph's favour is desirous of having the power of expressing *it* more largely than is possible through this channel. If still intitled to protection, begs to be informed, how a private letter may reach his hand."

I have not leisure nor inclination to make a long digression, or would tell you, the St. James's is a news-paper which is the fashionable vehicle of intelligence; and from the circumstance alone of its admission into all families, and meeting all eyes, I chose it to convey my wishes to the Sylph. The next evening I had the satisfaction of finding those wishes answered; and the further pleasure (as you will see by the enclosed copy) of being assured of his approbation of the step I have taken.

And now for a little of family-affairs. You know I have a certain allowance, of what is called pin-money;—my quarter having been due for some time, I thought I might as well have it in my own possession,—not that I am poor, for I assure you, on the contrary, I have generally a quarter in hand, though I am not in debt. I sent Win to Harris's the steward, for my stipend. She returned, with his duty to me, acquainting me, it was not in his power at present to honour my note, not having any cash in hand. Surprized at his inability of furnishing a hundred and fifty pounds, I desired to speak with him; when he gave me so melancholy a detail of his master's circumstances, as makes me dread the consequences. He is surrounded with Jew-brokers; for, in this Christian land, Jews are the money-negotiators; and such wretches as you would tremble to behold are admitted into the private recesses of the Great, and caressed as their better-angels. These infernal agents procure them money; for which they pay fifty, a hundred, and sometimes two hundred *per Cent*. Am I wrong in styling them *infernal?* Do they not make the silly people who trust in them pay very dear for the means of accomplishing their own destruction? Like those miserable beings they used to call *Witches*, who were said to sell their souls to the Devil for everlasting, to have the power of doing temporary mischief upon earth.

These now form the bosom-associates of my husband. Ah! wonder not the image of thy sister is banished thence! rather rejoice with me, that he pays that reverence to virtue and decency as to distinguish me from that dreadful herd of which his chief companions are composed.

I go very little from home—In truth, I have no creature to go with.—I avoid Lord Biddulph, because I hate him; and (dare I whisper it to my Louisa?) I estrange myself from the Baron, lest I should be too partial to the numerous good qualities I cannot but see, and yet which it would be dangerous to contemplate too often. Oh, Louisa! why are there not many such men? His merit would not so forcibly strike me, if I could find any one in the circle of my acquaintance who could come in competition with him; for, be assured, it is not the tincture of the skin which I admire; not because *fairest*, but *best*. But where shall a married-woman find excuse to seek for, and admire, merit in any other than her husband? I will banish this too, too amiable man from my thoughts. As my Sylph says, such men (under the circumstances I am in) are infinitely more dangerous than a Biddulph. Yet, can one fall by the hand of virtue?—Alas! this is deceitful sophistry. If I give myself up to temptation, how dare I flatter myself I shall *be delivered from evil?*

Could two men be more opposite than what Sir William appeared at Woodley-vale, and what he now is?—for too surely, *that* was appearance—*this* reality. Think of him then sitting in your library, reading by turns with my dear father some instructive and amusing author, while *we* listened to their joint comments; what lively sallies we discovered in him; and how we all united in approving the natural flow of good spirits, chastened as we thought with the principles of virtue! See him now—But my pen refuses to draw the pain-inspiring portrait. Alas! it would but be a copy of what I have so repeatedly traced in my frequent letters; a copy from which we should turn with disgust, bordering on contempt. This we should do, were the character unknown or indifferent to us. But how must that woman feel—who sees in the picture the well-known features of a man, whom she is bound by her vows to love, honour, and obey? Your tenderness, my sister, will teach you to pity so unhappy a wretch. I will not, however, tax that tenderness too much. I will not dwell on the melancholy theme.

But I lose sight of my purpose, in thus contrasting Sir William *to himself*; I meant to infer, from the total change which seems to have taken place in him, that other men may be the same, could the same opportunity of developing their characters present itself. Thus, though the Baron wears this semblance of an angel—yet it may be assumed. What will not men do to carry a favourite point? He saw the open and avowed principles of libertinism in Lord Biddulph disgusted me from the first. He, therefore, may conceal the same invidious intention under the seducing form of every virtue. The simile of the robber and the beggar, in the Sylph's first letter, occurs to my recollection. Yet, perhaps, I am injuring the Baron by my suspicion. He may have had virtue enough to suppress those feelings in my favour, which my situation should certainly destroy in a virtuous breast.—Nay, I believe, I may make myself wholly easy on that head. He has, for some time, paid great attention to Miss Finch, who, I find, has totally broke with Colonel Montague. Certainly, if we should pay any deference to appearance, she will make a much better election by chusing Baron Ton-hausen, than the Colonel. She has lately—Miss Finch, I should say—has lately spent more time with me than any other lady—for my two first companions I have taken an opportunity of civilly dropping. I took care to be from home whenever they called by *accident*—and always to have some *prior* engagement when they proposed meeting by *design.*

Miss Finch is by much the least reprehensible character I have met with.—But, as Lady Besford once said, one can form no opinion of what a woman is while she is single. *She* must keep within the rules of decorum. The single state is not a state of freedom. Only the married ladies have that privilege. But, as far as one can judge, there is no danger in the acquaintance of Miss Finch. I own, I like her, for having refused Colonel Montague, and yet, (Oh! human nature!) on looking over what I have written, I have expressed myself disrespectfully, on the supposition that she saw Ton-hausen with the same eyes as a certain foolish creature that shall be nameless.

LETTER XXV.

Enclosed in the foregoing.
TO Lady STANLEY.

The satisfaction of a benevolent heart will ever be its own recompense; but not its *only* reward, as you have sweetly assured me, by the advertisement that blessed my eyes last night. I beheld, with pleasure, that my admonitions have not lost their intended effect. I should have been most cruelly disappointed, and have given up my knowledge of the human heart as imperfect, had I found you incorrigible to my advice. But I have heretofore told you, I was thoroughly acquainted with the excellencies of your mind. Your renunciation of your favourite game, and cards in general, give every reason to justify my sentiments of you. I have formed the most exalted idea of you.—And you alone can destroy the altar I have raised to your divinity. All the incense I dare hope to receive from you, is a just and implicit observance of my dictates, while *they* are influenced by virtue, of which none but you can properly judge, since to none but yourself they are addressed. Doubts, I am convinced, may arise in your mind concerning this invisible agency. As far as is necessary, I will satisfy those doubts. But to be for ever concealed from your knowledge as to identity, your own good sense will see too clearly the necessity of, to need any illustration from my pen. If I admired you before—how much has that admiration encreased from the chearful acquiescence you have paid to my injunctions! Go on, then, my beloved charge! Pursue the road of *virtue*; and be assured, however rugged the path, and tedious the way, you will, one day, arrive at the goal, and find *her* "in her own form—how lovely!" I had almost said, as lovely as yourself.

Perhaps, you will think this last expression too warm, and favouring more of the man—than the Rosicrusian philosopher.—But be not alarmed. By the most rigid observance of virtue it is we attain this superiority over the rest of mankind; and only by this course can we maintain it—we are not, however, divested of our sensibilities; nay, I believe, as they have not been vitiated by contamination, they are more *tremblingly alive* than other mortals usually are. In the human character, I could be of no use to you; in the Sylphiad, of the utmost. Look on me, then, only in the light of a preternatural being—and if my sentiments should sometimes flow in a more earthly stile—yet, take my word as a Sylph, they shall never be such as shall corrupt your heart. To guard it from the corruptions of mortals, is my sole view in the lectures I have given, or shall from time to time give you.

I saw and admired the laudable motive which induced you to give up part of your settlement. Would to heaven, for your sake, it had been attended with the happy consequences you flattered yourself with seeing. Alas! all the produce of that is squandered after the rest. Beware how you are prevailed on to resign any more; for, I question not, you will have application made you very soon for the remainder, or at least part of it: but take this advice of your true and disinterested friend. The time may come, and from the unhappy propensities of Sir William, I must fear it will not be long ere it does come, when both he and you may have no other resource than what your jointure affords you. By this ill-placed benevolence you will deprive yourself of the means of supporting him, when all other means will have totally failed. Let this be your plea to resist his importunities.

When you shall be disposed to make me the repository of your confidential thoughts, you may direct to A.B. at Anderton's coffee-house. I rely on your prudence, to take no measures to discover me. May you be as happy as you deserve, or, in one word, as I wish you!

Your careful
SYLPH.

LETTER XXVI.

To THE SYLPH.

It is happy for me, if my actions have stood so much in my favour, as to make any return for the obligations, which I feel I want words to express. Alas! what would have become of me without the friendly, the paternal admonitions of my kind Sylph! Spare me not, tell me all my faults—for, notwithstanding your partiality, I find them numerous. I feel the necessity of having those admonitions often inforced; and am apprehensive I shall grow troublesome to you.

Will, then, my friend allow me to have recourse to him on any important occasion— or what may appear so to me? Surely an implicit observance of his precepts will be the least return I can make for his disinterested interposition in my favour—and thus, as it were, stepping in between me and ruin. Believe me, my heart overflows with a grateful sense of these unmerited benefits—and feels the strongest resolution to persevere in the paths of rectitude so kindly pointed out to me by the hand of Heaven.

I experience a sincere affliction, that the renunciation of part of my future subsistence should not have had the desired effect; but *none* that I have parted with it. My husband is young, and blest with a most excellent constitution, which even *his* irregularities have not injured. I am young likewise, but of a more delicate frame, which the repeated hurries I have for many months past lived in (joined to a variety of other causes, from anxieties and inquietude of mind) have not a little impaired; so that I have not a remote idea of living to want what I have already bestowed, or may hereafter resign, for the benefit of my husband's creditors. Yet in this, as well as every thing else, I will submit to your more enlightened judgment—and abide most chearfully by your decision.

Would to Heaven Sir William would listen to such an adviser! He yet might retrieve his affairs. We yet might be happy. But, alas! he will not suffer his reason to have any sway over his actions. He hurries on to ruin with hasty strides—nor ever casts one look behind.

The perturbation these sad reflections create in my bosom will apologize to my worthy guide for the abruptness of this conclusion, as well as the incorrectness of the whole. May Heaven reward you! prays your ever grateful,
JULIA STANLEY.

VOLUME II

LETTER XXVII.

To Miss GRENVILLE.

I feel easier in my mind, my dearest Louisa, since I have established a sort of correspondence with the Sylph. I can now, when any intricate circumstance arises, which your distance may disable you from being serviceable in, have an almost immediate assistance in, or at least the concurrence of—my Sylph, my guardian angel!

In a letter I received from him the other day, he told me, "a time might come when he should lose his influence over me; however remote the period, as there was a possibility of his living to see it, the *idea* filled his mind with sorrow. The only method his skill could divine, of still possessing the privilege of superintending my concerns, would be to have some pledge from me. He flattered himself I should not scruple to indulge this only weakness of *humanity* he discovered, since I might rest assured he had it neither in his will or inclination to make an ill use of my condescension." The rest of the letter contained advice as usual. I only made this extract to tell you my determination on this head. I think to send a little locket with my hair in it. The *design* I have formed in my own mind, and, when it is compleated, will describe it to you.

I have seriously reflected on what I had written to you in my last concerning Miss Finch and (let me not practice disingenuity to my beloved sister) the Baron Ton-hausen.

56

Miss Finch called on me yesterday morning—she brought her work. "I am come," said she, "to spend some hours with you." "I wish," returned I, "you would enlarge your plan, and make it the whole day."

"With all my heart," she replied, "if you are to be alone; for I wish to have a good deal of chat with you; and hope we shall have no male impertinents break-in upon our little female *tête-à-tête*." I knew Sir William was out for the day, and gave orders I should not be at home to any one.

As soon as we were quite by ourselves, "Lord!" said she, "I was monstrously flurried coming hither, for I met Montague in the Park, and could hardly get clear of him—I was fearful he would follow me here." As she first mentioned him, I thought it gave me a kind of right to ask her some questions concerning that gentleman, and the occasion of her rupture with him. She answered me very candidly—"To tell you the truth, my dear Lady Stanley, it is but lately I had much idea that it was necessary to love one's husband, in order to be happy in marriage." "You astonish me," I cried. "Nay, but hear me. Reflect how we young women, who are born in the air of the court, are bred. Our heads filled with nothing but pleasure—let the means of procuring it be, almost, what you will. We marry—but without any notion of its being an union for life—only a few years; and then we make a second choice. But I have lately thought otherwise; and in consequence of these my more serious reflections, am convinced Colonel Montague and I might make a fashionable couple, but never a happy one. I used to laugh at his gaieties, and foolishly thought myself flattered by the attentions of a man whom half my sex had found dangerous; but I never loved him; that I am now more convinced of than ever: and as to reforming his morals—oh! it would not be worth the pains, if the thing was possible.

"Let the women be ever so exemplary, their conduct will have no influence over these professed rakes; these rakes upon principle, as that iniquitous Lord Chesterfield has taught our youth to be. Only look at yourself, I do not mean to flatter you; what effect has your mildness, your thousand and ten thousand good qualities, for I will not pretend to enumerate them, had over the mind of your husband? None. On my conscience, I believe it has only made him worse; because he knew he never should be censured by such a pattern of meekness. And what chance should such an one as I have with one of these *modern* husbands? I fear me, I should become a *modern* wife. I think I am not vainglorious, when I say I have not a bad heart, and am ambitious of emulating a good example. On these considerations alone, I resolved to give the Colonel his dismission. He pretended to be much hurt by my determination; but I really believe the loss of my fortune is his greatest disappointment, as I find he has two, if not more, mistresses to console him."

"It would hardly be fair," said I, "after your candid declaration, to call any part in question, or else I should be tempted to ask you, if you had really no other motive for your rejection of the Colonel's suit?"

"You scrutinize pretty closely," returned Miss Finch, blushing; "but I will make no concealments; I have a man in my eye, with whom, I think, the longer the union lasted, the happier I, at least, should be."

"Do I know the happy man?"

"Indeed you do; and one of some consequence too."

"It cannot be Lord Biddulph?"

"Lord Biddulph!—No, indeed!—not Lord Biddulph, I assure your Ladyship; though *he* has a title, but not an English one."

To you, my dear Louisa, I use no reserve. I felt a sickishness and chill all over me; but recovering instantly, or rather, I fear, desirous of appearing unaffected by what she said, I immediately rejoined—"So then, I may wish the *Baron* joy of his conquest." A faint smile, which barely concealed my anguish, accompanied my speech.

"Why should I be ashamed of saying I think the Baron the most amiable man in the world? though it is but lately I have allowed his superior merit the preference; indeed, I did not know so much of him as within these few weeks I have had opportunity."

"He is certainly very amiable," said I. "But don't you think it very close?" (I felt ill.) "I believe I must open the window for a little air. Pursue your panegyric, my dear Miss Finch. I was rather overcome by the warmth of the day; I am better now—pray proceed."

"Well then, it is not because he is handsome that I give him this preference; for I do not know whether Montague has not a finer person. observe, I make this a doubt, for I think those marks of the small-pox give an additional expression to his features. What say you?"

"I am no competent judge;" I answered, "but, in my opinion, those who do most justice to Baron Ton-hausen, will forget, or overlook, the graces of his person, in the contemplation of the more estimable, because more permanent, beauties of his mind."

"What an elegant panegyrist you are! in three words you have comprized his eulogium, which I should have spent hours about, and not so compleated at last. But the opportunity I hinted at having had of late, of discovering more of the Baron's character, is this: I was one day walking in the Park with some ladies; the Baron joined us; a well-looking old man, but meanly dressed, met us; he fixed his eyes on Ton-hausen; he started, then, clasping his hands together, exclaimed with eagerness, 'It is, it must be he! O, Sir! O, thou best of men!' 'My good friend,' said the Baron, while his face was crimsoned over, 'my good friend, I am glad to see you in health; but be more moderate.' I never before thought him handsome; but such a look of benevolence accompanied his soft accents, that I fancied him something more than mortal. 'Pardon my too lively expressions,' the old man answered, 'but gratitude—oh for such benefits! you, Sir, may, and have a right to command my lips; but my eyes—my eyes will bear testimony.' His voice was now almost choaked with sobs, and the tears flowed plentifully. I was extremely moved at this scene, and had likewise a little female curiosity excited to develope this mystery. I saw the Baron wished to conceal his own and the old man's emotions, so walked a little aside with him. I took that opportunity of whispering my servant to find out, if possible, where this man came from, and discover the state of this adventure. The ladies and myself naturally were chatting on this subject, when the Baron rejoined our party. 'Poor fellow', said he, 'he is so full of gratitude for my having rendered a slight piece of service to his family, and fancies he owes every blessing in life to me, for having placed two or three of his children out in the world.' We were unanimous in praising the generosity of the Baron, and were making some hard reflections on the infrequency of such examples among the affluent, when Montague came up; he begged to know on whom we were so severe; I told him in three words—and pointed to the object of the Baron's bounty. He looked a little chagrined, which I attributed to my commendations of this late instance of worth, as, I believe, I expressed myself with that generous warmth which a benevolent action excites in a breast capable of feeling, and wishing to emulate, such patterns. After my return home, my servant told me he had followed the old man to his lodgings, which were in an obscure part of the town, where he saw him received by a woman nearly his own age, a beautiful girl of eighteen, and two little boys. James, who is really an *adroit* fellow, farther said, that, by way of introduction, he told them to whom he was servant; that his lady was attached to their interest from something the Baron had mentioned concerning them, and had, in earnest of her future intentions, sent them a half-guinea. At the name of the Baron, the old folks lifted up their hands and blessed him; the girl blushed, and cast down her eyes; and, said James, 'I thought, my lady, she seemed to pray for him with greater fervour than the rest.' 'He is the noblest of men!' echoed the old pair. 'He is indeed!' sighed the young girl. 'My heart, my lady, ran over at my eyes to see the thankfulness of these poor people. They begged me to make their grateful acknowledgments to your ladyship for your bounty, and hoped the worthy Baron would convince you it was not thrown away on base or forgetful folks.' James was not farther inquisitive about their affairs, judging, very properly, that I should chuse to make some inquiries myself.

"The next day I happened to meet the Baron at your house. I hinted to him how much my curiosity had been excited by the adventure in the Park. He made very light of it, saying, his services were only common ones; but that the object having had a tolerable education, his expressions were rather adapted to his own feelings than to the merit of the benefit. 'Ah! Baron,' I cried, 'there is more in this affair than you think proper to communicate. I shall not cease persecuting you till you let me a little more into it. I feel myself interested, and you must oblige me with a recital of the circumstances; for which purpose I will set you down in my *vis-à-vis*.' 'Are you not aware, my dear Miss Finch, of the pain you will put me to in resounding my own praise?—What can be more perplexing to a modest man?' 'A truce with your modesty in this instance,' I replied; 'be *just* to yourself, and *generously indulgent* to me.' He bowed, and promised to gratify my desire. When we were seated, 'I will now obey you, Madam,' said the Baron. 'A young fellow, who was the lover of the daughter to the old man you saw yesterday, was inveigled by some soldiers to inlist in Colonel Montague's regiment. The present times are so critical, that the idea of a soldier's life is full of terror in the breast of a tender female. Nancy Johnson was in a state of distraction, which the consciousness of her being rather too severe in a late dispute with her lover served to heighten, as she fancied herself the cause of his resolution. Being a fine young man of six feet, he was too eligible an object for the Colonel to wish to part from. Great intercession, however, was made, but to no effect, for he was ordered to join the regiment. You must conceive the distress of the whole family; the poor girl broken-hearted; her parents hanging over her in anguish, and, ardent to restore the peace of mind of their darling, forming the determination of coming up to town to solicit his discharge from the Colonel. By accident I became acquainted with their distressed situation, and, from my intimacy with Montague, procured them the blessing they sought for. I have provided him with a small place, and made a trifling addition to her portion. They are shortly to be married; and of course, I hope, happy. And now, madam,' he continued, 'I have acquitted myself of my engagement to you.' I thanked him for his recital, and said, 'I doubted not his pleasure was near as great as theirs; for to a mind like his, a benevolent action must carry a great reward with it.' 'Happiness and pleasure,' he answered, 'are both comparative in some degree; and to feel them in their most exquisite sense, must be after having been deprived of them for a long time—we see ourselves possessed of them when hope had forsaken us. When the happiness of man depends on relative objects, he will be frequently liable to disappointment. I have found it so. I have seen every prop, on which I had built my schemes of felicity, sink one after the other; no other resource was then left, but to endeavor to form that happiness in others, which fate had for ever prevented my enjoying; and when I succeed, I feel a pleasure which for a moment prevents obtruding thoughts from rankling in my bosom. But I ask your pardon—I am too serious—tho' my *tête-à-têtes* with the ladies are usually so.' I told him, such reflections as his conversation gave rise to, excited more heart-felt pleasure than the broadest mirth could e'er bestow; that *I* too was serious, and I hoped should be a better woman as long as I lived, from the resolution I had formed of attending, for the future, to the happiness of others more than I had done. Here our conversation ended, for we arrived at his house. I went home full of the idea of the Baron and his recital; which, tho' I gave him credit for, I did not implicitly believe, at least as to circumstance, tho' I might to substance. I was kept waking the whole night, in comparing the several parts of the Baron's and James's accounts. In short, the more I ruminated, the more I was convinced there was more in it than the Baron had revealed; and Montague being an actor in the play, did not a little contribute to my desire of *peeping behind the curtain*, and having the whole *drama* before me. Accordingly, as soon as I had breakfasted, I ordered my carriage, and took James for my guide. When we came to the end of the street, I got out, and away I tramped to Johnson's lodgings. I made James go up first, and apprize them of my coming; and, out of the goodness of his heart, in order to relieve their minds from the perplexity which inferiority always excites, James told them, I was the best lady in the world, and might, for charity, pass for the Baron's sister. I heard this as I ascended the stair-case. But, when I entered, I was really struck with the figure of the young girl. Divested of all ornament—without the aid of dress, or any external advantage, I think I never beheld a more beautiful object. I apologized for the abruptness of my appearance amongst them, but added, I doubted not, as a friend of the Baron's and an encourager of merit, I should not be unwelcome. I begged them to go on with their several employments. They received me with that kind of embarrassment which is usual with people circumstanced as they are, who fancy themselves under obligations to the affluent for treating them with common civility. That they might recover their spirits, I addressed myself to the two little boys, and emptied my pockets to amuse them. I told the good old pair what the Baron had related to me; but fairly added I did not believe he had told me all the truth, which I attributed to his delicacy. 'Oh!' said the young girl, 'with the best and most noble of minds, the Baron possesses the greatest delicacy; but I need not tell you so; you, Madam, I doubt not, are acquainted with his excellencies; and may he, in you, receive his earthly reward for the good he has done to us! Oh, Madam! he has saved me, both soul and body; but for him, I had been the most undone of all creatures. Sure he was our better angel, sent down to stand between us and destruction.'

'Wonder not, madam,' said the father, 'at the lively expressions of my child; gratitude is the best master of eloquence; she feels, Madam—we all feel the force of the advantages we derive from that worthy man. Good God! what had been our situation at this moment, had we not owed our deliverance to the Baron!' 'I am not,' said I, 'entirely acquainted with the whole of your story; the Baron, I am certain, concealed great part; but I should be happy to hear the particulars.'

"The old man assured me he had a pleasure in reciting a tale which reflected so much honour on the Baron; 'and let me,' said he, 'in the pride of my heart, let me add, no disgrace on me or mine; for, Madam, poverty, in the eye of the right-judging, is no disgrace. Heaven is my witness, I never repined at my lowly station, till by that I was deprived of the means of rescuing my beloved family from their distress. But what would riches have availed me, had the evil befallen me from which that godlike man extricated us? Oh! Madam, the wealth of worlds could not have conveyed one ray of comfort to my heart, if I could not have looked all round my family, and said, tho' we are poor, we are virtuous, my children.

'It would be impertinent to trouble you, Madam, with a prolix account of my parentage and family. I was once master of a little charity-school, but by unavoidable misfortunes I lost it. My eldest daughter, who sits there, was tenderly beloved by a young man in our village, whose virtues would have reflected honour on the most elevated character. She did ample justice to his merit. We looked forward to the *happy* hour that was to render our child so, and had formed a thousand little schemes of rational delight, to enliven our evening of life; in one short moment the sun of our joy was overcast, and promised to set in lasting night. On a fatal day, my Nancy was seen by a gentleman in the army, who was down on a visit to a neighbouring squire, my landlord; her figure attracted his notice, and he followed her to our peaceful dwelling. Her mother and I were absent with a sick relation, and her protector was out at work with a farmer at some distance. He obtruded himself into our house, and begged a draught of ale; my daughter, whose innocence suspected no ill, freely gave him a mug, of which he just sipped; then, putting it down, swore he would next taste the nectar of her lips. She repelled his boldness with all her strength, which, however, would have availed her but little, had not our next-door neighbour, seeing a fine-looking man follow her in, harboured a suspicion that all was not right, and took an opportunity of coming in to borrow something. Nancy was happy to see her, and begged her to stay till our return, pretending she could not procure her what she wanted till then. Finding himself disappointed, Colonel Montague (I suppose, Madam, you know him), went away, when Nancy informed our neighbour of his proceedings. She had hardly recovered herself from her perturbation when we came home. I felt myself exceedingly alarmed at her account; more particularly as I learnt the Colonel was a man of intrigue, and proposed staying some time in the country. I resolved never to leave my daughter at home by herself, or suffer her to go out without her intended husband. But the vigilance of a fond father was too easily eluded by the subtilties of an enterprising man, who spared neither time nor money to compass his illaudable schemes. By presents he corrupted *that* neighbour, whose timely interposition had preserved my child inviolate. From the friendship she had expressed for us, we placed the utmost confidence in her, and, next to ourselves, intrusted her with the future welfare of our daughter. When the out-posts are corrupted, what *fort* can remain unendangered? It is, I believe, a received opinion, that more women are seduced from the path of virtue by their own sex, than by ours. Whether it is, that the unlimited faith they are apt to put in their own sex weakens the barriers of virtue, and renders them less powerful against the attacks of the men, or that, suspecting no sinister view, they throw off their guard; it is certain that an artful and vicious woman is infinitely a more to be dreaded companion, than the most abandoned libertine. This false friend used from time to time to administer the poison of flattery to the tender unsuspicious daughter of innocence. What female is free from the seeds of vanity? And unfortunately, this bad woman was but too well versed in this destructive art. She continually was introducing instances of handsome girls who had made their fortunes merely from that circumstance. That, to be sure, the young man, her sweetheart, had merit; but what a pity a person like her's should be lost to the world! That she believed the Colonel to be too much a man of honour to seduce a young woman, though he might like to divert himself with them. What a fine opportunity it would be to raise her family, like *Pamela Andrews*; and accordingly placed in the hands of my child those pernicious volumes. Ah! Madam, what wonder such artifices should prevail over the ignorant mind of a young rustic! Alas! they sunk too deep. Nancy first learnt to disrelish the honest, artless effusions of her first lover's heart. His language was insipid after the luscious speeches, and ardent but dishonourable warmth of Mr. B—, in the books before-mentioned. Taught to despise simplicity, she was easily led to suffer the Colonel to plead for pardon for his late boldness. My poor girl's head was now completely turned, to see such an accomplished man kneeling at her feet suing for forgiveness and using the most refined expressions; and elevating her to a Goddess, that he may debase her to the lowest dregs of human kind. Oh! Madam, what have not such wretches to answer for! The Colonel's professions, however, at present, were all within the bounds of honour. A man never scruples to make engagements which he never purposes to fulfill, and which he takes care no one shall ever be able to claim. He was very profuse of promises, judging it the most likely method of triumphing over her virtue by appearing to respect it. Things were proceeding thus; when, finding the Colonel's continued stay in our neighbourhood, I became anxious to conclude my daughter's union, hoping, that when he should see her married, he would entirely lay his schemes aside; for, by his hovering about our village, I could not remain satisfied, or prevent disagreeable apprehensions arising. My daughter was too artless to frame any excuse to protract her wedding, and equally *so*, not to discover, by her confusion, that her sentiments were changed. My intended son-in-law saw too clearly that *change*; perhaps he had heard more than I had. He made rather a too sharp observation on the alteration in his mistress's features. Duty and respect kept her silent to me, but to him she made an acrimonious reply. He had been that day at market, and had taken a too free draught of ale. His spirits had been elevated by my information, that I would that evening fix his wedding-day. The damp on my daughter's brow had therefore a greater effect on him. He could not brook her reply, and his answer to it was a sarcastic reflection on those women who were undone by the *red-coats*. This touched too nearly; and, after darting a look of the most ineffable contempt on him, Nancy declared, whatever might be the consequence, she would never give her hand to a man who had dared to treat her on the eve of her marriage with such unexampled insolence; so saying, she left the room. I was sorry matters had gone so far, and wished to reconcile the pair, but both were too haughty to yield to the intercessions I made; and he left us with a fixed resolution of making her repent, as he said. As is too common in such cases, the public-house seemed the properest asylum for the disappointed lover. He there met with a recruiting serjeant of the Colonel's, who, we since find, was sent on purpose to our village, to get Nancy's future husband out of the way. The bait unhappily took, and before morning he was enlisted in the king's service. His father and mother, half distracted, ran to our house, to learn the cause of this rash action in their son. Nancy, whose virtuous attachment to her former lover had only been lulled to sleep, now felt it rouze with redoubled violence. She pictured to herself the dangers he was now going to encounter, and accused herself with being the cause. Judging of the influence she had over the Colonel, she flew into his presence; she begged, she conjured him, to give the precipitate young soldier his discharge. He told her, 'he could freely grant any thing to her petition, but that it was too much his interest to remove the only obstacle to his happiness out of the way, for him to be able to comply with her request. However,' continued he, taking her hand, 'my Nancy has it in her power to preserve the young man.' 'Oh!' cried she, 'how freely would I exert that power!' 'Be mine this moment,' said he, 'and I will promise on my honour to discharge him.' 'By that sacred word,' said Nancy, 'I beg you, Sir, to reflect on the cruelty of your conduct to me! what generous professions you have made voluntarily to me! how sincerely have you promised me your friendship! and does all this end in a design to render me the most criminal of beings?' 'My angel,' cried the Colonel, throwing his arms round her waist, and pressing her hand to his lips, 'give not so harsh a name to my intentions. No disgrace shall befall you. You are a sensible girl; and I need not, I am sure, tell you, that, circumstanced as *I* am in life, it would be utterly impossible to marry you. I adore you; you know it; do not then play the sex upon me, and treat me with rigour, because I have candidly confessed I cannot live without you. Consent to bestow on me the possession of your charming person, and I will hide your lovely blushes in my fond bosom; while you shall whisper to my enraptured ear, that I shall still have the delightful privilege of an husband, and Will Parker shall bear the name. This little delicious private treaty shall be known only to ourselves. Speak, my angel, or rather let me read your willingness in your lovely eyes.' 'If I have been silent, Sir,' said my poor girl, 'believe me, it is the horror which I feel at your proposal, which struck me dumb. But, thus called upon, let me say, I bless Heaven, for having allowed me to see your cloven-foot, while yet I can be out of its reach. You may wound me to the soul, and (no longer able to conceal her tears) you have most sorely wounded me through the side of William; but I will never consent to enlarge him at the price of my honour. We are poor people. He has not had the advantages of education as you have had; but, lowly as his mind is, I am convinced he would first die, before I should suffer for his sake. Permit me, Sir, to leave you, deeply affected with the disappointments I have sustained; and more so, that in part I have brought them on myself.' Luckily at this moment a servant came in with a letter. 'You are now engaged, Sir,' she added, striving to hide her distress from the man. 'Stay, young woman,' said the Colonel, 'I have something more to say to you on this head.' 'I thank you Sir,' said she, curtseying, 'but I will take the liberty of sending my father to hear what further you may have to say on this subject.' He endeavoured to detain her, but she took this opportunity of escaping. On her return, she threw her arms round her mother's neck, unable to speak for sobs. Good God! what were our feelings on seeing her distress! dying to hear, yet dreading to enquire. My wife folded her speechless child to her bosom, and in all the agony of despair besought her to explain this mournful silence. Nancy slid from her mother's incircling arms, and sunk upon her knees, hiding her face in her lap: at last she sobbed out, 'she was undone for ever; her William would be hurried away, and the Colonel was the basest of men.' These broken sentences served but to add to our distraction. We urged a full account; but it was a long time before we could learn the whole particulars. The poor girl now made a full recital of all her folly, in having listened so long to the artful addresses of Colonel Montague, and the no less artful persuasions of our perfidious neighbour; and concluded, by imploring our forgiveness. It would have been the height of cruelty, to have added to the already deeply wounded Nancy. We assured her of our pardon, and spoke all the comfortable things we could devise. She grew tolerably calm, and we talked composedly of applying to some persons whom we hoped might assist us. Just at this juncture, a confused noise made us run to the door, when we beheld some soldiers marching, and dragging with them the unfortunate William loaded with irons, and hand-cuffed. On my hastily demanding why he was thus treated like a felon, the serjeant answered, he had been detected in an attempt to desert; but that he would be tried to-morrow, and might escape with five hundred lashes; but, if he did not mend his manners for the future, he would be shot, as all such cowardly dogs ought to be; and added, they were on the march the regiment. Figure to yourself, Madam, what was now the situation of poor Nancy. Imagination can hardly picture so distressed an object. A heavy stupor seemed to take intire possession of all her faculties. Unless strongly urged, she never opened her lips, and then only to breathe out the most heart-piercing complaints. Towards the morning, she appeared inclinable to doze; and her mother left her bed-side, and went to her own. When we rose, my wife's first business was to go and see how her child fared; but what was her grief and astonishment, to find the bed cold, and her darling fled! A small scrap of paper, containing these few distracted words, was all the information we could gain:

'My dearest father and mother, make no inquiry after the most forlorn of all wretches. I am undeserving of your least *regard*. I fear, I have forfeited *that* of Heaven. Yet pray for me: I am myself unable, as I shall prove myself unworthy. I am in despair; what that despair may lead to, I dare not tell: I dare hardly think. Farewell. May my brothers and sisters repay you the tenderness which has been thrown away on A. Johnson!' My wife's shrieks reached my affrighted ears; I flew to her, and felt a thousand conflicting passions, while I read the dreadful scroll. We ran about the yard and little field, every moment terrified with the idea of seeing our beloved child's corpse; for what other interpretation could we put on the alarming notice we had received, but that to destroy herself was her intention? All our inquiry failed. I then formed the resolution of going up to London, as I heard the regiment was ordered to quarters near town, and *hoped* there. After a fruitless search of some days, our strength, and what little money we had collected, nearly exhausted, it pleased the mercy of heaven to raise us up a friend; one, who, like an angel, bestowed every comfort upon us; in short, all comforts in one—our dear wanderer: restored her to us pure and undefiled, and obtained us the felicity of looking forward to better days. But I will pursue my long detail with some method, and follow my poor distressed daughter thro' all the sad variety of woe she was doomed to encounter. She told us, that, as soon as her mother had left her room, she rose and dressed herself, wrote the little melancholy note, then stole softly out of the house, resolving to follow the regiment, and to preserve her lover by resigning herself to the base wishes of the Colonel; that she had taken the gloomy resolution of destroying herself, as soon as his discharge was signed, as she could not support the idea of living in infamy. Without money, she followed them, at a painful distance, on foot, and sustained herself from the springs and a few berries; she arrived at the market-town where they were to take up their quarters; and the first news that struck her ear was, that a fine young fellow was just then receiving part of five hundred lashes for desertion; her trembling limbs just bore her to the dreadful scene; she saw the back of her William streaming with blood; she heard his agonizing groans! she saw—she heard no more! She sunk insensible on the ground. The compassion of the crowd around her, soon, too soon, restored her to a sense of her distress. The object of it was, at this moment, taken from the halberts, and was conveying away, to have such applications to his lacerated back as should preserve his life to a renewal of his torture. He was led by the spot where my child was supported; he instantly knew her. 'Oh! Nancy,' he cried, 'what do I see?' 'A wretch,' she exclaimed, 'but one who will do you justice. Should my death have prevented this, freely would I have submitted to the most painful. Yes, my William, I would have died to have released you from those bonds, and the exquisite torture I have been witness to; but the cruel Colonel is deaf to intreaty; nothing but my everlasting ruin can preserve you. Yet you shall be preserved; and heaven will, I hope, have that mercy on my poor soul, which, this basest of men will not shew.' The wretches, who had the care of poor William, hurried him away, nor would suffer him to speak. Nancy strove to run after them, but fell a second time, through weakness and distress of mind. Heaven sent amongst the spectators that best of men, the noble-minded Baron. Averse to such scenes of cruel discipline, he came that way by accident; struck with the appearance of my frantic daughter, he stopped to make some inquiry. He stayed till the crowd had dispersed, and then addressed himself to this forlorn victim of woe. Despair had rendered her wholly unreserved; and she related, in few words, the unhappy resolution she was obliged to take, to secure her lover from a repetition of his sufferings. 'If I will devote myself to infamy to Colonel Montague,' said she, 'my dear William will be released. Hard as the terms are, I cannot refuse. See, see!' she screamed out, 'how the blood runs! Oh! stop thy barbarous hand!' She raved, and then fell into a fit again. The good Baron intreated some people, who were near, to take care of her. They removed the distracted creature to a house in the town, where some comfortable things were given her by an apothecary, which the care of the Baron provided.

'By his indefatigable industry, the Baron discovered the basest collusion between the Colonel and serjeant; that, by the instigation of the former, the latter had been tampering with the young recruit, about procuring his discharge for a sum of money, which he being at that time unable to advance, the serjeant was to connive at his escape, and receive the stipulated reward by instalments. This infamous league was contrived to have a plea for tormenting poor William, hoping, by that means, to effect the ruin of Nancy. The whole of this black transaction being unravelled, the Baron went to Colonel Montague, to whom he talked in pretty severe terms. The Colonel, at first, was very warm, and wanted much to decide the affair, as he said, in an honourable way. The Baron replied, 'it was too *dishonourable* a piece of business to be thus decided; that he went on sure grounds; that he would prosecute the serjeant for wilful and corrupt perjury; and how honourably it would sound, that the Colonel of the regiment had conspired with such a fellow to procure an innocent man so ignominious a punishment.' As this was not an affair of common gallantry, the Colonel was fearful of the exposure of it; therefore, to hush it up, signed the discharge, remitted the remaining infliction of discipline, and gave a note of two hundred pounds for the young people to begin the world with. The Baron generously added the same sum. I had heard my daughter was near town; the circumstances of her distress were aggravated in the accounts I had received. Providence, in pity to my age and infirmities, at last brought us together. I advertised her in the papers: and our guardian angel used such means to discover my lodgings, as had the desired effect. My children are now happy; they were married last week. Our generous protector gave Nancy to her faithful William. We propose leaving this place soon; and shall finish our days in praying for the happiness of our benefactor.'

"You will suppose," continued Miss Finch, "my dear Lady Stanley, how much I was affected with this little narrative. I left the good folks with my heart filled with resentment against Montague, and complacency towards Ton-hausen. You will believe I did not hesitate long about the dismission of the former; and my frequent conversations on this head with the latter has made him a very favourable interest in my bosom. Not that I have the vanity to think he possesses any predilection in my favour; but, till I see a man I like as well as him, I will not receive the addresses of any one."

We joined in our commendation of the generous Baron. The manner in which he disclaimed all praise, Miss Finch said, served only to render him still more praise-worthy. He begged her to keep this little affair a secret, and particularly from me. I asked Miss Finch, why he should make that request? "I know not indeed," she answered, "except that, knowing I was more intimate with you than any one beside, he might mention your name by way of enforcing the restriction." Soon after this, Miss Finch took leave.

Oh, Louisa! dare I, even to your indulgent bosom, confide my secret thoughts? How did I lament not being in the Park the day of this adventure. *I* might then have been the envied*confidante* of the amiable Ton-hausen. They have had frequent conversations in consequence. The softness which the melancholy detail gave to Miss Finch's looks and expressions, have deeply impressed the mind of the Baron. Should I have shewn less sensibility? I have, indeed, rather sought to conceal the tenderness of my soul. I have been constrained to do so. Miss Finch has given her's full scope, and has riveted the chain which her beauty and accomplishments first forged. But what am I doing? Oh! my sister, chide me for thus giving loose to such expressions. How much am I to blame! How infinitely more prudent is the Baron! He begged that *I*, of all persons, should not know his generosity. Heavens! what an idea does that give birth to! He has seen—Oh! Louisa, what will become of me, if he should have discovered the struggles of my soul? If he should have searched into the recesses of my heart, and developed the thin veil I spread over the feelings I have laboured incessantly to overcome! He then, perhaps, wished to conceal his excellencies from me, lest I should be too partial to them. I ought then to copy his discretion. I will do so; Yes, Louisa, I will drive his image from my bosom! I ought—I know it would be my interest to wish him married to Miss Finch, or any one that would make him happy. I am culpable in harbouring the remotest desire of his preserving his attachment to me. He has had virtue enough. to conquer so *improper* an attachment; and, if improper in him, how infinitely more so in me! But I will dwell no longer on this forbidden subject; let me set bounds to my pen, as an earnest that I most truly mean to do so to my thoughts.

Think what an enormous packet I shall send you. Preserve your affection for me, my dearest sister; and, trust to my asseverations, you shall have no cause to blush for

JULIA STANLEY.

LETTER XXVIII.

TO Miss GRENVILLE.

This morning I dispatched to Anderton's Coffee-house the most elegant locket in hair that you ever saw. May I be permitted to say thus much, when the design was all my own? Yet, why not give myself praise when I can? The locket is in the form and size of that bracelet I sent you; the device, an altar, on which is inscribed these words, *To Gratitude*, an elegant figure of a woman making an offering on her knees, and a winged cherub bearing the incense to heaven. A narrow plait of hair, about the breadth of penny ribbon, is fastened on each side the locket, near the top, by three diamonds, and united with a bow of diamonds, by which it may hang to a ribbon. I assure you, it is exceedingly pretty. I hope the Sylph will approve of it. I forget to tell you, as the hair was taken from my head by your dear hand before I married, I took the fancy of putting the initials J. G. instead of J. S. It was a whim that seized me, because the hair did never belong to J.S.

Adieu!

JULIA.

LETTER XXIX.

From the SYLPH to Lady STANLEY.

Will my amiable charge be ever thus encreasing my veneration, my almost adoration of her perfections? Yes, Julia; still pursue these methods, and my whole life will be too confined a period to render you my acknowledgments. Its best services have, and ever shall be, devoted to your advantage. I have no other business, and, I am sure, no other pleasure, in this world, than to watch over your interest; and, if I should at any time be so fortunate as to have procured you the smallest share of felicity, or saved you from the minutest inquietude, I shall feel myself amply repaid; repaid! Where have I learnt so cold an expression? from the earth-born sons of clay? I shall feel a bliss beyond the sensation of a mortal!

None but a mind delicate as your own can form an idea of the sentimental joy I experienced on seeing the letters J.G. on the most elegant of devices, an emblem of the lovely giver! There was a purity, a chasteness of thought, in the design, which can only be conceived; all expression would be faint; even my Julia can hardly define it. Wonder not at my boundless partiality to you. You know not, you see not, yourself, as I *know* and *see* you. I pierce through the recesses of your soul; each fold expands itself to my eye; the struggles of your mind are open to my view; I see how nobly your virtue towers over the involuntary tribute you pay to concealed merit. But be not uneasy. Feel not humiliated, that the secret of your mind is discovered to me. Heaven sees our thoughts, and reads our hearts; we know it; but feel no restraint therefrom. Consider me as Heaven's agent, and be not dismayed at the idea of having a window in your breast, when only the sincerest, the most disinterested of your friends, is allowed the privilege of looking through it. Adieu! May the blest above (thy only superiors), guard you from ill! So prays your

SYLPH.

LETTER XXX.

To the SYLPH.

Though encouraged by the commendations of my Sylph, I tremble when you tell me the most retired secrets of my soul are open to your view. You say you have seen its struggles. Oh! that you alone have seen them! Could I be assured, that one *other* is yet a stranger to those struggles, I should feel no more humiliated (though that word is not sufficiently strong to express my meaning), than I do in my confessions to Heaven; because I am taught to believe, that our thoughts are involuntary, and that we are not answerable for them, unless they tend to excite us to evil actions. Mine, thank God! have done me no other mischief, than robbing me of that *repose*, which, perhaps, had I been blest with insensibility, might have been my portion. But a very large share of insensibility must have been dealt out to me, to have guarded me from my sense of merit in one person, and my feeling no affliction at the want of it in another, that *other* too, with whose fate mine is unavoidably connected. I must do myself that justice to say, my heart would have remained fixed with my hand, had my husband remained the same. Had *he* known no change, my affections would have centered in him; that is, I should have passed through life a duteous and observant partner of his cares and pleasures. When I married, I had never loved any but my own relations; indeed I had seen no *one* to love. The language, and its emotions, were equally strangers to my ears or heart. Sir William Stanley was the first man who used the one, and consequently, in a bosom so young and inexperienced as mine, created the other. He told me, he loved. I blushed, and felt confused; unhappily, I construed these indications of self-love into an attachment for him. Although this bore but a small relation to love, yet, in a breast where virtue and a natural tenderness resided, it would have been sufficient to have guarded my heart from receiving any other impression. He did so, till repeated slights and irregularities on one hand, and on the other all the virtues and graces that can adorn and beautify the mind, raised a conflict in my bosom, that has destroyed my peace, and hurt my constitution. I have a beloved sister, who deserves all the affection I bear her; from her I have concealed nothing. She has read every secret of my heart; for, when I wrote to her, reserve was banished from my pen. This unfortunate predilection, which, believe me, I have from the first combated with all my force, has given my Louisa, who has the tenderest soul, the utmost uneasiness. I have very lately assured her, my resolves to conquer this fatal attachment are fixed and permanent. I doubt (and she thinks perhaps) I have too often indulged myself in dwelling upon the dangerous subject in my frequent letters. I have given my word I will mention him no more. Oh! my Sylph! how has he risen in my esteem from a recent story I have heard of him! How hard is my fate (you can read my thoughts, so that to endeavour to soften the expression would be needless), that I am constrained to obey the man I can neither love nor honour! and, alas! love the man, who is not, nor can be, any thing to me.

I have vowed to my sister, myself, and now to you, that, however hardly treated, yet virtue and rectitude shall be my guide. I arrogate no great merit to myself in still preserving myself untainted in this vortex of folly and vice. No one falls all at once; and I have no temptation to do so. The man I esteem above all others is superior to all others. His manners refined, generous, virtuous, humane; oh! when shall I fill the catalogue of his excellent qualities? He pays a deference to me, at least used to do, because I was not tinctured with the licentious fashion of the times; he would lose that esteem for me, were I to act without decency and discretion; and I hope I know enough of my heart, to say, I should no longer feel an attachment for him, did he countenance vice. Alas! what is to be inferred from this, but that I shall carry this fatal preference with me to the grave! Let me, however, descend to *it*, without bringing disgrace on myself, sorrow on my beloved relations, and repentance on my Sylph, for having thrown away his counsels on an ingrate; and I will peacefully retire from a world for whose pleasures I have very little taste. Adieu.
JULIA STANLEY.

LETTER XXXI.

TO Lady STANLEY.
My dearest Sister,

It is with infinite pleasure I receive your promise, of no longer indulging your pen with a subject which has too much engaged your thoughts of late; a pleasure, heightened by the assurance, that your silence in future shall be an earnest of banishing an image from your idea, which I cannot but own, from the picture you have drawn, is very amiable, and, for that reason, very dangerous. I will, my Julia, emulate your example; this shall be the last letter that treats on this to-be-forbidden theme. Permit me, therefore, to make some comment on your long letter. Sure never two people were more strongly contrasted than the Baron and the Colonel. The one seems the kindly sun, cherishing the tender herbage of the field; the other, the blasting mildew, breathing its pestiferous venom over every beautiful plant and flower. However, do you, my love, only regard them as virtue and vice personified; look on them as patterns and examples; view them in no other light; for in *no other* can they be of any advantage to you. You are extremely reprehensible (I hope, and believe, I shall never have occasion to use such harsh language again) in your strictures on the supposed change in the Baron's sentiments. You absolutely seem to regret, if not express anger, that *he* has had virtue sufficient to resist the violence of an improper attachment. The efforts he has made, and my partiality for you supposes them not to have been easily made, ought to convince you, the conquest over ourselves is possible, though oftentimes difficult. It is, I believe, (and I may say I am certain from my own experience) a very mistaken notion, that we nourish our afflictions, by keeping them to ourselves. I said, I know so experimentally. While I indulged myself, and your tenderness induced you to do the same, in lamenting in the most pathetic language the perfidy of Mr. Montgomery and Emily Wingrove, I increased the wounds which that *perfidy* occasioned; but, when I took the resolution of never mentioning their names, or ever suffering myself to dwell on former scenes, burning every letter I had received from either; though these efforts cost me floods of tears, and many sleepless nights, yet, in time, my reflections lost much of their poignancy; and I chiefly attribute it to my steady adherence to my laudable resolution. He deserved not my tenderness, even if only because he was married to another. This is the first time I have suffered my pen to write his name since that determination; nor does he now ever mix with my thoughts unless by chance, and then quite as an indifferent person. I have recalled his idea for no other reason, than to convince you, that, although painful, yet self-conquest is attainable. You will not think I am endued with less sensibility than you are; and I had long been authorized to indulge my attachment to this ingrate, and had long been cruelly deceived into a belief, that his regard was equal to mine; while, from the first, *you* could have no *hope* to lead you on by flowery footsteps to the confines of *disappointment* and *despair*; for to those goals does that fallacious phantom too frequently lead. You envy Miss Finch the distinction which accident induced the Baron to pay her, by making her his *confidante*. Had you been on the spot, it is possible you might have shared his confidence; but, believe me, I am thankful to Heaven, that chance threw you not in his way; with your natural tenderness, and your unhappy predilection, I tremble for what might have been the consequence of frequent conversations, in which pity and compassion bore so large a share, as perhaps might have superseded every other consideration. I wish from my soul, and hope my Julia will soon join my wish, that the Baron may be in earnest in his attention to Miss Finch. I wish to have him married, that his engagements may increase, and prevent your seeing him so often, as you now do, for undoubtedly your difficulty will be greater; but consider, my dear Julia, your triumph will be *greater* likewise. It is sometimes harder to turn one's eyes from a pleasing object than one's thoughts; yet there is nothing which may not be achieved by resolution and perseverance; both of which, I question not, my beloved will exert, if it be but to lighten the oppressed mind of her faithful

LOUISA GRENVILLE.

LETTER XXXII.

To the SYLPH.

Will my kind guardian candidly inform me if he thinks I may comply with the desire of Sir William, in going next Thursday to the masquerade at the Pantheon? Without your previous advice, I would not willingly consent. Is it a diversion of which I may participate without danger? Though I doubt there is hardly decency enough left in this part of the world, that *vice* need wear a mask; yet do not people give a greater scope to their licentious inclinations while under that veil? However, if you think I may venture with safety, I will indulge my husband, who seems to have set his mind on my accompanying his party thither. Miss Finch has promised to go if I go; and, as she has been often to those motley meetings, assures me she will take care of me. Sir William does not know of my application to that lady; but I did so, merely to gain time to inform you, that I might have your sanction (or be justified by your advising the contrary), either to accept or reject the invitation.

I am ever your obliged,

J.S.

LETTER XXXIII.

From the SYLPH.

When the face is masked, the mind is uncovered. From the conduct and language of those who frequent masquerades, we may judge of the principles of their souls. A modest woman will blush in the dark; and a man of honour would scorn to use expressions while behind a vizor, which he would not openly avow in the face of day. A masquerade is then the criterion, by which you should form your opinion of people; and, as I believe I have before observed to my Julia, that female companions are either the safest or most dangerous of any, you may make this trial, whether Miss F. is, or is not, one in whom you may confide. When I say *confide*, I would not be understood that you should place an unlimited confidence in her; there is no occasion to lay our hearts bare to the inspection of all our intimates; we should lessen the compliment we mean to pay to our particular friends, by destroying that distinguishing mark. But you want a female companion. Indeed, for your sake, I should wish you one older than Miss F. and a married woman; yet, unless she was very prudent, *you* had better be the *leader* than the *led*; therefore, upon the whole, perhaps it is as well as it is.

67

I shall never enough admire your amiable condescension, in asking (in a manner) my permission to go to the Pantheon. And at the same time I feel the delicacy of your situation, and the effect it must have on a woman of your exquisite sensibility, to be constrained to appeal to another in an article wherein her husband ought to be the properest guide. Unhappily for you, Sir William will find so many engagements, that the protection of his wife must be left either to her own discretion, or to strangers. But your Sylph, my Julia, will never desert you. You request my leave to go thither. I freely grant that, and even more than you desire. I will meet my charge among the motley groupe. I do not demand a description of your dress; for, oh! what disguise can conceal you from him whose heart only vibrates in union with yours? I will not inform you how I shall be habited that night, as I have not a doubt but that I shall soon be discovered by you, though I shall be invisible to all beside. Only you will see me; and I, of course, shall only see *you*; you, who are all and every thing in this world to your faithful attendant

SYLPH.

LETTER XXXIV.

To the SYLPH.

Will you ever thus be adding to my weight of obligation! Yes! my Sylph! be still thus kind, thus indulgent; and be assured your benevolence shall be repaid by my steady adherence to your virtuous counsel. Adieu! Thursday is eagerly wished for by your's,

J.S.

LETTER XXXV.

TO Miss GRENVILLE.

Enclosed my Louisa will find some letters which have passed between the Sylph and your Julia. I have sent them, to inform you of my being present at a masquerade, in compliance with the taste of Sir William, who was very desirous of my exhibiting myself there. As he has of late never intimated an inclination to have me in any of his parties till this whim seized him, I thought it would not become me to refuse my consent. You will find, however, I was not so dutiful a wife as to pay an implicit obedience to his mandate, without taking the concurrence of my guardian angel on the subject. My dear, you must be first circumstanced as I am (which Heaven forbid!), before you can form an idea of the satisfaction I felt on the assurances of my Sylph's being present. No words can convey it to you. It seemed as if I was going to enjoy the ultimate wish of my heart. As to my dress, I told Sir William I would leave the choice of it to him, not doubting, in matters of elegant taste, he would be far superior to me. I made him this compliment, as I have been long convinced he has no other pleasure in possessing me, than what is excited by the admiration which other people bestow on me. Nay, he has said, unless he heard every body say his wife was one of the handsomest women at court, he would never suffer her to appear there, or any where else.

That I might do credit to his taste, I was to be most superbly brilliant; and Sir William desired to see my jewels. He objected to their manner of being set, though they were quite new-done when he married. But now these were detestable, horridly *outré*, and so barbarously antique, that I could only appear as Rembrandt's Wife, or some such relic of ancient history. As I had promised to be guided by him, I acquiesced in what I thought a very unnecessary expense; but was much laughed at, when I expressed my amazement at the jeweller's saying the setting would come to about two hundred pounds. This is well worth while for an evening's amusement, for they are now in such whimsical forms, that they will be scarce fit for any other purpose. And oh! my Louisa! do you not think I was cut to the soul when I had this painful reflection to make, that many honest and industrious tradesmen are every day dunning for their lawful demands, while we are thus throwing away hundreds after hundreds, without affording the least heartfelt satisfaction?

Well, at last my dress was completed; but what character I assumed I know not, unless I was the epitome of the folly of this world. I thought myself only an agent to support all the frippery and finery of *Tavistock-street*; but, however, I received many compliments on the figure I made; and some people of the first fashion pronounced me to be quite the thing.

They say, one may believe the women when they praise one of their own sex, and Miss Finch said, I had contrived to heighten and improve every charm with which Nature had endowed me. Sir William seemed to tread on air, to see and hear the commendations which were lavished on me from all sides. To a man of his taste, I am no more than any fashionable piece of furniture or new equipage; or, what will come nearer our idea of things, a beautiful prospect, which a man fancies he shall never be tired of beholding, and therefore builds himself an house within view of it; by that time he is fixed, he hardly remembers what was his motive, nor ever feels any pleasure but in pointing out its various perfections to his guests; his vanity is awhile gratified, but even that soon loses its *goût*; and he wonders how others can be pleased with objects now grown familiar, and, consequently, indifferent to him. But I am running quite out of the course. Suppose me now dressed, and mingling with a fantastic groupe of all kinds of forms and figures, striving to disengage my eyes from the throng, to single out my Sylph. Our usual party was there; Miss Finch, Lady Barton, a distant relation of her's, the Baron, Lord Biddulph, and some others; but it was impossible to keep long together. Sometimes I found myself with one; then they were gone, and I was *tête-à-tête* with somebody else; for a good while I observed a mask, who looked like a fortune-teller, followed me about, particularly when the Baron and Miss Finch were with me. I thought I must say something, so I asked him if he would tell me my fortune. "Go into the next room," said he, in a whisper, "and you shall see one more learned in the occult science than you think; but I shall say no more while you are surrounded with so many observers." Nothing is so easy as to get away from your company in a crowd: I slipped from them, and went into a room which was nearly empty, and still followed by the conjuror. I seated myself on a sopha, and just turned my head round, when I perceived the most elegant creature that imagination can form placed by me. I started, half-breathless with surprize. "Be not alarmed, my Julia," said the phantom, (for such I at first thought it) "be not alarmed at the appearance of your Sylph." He took my hand in his, and, pressing it gently, speaking all the while in a soft kind of whisper, "Does my amiable charge repent her condescension in teaching me to believe she would be pleased to see her faithful adherent?" I begged him to attribute my tremor to the hurry of spirits so new a scene excited, and, in part, to the pleasure his presence afforded me. But, before I proceed, I will describe his dress: his figure in itself seems the most perfect I ever saw; the finest harmony of shape; a waistcoat and breeches of silver tissue, exactly fitted to his body; buskins of the same, fringed, &c.; a blue silk mantle depending from one shoulder, to which it was secured by a diamond epaulette, falling in beautiful folds upon the ground; this robe was starred all over with plated silver, which had a most brilliant effect; on each shoulder was placed a transparent wing of painted gauze, which looked like peacocks feathers; a cap, suitable to the whole dress, which was certainly the most elegant and best contrived that can be imagined. I gazed on him with the most perfect admiration. Ah! how I longed to see his face, which the envious mask concealed. His hair hung in sportive ringlets; and just carelessly restrained from wandering too far by a white ribband. In more, the most luxuriant fancy could hardly create a more captivating object. When my astonishment a little subsided, I found utterance. "How is it possible I should be so great a favourite of fortune as to interest you in my welfare?" "We have each our task allotted us," he answered, "from the beginning of the world, and it was my happy privilege to watch over your destiny." "I speak to you as a man," said I, "but you answer only as a Sylph."

"Believe me," he replied, "it is the safest character I can assume. I must divest myself of my feelings as a *man*, or I should be too much enamoured to be serviceable to you: I shut my eyes to the beauties of your person, which excites tumultuous raptures in the chastest bosom, and only allow myself the free contemplation of your interior perfections. There your virtue secures me, and renders my attachment as pure as your own pure breast. I could not, however, resist this opportunity of paying my personal *devoir* to you, and yet I feel too sensibly I shall be a sufferer from my indulgence; but I will never forget that I am placed over you as your guardian-angel and protector, and that my sole business on earth is to secure you from the wiles and snares which are daily practised against youth and beauty. What does my excellent pupil say? Does she still chearfully submit herself to my guidance?" While he spoke this, he had again taken my hand, and pressed it with rapture to his bosom, which, beating with violence, I own caused no small emotion in mine. I gently withdrew my hand, and said, with as composed a voice as I could command, "Yes, my Sylph, I do most readily resign myself to your protection, and shall never feel a wish to put any restriction on it, while I am enabled to judge of you from your own criterion; while virtue presides over your lessons; while your instructions are calculated to make me a good and respectable character, I can form no wish to depart from them." He felt the delicacy of the reproof, and, sighing, said, "Let me never depart from that sacred character! Let me still remember I am your Sylph! But I believe I have before said, a time may come when you will no longer stand in need of my interposition. Shall I own to you, I sicken at the idea of my being useless to you?" "The time can never arrive in which you will not be serviceable to me, or, at least, when I shall not be inclined to ask and follow your advice." "Amiable Julia! may I venture to ask you this question? If fate should ever put it in your power to make a second choice, would you consult your Sylph?" "Hear me," cried I, "while I give you my hand on it, and attest heaven to witness my vow: that if I should have the fate (which may that heaven avert!) to outlive Sir William, I will abide by your decision; neither my hand nor affections shall be disposed of without your concurrence. My obligations to you are unbounded; my confidence in you shall likewise be the same; I can make no other return than to resign myself solely to your guidance in that and every other concern of moment to me."

"Are you aware of what you have said, Lady Stanley?"

"It is past recall," I answered; "and if the vow could return again into my bosom, it should only be to issue thence more strongly ratified."

"Oh!" cried he, clasping his hands together, "Oh! thou merciful Father, make me but worthy of this amiable, and most excellent of all thy creatures' confidence! None but the most accurst of villains could abuse such goodness. The blameless purity and innocent simplicity of your heart would make a convert of a libertine." "Alas!" said I, "that, I fear, is impossible; but how infinitely happy should I be, if my utmost efforts could work the least reformation in my husband! Could I but prevail on him to quit this destructive place, and retire into the peaceful country, I should esteem myself a fortunate woman."

"And could you really quit these gay scenes, nor *cast one longing lingering look behind?*"

"Yes," I replied with vivacity, "nor even cast a thought on what I had left behind!"

"Would no one be remembered with a tender regret? Would your Sylph be entirely forgotten?"

"My Sylph," I answered, "is possessed of the power of omnipresence; he would still be with me, wherever I went."

"And would no other ever be thought of? You blush, Lady Stanley; the face is the needle which points to the polar-star, the heart; from that information, may I not conclude, some one, whom you would leave behind, would mix with your ideas in your retirement, and that, even in solitude, you would not be alone?"

I felt my cheeks glow while he spoke; but, as I was a mask, I did not suppose the Sylph could discover the emotion his discourse caused. "Since," said I in a faultering voice, "you are capable of reading my heart, it is unnecessary to declare its sentiments to you; but it would be my purpose, in retirement, to obliterate every idea which might conduce to rob my mind of peace; I should endeavour to reform as well as my husband; and if he would oblige me by such a compliance to my will, I should think I could do no less than seek to amuse him, and should, indeed, devote my whole time and study to that purpose."

"You may think I probe too deep: but is not your desire of retirement stronger, since you have conceived the idea of the Baron's entertaining a *penchant* for Miss Finch, than it has been heretofore?"

I sighed—"Indeed you do probe very deep; and the pain you cause is exquisite: but I know it is your friendly concern for me; and it proves how needful it is to apply some remedy for the wound, the examination of which is so acute. Instruct me, ought I to wish him married? Should I be happier if he was so? And if he married Miss Finch, should I not be as much exposed to danger as at present, for his amiable qualities are more of the domestic kind?"

"I hardly know how to answer to these interrogatories; nor am I a judge of the heart and inclinations of the Baron; only thus much: if you have ever had any cause to believe him impressed with your idea, I cannot suppose it possible for Miss Finch, or any other woman, to obliterate that idea. But, *the heart of man is deceitful above all things*. For the sake of your interest, I wish Sir William would adopt your plan, though I have my doubts that his affairs are not in the power of any ceconomy to arrange; and this consideration urges me to enforce what I have before advised, that you do not surrender up any farther part of your jointure, as *that* may, too soon, be your sole support; and I have seen a recent proof of what mean subterfuges some men are necessitated to fly to, in order to extricate themselves for a little time. But the room fills; our conversation may be noticed; and, in this age of dissipation and licentiousness, to escape censure we must not stray within the limits of impropriety. Your having been so long *tête-à-tête* with any character will be observed. Adieu therefore for the present—see, Miss Finch is approaching." I turned my eye towards the door; the Sylph rose—I did the same—he pressed my hand on his quitting it; I cast my eye round, but I saw him no more; how he escaped my view I know not. Miss Finch by this time bustled through the crowd, and asked me where I had been, and whether I had seen the Baron, whom she had dispatched to seek after me?

The Baron then coming up, rallied me for hiding myself from the party, and losing a share of merriment which had been occasioned by two whimsical masks making themselves very ridiculous to entertain the company. I assured them I had not quitted that place after I missed them in the great room; but, however, adding, that I had determined to wait there till some of the party joined me, as I had not courage to venture a *tour* of the rooms by myself. To be sure all this account was not strictly true; but I was obliged to make some excuse for my behaviour, which otherwise might have caused some suspicion. They willingly accompanied me through every room, but my eyes could no where fix on the object they were in search of, and therefore returned from their survey dissatisfied. I complained of fatigue, which was really true, for I had no pleasure in the hurry and confusion of the multitude, and it grew late. I shall frighten you, Louisa, by telling you the hour; but we did not go till twelve at night. I soon met with Sir William, and on my expressing an inclination to retire, to my great astonishment, instead of censuring, he commended my resolution, and hasted to the door to procure my carriage. When you proceed, my dear Louisa, you will wonder at my being able to pursue, in so methodical a manner, this little narrative; but I have taken some time to let my thoughts subside, that I might not anticipate any circumstance of an event that may be productive of very serious consequences. Well then, pleased as I was with Sir William's ready compliance with my request of returning, suppose me seated in my chair, and giving way to some hopes that he would yet see his errors, and some method be pitched on to relieve all. He was ready to hand me out of the chair, and led me up stairs into my dressing-room. I had taken off my mask, as it was very warm; he still kept his on, and talked in the same kind of voice he practised at the masquerade. He paid me most profuse compliments on the beauty of my dress, and, throwing his arms round my waist, congratulated himself on possessing such an angel, at the same time kissing my face and bosom with such a strange kind of eagerness as made me suppose he was intoxicated; and, under that idea, being very desirous of disengaging myself from his arms, I struggled to get away from him. He pressed me to go to bed; and, in short, his behaviour was unaccountable: at last, on my persisting to intreat him to let me go, he blew out one of the candles. I then used all my force, and burst from him, and at that instant his mask gave way; and in the dress of my husband, (Oh, Louisa! judge, if you can, of my terror) I beheld that villain Lord Biddulph.

"Curse on my folly!" cried he, "that I could not restrain my raptures till I had you secure."

"Thou most insolent of wretches!" said I, throwing the most contemptuous looks at him, "how dared you assume the dress of my husband, to treat me with such indignity?" While I spoke, I rang the bell with some violence.

He attempted to make some apology for his indiscretion, urging the force of his passion, the power of my charms, and such stuff.

I stopped him short, by telling him, the only apology I should accept would be his instantly quitting the house, and never insulting me again with his presence. With a most malignant sneer on his countenance, he said, "I might indeed have supposed my caresses were disagreeable, when offered under the character of an husband; I had been more blest, at least better received, had I worn the dress of the Baron. All men, Lady Stanley, are not so blind as Sir William." I felt myself ready to expire with confusion and anger at his base insinuation.

"Your hint," said I, "is as void of truth as you are of honour; I despise both equally; but would advise you to be cautious how you dare traduce characters so opposite to your own."

By this time a servant came in; and the hateful wretch walked off, insolently wishing me a good repose, and humming an Italian air, though it was visible what chagrin was painted on his face. Preston came into the room, to assist me in undressing:—she is by no means a favourite of mine; and, as I was extremely fatigued and unable to sit up, I did not chuse to leave my door open till Sir William came home, nor did I care to trust her with the key. I asked for Winifred. She told me, she had been in bed some hours. "Let her be called then," said I. "Can't I do what your ladyship wants?"

"No; I chuse to have Win sit with me." "I will attend your ladyship, if you please."

"It would give me more pleasure if you would obey, than dispute my orders." I was vexed to the soul, and spoke with a peevishness unusual to me. She went out of the room, muttering to herself. I locked the door, terrified lest that monster had concealed himself somewhere in the house; nor would I open it till I heard Win speak. Poor girl! she got up with all the chearfulness in the world, and sat by my bed-side till morning, Sir William not returning the whole night. My fatigue, and the perturbation of mind I laboured under, together with the total deprivation of sleep, contributed to make me extremely ill. But how shall I describe to you, my dear Louisa, the horror which the reflection of this adventure excited in me?

Though I had, by the mercy of heaven, escaped the danger, yet the apprehension it left on my mind is not, to be told; and then the tacit apprehension which the base wretch threw on my character, by daring to say, he had been more *welcome* under another appearance, struck so forcibly on my heart, that I thought I should expire, from the fears of his traducing my fame; for what might I not expect from such a consummate villain, who had so recently proved to what enormous lengths he could go to accomplish his purposes? The blessing of having frustrated his evil design could hardly calm my terrors; I thought I heard him each moment, and the agitation of my mind operated so violently on my frame, that my bed actually shook under me. Win suffered extremely from her fears of my being dangerously ill, and wanted to have my leave to send for a physician; but I too well knew it was not in the power of medicine to administer relief to my feelings; and, after telling her I was much better, begged her not to quit my room at any rate.

About eleven I rose, so weak and dispirited, that I could hardly support myself. Soon after, I heard Sir William's voice; I had scarce strength left to speak to him; he looked pale and forlorn. I had had a conflict within myself, whether I should relate the behaviour of Lord Biddulph to my husband, lest the consequences should be fatal; but my spirits were so totally exhausted, that I could not articulate a sentence without tears. "What is the matter, Julia, with you," said he, taking my hand; "you seem fatigued to death. What a poor rake you are!"

"I have had something more than *fatigue* to discompose me," answered I, sobbing; "and I think I have some reproaches to make you, for not attending me home as you promised."

"Why Lord Biddulph promised to see you home. I saw him afterwards; and he told me, he left you at your own house."

"Lord Biddulph!" said I, with the most scornful air; "and did he tell you likewise of the insolence of his behaviour? Perhaps he promised you too, that he would insult me in my own house."

"Hey-day, Julia! what's in the wind now? Lord Biddulph insult you! pray let me into the whole of this affair?" I then related the particulars of his impudent conduct, and what I conceived his design to be, together with the repulse I had given him.

Sir William seemed extremely *chagrined*; and said, he should talk in a serious manner on the occasion to Lord Biddulph; and, if his answers were not satisfactory, he should lie under the necessity of calling him to account in the field. Terrified lest death should be the consequence of a quarrel between this infamous Lord and my husband, I conjured Sir William not to take any notice of the affair, any otherwise than to give up his acquaintance; a circumstance much wished for by me, as I have great reason to believe, Sir William's passion for play was excited by his intimacy with him; and, perhaps, may have led him to all the enormities he has too readily, and too rapidly, plunged himself into. He made no scruple to assure me, that he should find no difficulty in relinquishing the acquaintance; and joined with me, that a silent contempt would be the most cutting reproof to a man of his cast. On my part, I am resolved my doors shall never grant him access again; and, if Sir William should entirely break with him (which, after this atrocious behaviour, I think he must), I may be very happy that I have been the instrument, since I have had such an escape.

But still, Louisa, the innuendo of Lord Biddulph disturbs my peace. How shall I quiet my apprehensions? Does he dare scrutinize my conduct, and harbour suspicions of my predilection for a certain unfortunate? Base as is his soul, he cannot entertain an idea of the purity of a virtuous attachment! Ah! that speech of his has sunk deep in my memory; no time will efface it. When I have been struggling too—yes, Louisa, when I have been combating this fatal—But what am I doing? Why do I use these interdicted expressions? I have done. Alas! what is become of my boasting? If I cannot prescribe rules to a pen, which I can, in one moment, throw into the fire; how shall I restrain the secret murmurings of my mind, whose thoughts I can with difficulty silence, or even control? Adieu! your's, more than her own,

JULIA STANLEY.

LETTER XXXVI.

TO Miss GRENVILLE.

Alas! Louisa, fresh difficulties arise every day; and every day I find an exertion of my spirits more necessary, and myself less able to exert them. Sir William told me this morning, that he had lost frequent sums to Lord Biddulph (it wounds my soul to write his detested name); and since it was prudent to give up the acquaintance, it became highly incumbent on him to discharge these play-debts, for which purpose he must have recourse to me, and apprehended he should find no difficulty, as I had expressed my wish of his breaking immediately with his lordship. This was only the prelude to a proposal of my resignation of my marriage articles. My ready compliance with his former demands emboldened him to be urgent with me on this occasion. At first, I made some scruples, alledging the necessity there was of keeping something by us for a future day, as I had too much reason to apprehend, that what I could call my own would be all we should have to support us. This remonstrance of mine, however just, threw Sir William into a rage; he paced about the room like a madman; swore that his difficulties proceeded from my damned prudery; and that I should extricate him, or abide by the consequences. In short, Louisa, he appeared in a light entirely new to me; I was almost petrified with terror, and absolutely thought once he would beat me, for he came up to me with such fierce looks, and seized me by the arm, which he actually bruised with his grasp, and bade me, at my peril, refuse to surrender the writings to him. After giving me a violent shake, he pushed me from him with such force that I fell down, unable to support myself, from the trembling with which my whole frame was possessed.

"Don't think to practise any of the cursed arts of your sex upon me; don't pretend to throw yourself into fits."

"I scorn your imputation, Sir William," said I, half fainting and breathless, "nor shall I make any resistance or opposition to your leaving me a beggar. I have now reason to believe I shall not live to want what you are determined to force from me, as these violent methods will soon deprive me of my existence, even if *you* would withhold the murderous knife."

"Come, none of your damned whining; let me have the papers; and let us not think any more about it." He offered to raise me. "I want not your assistance," said I. "Oh! you are sulky, are you; but I shall let you know, Madam, these airs will not do with me." I had seated myself on a chair, and leaned my elbow on a table, supporting my head with my hand; he snatched my hand away from my face, while he was making the last speech. "What the devil!

73

am I to wait all day for the papers? Where are the keys?" "Take them," said I, drawing them from my pocket; "do what you will, provided you leave me to myself." "Damned sex!" cried he. "Wives or mistresses, by Heaven! you are all alike." So saying, he went out of the room, and, opening my bureau, possessed himself of the parchment so much desired by him. I have not seen him since, and now it is past eleven. What a fate is mine! However, I have no more to give up; so he cannot storm at, or threaten me again, since I am now a beggar as well as himself. I shall sit about an hour longer, and then I shall fasten my door for the night; and I hope he will not insist on my opening it for him. I make Win lie in a little bed in a closet within my room. She is the only domestic I can place the least confidence in. She sees my eyes red with weeping; she sheds tears, but asks no questions. Farewell, my dearest Louisa: pity the sufferings of thy sister, who feels every woe augmented by the grief she causes in your sympathizing breast.

Adieu! Adieu!

J.S.

LETTER XXXVII.

From the SYLPH.

I find my admonitions have failed, and my Julia has relinquished all her future dependence. Did you not promise an implicit obedience to my advice? How comes it then, that your husband triumphs in having the power of still visiting the gaming-tables, and betting with the utmost *éclat?* Settlements, as the late Lord Hardwicke used to say, are the foolishest bonds in nature, since there never yet was a woman who might not be kissed or kicked out of it: which of those methods Sir William has adopted, I know not; but it is plain it was a successful one. I pity you, my Julia; I grieve for you; and much fear, now Sir William has lost all restraint, he will lose the appearance of it likewise. What resource will he pursue next? Be on your guard, my most amiable friend; my foresight deceives me, or your danger is great. For when a man can once lose his humanity, so far as to deprive his wife of the means of subsisting herself, I much, very much fear he will so effectually lose his honour likewise, as to make a property of her's. May I judge too severely! May Sir William be an exception to my rule! And oh! may you, the fairest work of Heaven, be equally its care!

Adieu!

LETTER XXXVIII.

To the SYLPH.

Alas! I look for comfort when I open my kind Sylph's letters; yet in this before me you only point out the shoals and quicksands—but hold not out your sustaining hand, to guide me through the devious path. I have disobeyed your behest; but you know not how I have been urged, and my pained soul cannot support the repetition. I will ever be implicit in my obedience to you, as far as *I* am concerned only; as to this particular point, you would not have had me disobeyed my husband, I am sure. Indeed I could do no other than I did. If he should make an ill use of the sums raised, I am not answerable for it; but, if he had been driven to any fatal exigence through my refusal, my wretchedness would have been more exquisite than it now is, which I think would have exceeded what I could have supported. Something is in agitation now; but what I am totally a stranger to. I have just heard from one of my servants, that Mr. Stanley, an uncle of Sir William's, is expected in town. Would to Heaven he may have the will and power to extricate us! but I hear he is of a most morose temper, and was never on good terms with his nephew. The dangers you hint at, I hope, and pray without ceasing to Heaven, to be delivered from. Oh! that Sir William would permit me to return to my dear father and sister! in their kind embraces I should lose the remembrance of the tempests I have undergone; like the poor shipwrecked mariner, I should hail the friendly port, and never, never trust the deceitful ocean more. But ah! how fruitless this wish! Here I am doomed to stay, a wretch undone.

Adieu!

J.S.

LETTER XXXIX.

TO Miss GRENVILLE.

The Baron called here this morning. Don't be angry with me, my dearest Louisa, for mentioning *his* name, this will indeed be the last time. Never more will thy sister behold him. He is gone; yes, Louisa, I shall never see him again. But will his looks, his sighs, and tears, be forgotten? Oh! never, never! He came to bid me adieu, "Could I but leave you happy," he cried in scarce articulate accents—"Was I but blest with the remote hope of your having your merit rewarded in this world, I should quit you with less regret and anguish. Oh! Lady Stanley! best of women! I mean not to lay claim to your gratitude; far be such an idea from my soul! but for your sake I leave the kingdom."

"For mine!" I exclaimed, clasping my hands wildly together, hardly knowing what I said or did, "What! leave me! Leave the kingdom for my sake! Oh! my God! what advantage can accrue to me by losing"—I could not proceed; my voice failed me, and I remained the petrified statue of despair.

"Lady Stanley," said he with an assumed calmness, "be composed, and hear me. In an age like this, where the examples of vice are so many and so prevalent, though a woman is chaste as the icicle that hangs on Diana's temple, still she will be suspected; and, was the sun never to look upon her, yet she would be tainted by the envenomed breath of slander. Lady Anne Parker has dared in a public company to say, that the most virtuous and lovely of her sex will speedily find consolation for the infidelity of her husband, by making reprisals; her malevolence has farther induced her to point her finger to one, who adores all the virtues with which Heaven first endued woman in your form. A voluntary banishment on my side may wipe off this transient eclipse of the fairest and most amiable character in the world, and the beauties of it shine forth with greater lustre, like the diamond, which can only be sullied by the breath, and which evaporates in an instant, and beams with fresh brilliancy. I would not wish you to look into my heart," added he with a softened voice, "lest your compassion might affect you too much; yet you know not, you never can know, what I have suffered, and must for ever suffer.

"Condemn'd,   alas!   whole   ages   to   deplore,
And image charms I must behold no more."

I sat motionless during his speech; but, finding him silent, and, I believe, from his emotions, unable to proceed, "Behold," cried I, "with what a composed resignation I submit to my fate. I hoped I had been too inconsiderable to have excited the tongue of slander, or fix its sting in my bosom. But may you, my friend, regain your peace and happiness in your native country!"

"My native country!" exclaimed he, "What is my native country, what the whole globe itself, to that spot which contains all? But I will say no more. I dare not trust myself, I must not. Oh Julia! forgive me! Adieu, for ever!" I had no voice to detain him; I suffered him to quit the room, and my eyes lost sight of him—for ever!

I remained with my eyes stupidly fixed on the door. Oh! Louisa, dare I tell you? my soul seemed to follow him; and all my sufferings have been trivial to this. To be esteemed by him, to be worthy his regard, and read his approbation in his speaking eyes; this was my support, this sustained me, nor suffered my feet to strike against a stone in this disfigured path of destruction. He was my polar star. But he is gone, and knows not how much I loved him. I knew it not myself; else how could I promise never to speak, never to think of him again? But whence these wild expressions? Oh! pardon the effusions of phrenetic fancy. I know not what I have said. I am lost, lost!

J.S.

LETTER XL.

TO Colonel MONTAGUE.

Congratulate me, my dear Jack, on having beat the Baron out of the pit. He is off, my boy! and now I may play a safer game; for, between ourselves, I have as much inclination to sleep in a whole skin, as somebody else you and I know of. I have really been more successful than I could have flattered myself I should be; but the devil still stands my friend, which is but grateful to be sure, as the devil is in it if one good turn does not deserve another; and I have helped his sable divinity to many a good job in my day. The summit of my wishes was to remove this troublesome fellow; but he has taken himself clean out of the kingdom, lest the fame of his Dulcinea should suffer in the *Morning Post*. He, if any man could, would not scruple drubbing that *Hydra* of scandal; but then the stain would still remain where the blot had been made. I think you will be glad that he is punished at any rate for his impertinent interference in your late affair with the recruit's sweetheart. These delicate minds are ever contriving their own misery; and, from their exquisite sensibility, find out the method of refining on torture. Thus, in a fit of heroics, he has banished himself from the only woman he loves; and who in a short time, unless my ammunition fails, or my mine springs, too soon he might have a chance of being happy with, was he cast in mortal mould.—But I take it, he is one of that sort which Madame Sevigne calls "a pumkin fried in snow," or engendered between a Lapland sailor and a mermaid on the icy plains of Greenland. Even the charms of Julia can but just warm him. He does not burn like me. The consuming fire of Etna riots not in his veins, or he would have lost all consideration, but that of the completion of his whims. Mine have become ten times more eager from the resistance I have met with. Fool that I was! not to be able to keep a rein over my transports, till I had extinguished the lights! but to see her before me, my pulse beating with tumultuous passion, and my villainous fancy anticipating the tempting scene, all conspired to give such spirit to my caresses, as ill suited with the character I assumed of an indifferent husband. Like *Calista* of old, she soon discovered the God under the semblance of Diana. Heavens! how she fired up, and like the leopard, appeared more beauteous when heightened by anger? But in vain, my pretty trembler, in vain you struggle in the toils; thy price is paid, and thou wilt soon be mine. Stanley has lost every thing to me but his property in his wife's person; and though perhaps he may make a few wry faces, he must digest that bitter pill. He has obliged her to give up all her jointure, so she has now no dependance. What a fool he is! but he has ever been so; the most palpable cheat passes on him; and though he is morally certain, that to *play* and to *lose* is one and the same thing, yet nothing can cure his cursed itch of gaming. Notwithstanding all the *remonstrances* I have made, and the *dissuasives* I have daily used, he is bent upon his own destruction; and, since that is plainly the case, why may not I, and a few clever fellows like myself, take advantage of his egregious folly?

It was but yesterday I met him. "I am most consumedly in the flat key, Biddulph," said he; "I know not what to do with myself. For God's sake! let us have a little touch at billiards, picquet, or something, to drive the devil melancholy out of my citadel (touching his bosom), for, by my soul, I believe I shall make away with myself, if left to my own *agreeable* meditations." As usual, I advised him to reflect how much luck had run against him, and begged him to be cautious; that I positively had no pleasure in playing with one who never turned a game; that I should look out for some one who understood billiards well enough to be my conqueror. "What the devil!" cried he, "you think me a novice? come, come, I will convince you, to your sorrow, I know something of the game; I'll bet you five hundred, Biddulph, that I pocket your ball in five minutes."

"You can't beat me," said I, "and I will give you three."

"I'll be damned if I accept three; no, no, let us play on the square." So to it we went; and as usual it ended. The more he loses, the more impetuous and eager he is to play.

There will be a confounded bustle soon; his uncle, old Stanley, is coming up to town. In disposing of his wife's jointure, part of which was connected with an estate of Squaretoes, the affair has consequently reached his ears, and he is all fury upon the occasion. I believe there has been a little chicanery practised between Sir William and his lawyer, which will prove but an ugly business. However, thanks to my foresight in these matters, I am out of the scrape; but I can see the Baronet is cursedly off the hooks, from the idea of its transpiring, and had rather see the Devil than the Don. He has burnt his fingers, and smarts till he roars again. Adieu! dear Jack:

Remember thy old friend,
BIDDULPH.

LETTER XLI.

TO Miss GRENVILLE.

My storm of grief is now a little appeased; and I think I ought to apologize to my dearest Louisa, for making her so free a participator of my phrenzy; yet I doubt not of your forgiveness on this, as well as many occasions, reflecting with the liveliest gratitude on the extreme tenderness you have ever shewn me.

The morning after I had written that incoherent letter to you, Miss Finch paid me a visit. She took no notice of the dejection of my countenance, which I am convinced was but too visible; but, putting on a chearful air, though I thought she too looked melancholy when she first came in, "I am come to tell you, my dear Lady Stanley," said she, "that you must go to Lady D—'s route this evening; you know you are engaged, and I design you for my *chaperon*." "Excuse me, my dear," returned I, "I cannot think of going thither, and was just going to send a card to that purpose."

"Lady Stanley," she replied, "you must go indeed. I have a very particular reason for urging you to make your appearance there." "And I have as particular a reason," said I, turning away my head to conceal a tear that would unbidden start in my eye, "to prevent my going there or any where else at present."

Her eyes were moistened; when, taking my hand in her's, and looking up in my face with the utmost friendliness, "My amiable Lady Stanley, it grieves my soul, to think any of the licentious wretches in this town should dare asperse such excellence as your's; but that infamous creature, Lady Anne, said last night, in the coffee-room at the opera, that she had heard Lady Stanley took to heart (was her expression) the departure of Baron Ton-hausen; and that she and Miss Finch had quarrelled about their gallant. Believe me, I could sooner have lost the power of speech, than have communicated so disagreeable a piece of intelligence to you, but that I think it highly incumbent on you, by appearing with chearfulness in public with me, to frustrate the malevolence of that spightful woman as much as we both can."

"What have I done to that vile woman?" said I, giving a loose to my tears; "In what have I injured her, that she should thus seek to blacken my name?"

"Dared to be virtuous, while she is infamous," answered Miss Finch;—"but, however, my dear Lady Stanley, you perceive the necessity of contradicting her assertion of our having quarrelled on any account; and nothing can so effectually do it as our appearing together in good spirits."

"Mine," cried I, "are broken entirely. I have no wish to wear the semblance of pleasure, while my heart is bowed down with woe."

"But we must do disagreeable things sometimes to keep up appearances. That vile woman, as you justly call her, would be happy to have it in her power to spread her calumny; we may in part prevent it: besides, I promised the Baron I would not let you sit moping at home, but draw you out into company, at the same time giving you as much of mine as I could, and as I found agreeable to you."

"I beg you to be assured, my dear, that the company of no one can be more so than your's. And, as I have no doubts of your sincere wish for my welfare, I will readily submit myself to your discretion. But how shall I be able to confront that infamous Lady Anne, who will most probably be there?" "Never mind her; let conscious merit support you. Reflect on your own worth, nor cast one thought on such a wretch. I will dine with you; and in the evening we will prepare for this visit."

I made no enquiry why the Baron recommended me so strongly to Miss Finch. I thought such enquiry might lead us farther than was prudent; besides, I knew Miss Finch had a *tendre* for him, and therefore, through the course of the day, I never mentioned his name. Miss Finch was equally delicate as myself; our discourse then naturally fell on indifferent subjects; and I found I grew towards the evening much more composed than I had been for some time. The party was large; but, to avoid conversation as much as possible, I sat down to a quadrille table with Miss Finch; and, encouraged by her looks and smiles, which I believe the good girl forced into her countenance to give me spirits, I got through the evening tolerably well. The next morning, I walked with my friend into the Park. I never dine out, as I would wish always to be at home at meal-times, lest Sir William should chuse to give me his company, but that is very seldom the case; and as to the evenings, I never see him, as he does not come home till three or four in the morning, and often stays out the whole night. We have of course separate apartments. Adieu, my beloved! Would to God I could fly into your arms, and there forget my sorrows!

Your's, most affectionately,

J.S.

LETTER XLII.

TO Lord BIDDULPH.

For Heaven's sake, my dear Lord, let me see you instantly; or on second thoughts (though I am too much perplexed to be able to arrange them properly) I will lay before you the accursed difficulties with which I am surrounded, and then I shall beg the favour of you to go to Sir George Brudenel, and see what you can do with him. Sure the devil owes me some heavy grudge; every thing goes against me. Old Stanley has rubbed through a damned fit of the gout. Oh! that I could kill him with a wish! I then should be a free man again.

You see I make no scruple of applying to you, relying firmly on your professions of friendship; and assure yourself I shall be most happy in subscribing to any terms that you may propose for your own security; for fourteen thousand six hundred pounds I must have by Friday, if I pawn my soul twenty times for the sum. If you don't assist me, I have but one other method (you understand me), though I should be unwilling to be driven to such a procedure. But I am (except my hopes in you) all despair.

Adieu!

W. STANLEY.

LETTER XLIII.

Enclosed in the foregoing.

TO Sir WILLIAM STANLEY.

Sir,

I am extremely concerned, and as equally surprized, to find by my lawyer, that the Pemberton estate was not your's to dispose of. He tells me it is, after the death of your wife, the sole property of your uncle; Mr. Dawson (who is Mr. Stanley's lawyer) having clearly proved it to him by the deeds, which he swears he is possessed of. How then, Sir William, am I to reconcile this intelligence with the transactions between us? I have paid into your hands the sum of fourteen thousand six hundred pounds; and (I am sorry to write so harshly) have received a forged deed of conveyance. Mr. Dawson has assured Stevens, my lawyer, that his client never signed that conveyance. I should be very unwilling to bring you, or any gentleman, into such a dilemma; but you may suppose I should be as sorry to lose such a sum for nothing; nor, indeed, could I consent to injure my heirs by such a negligence. I hope it will suit you to replace the above sum in the hands of my banker, and I will not hesitate to conceal the writings now in my possession; but the money must be paid by Friday next. You will reflect on this maturely, as you must know in what a predicament you at present stand, and what must be the consequence of such an affair coming under the cognizance of the law.

I remain, Sir,

Your humble servant,

GEORGE BRUDENEL.

LETTER XLIV.

TO Miss GRENVILLE.

I write to you, my dearest Louisa, under the greatest agitation of spirits; and know no other method of quieting them, than communicating my griefs to you. But alas! how can you remedy the evils of which I complain? or how shall I describe them to you? How many times I have repeated, *how hard is my fate*! Yes, Louisa! and I must still repeat the same. In short, what have I to trust to? I see nothing before me but the effects of deep despair. I tremble at every sound, and every footstep seems to be the harbinger of some disaster.

Sir William breakfasted with me this morning, the first time these three weeks, I believe. A letter was brought him. He changed countenance on the perusal of it; and, starting up, traversed the room in great disorder. "Any ill news, Sir William?" I asked. He heeded me not, but rang the bell with violence. "Get the chariot ready directly—No, give me my hat and sword." Before they could be brought, he again changed his mind. He would then write a note. He took the standish, folded some paper, wrote, blotted, and tore many sheets, bit his lips, struck his forehead, and acted a thousand extravagances. I could contain myself no longer. "Whatever may be the consequence of your anger, Sir William," said I, "I must insist on knowing what sudden turn of affairs has occasioned this present distress. For Heaven's sake! do not refuse to communicate your trouble. I cannot support the agony your agitation has thrown me into."

"And you would be less able to support it, were I to communicate it."

"If you have any pity for me," cried I, rising, and going up to him, "I conjure you by that pity to disclose the cause of your disorder. Were I certain of being unable to bear the shock, yet I would meet it with calmness, rather than be thus kept in the most dreadful suspence."

"Suffice it then," cried he, throwing out his arm, "I am ruined for ever."

"Ruined!" I repeated with a faint voice.

"Yes!" he answered, starting on his feet, and muttering curses between his teeth. Then, after a fearful pause, "There is but one way, but one way to escape this impending evil."

"oh!" cried I, "may you fall on the right way! but, perhaps, things may not be so bad as you apprehend; you know I have valuable jewels; let me fetch them for you; the sale of them will produce a great deal of money."

"Jewels! O God! they are gone, you have no jewels."

"Indeed, my dear Sir William," I replied, shocked to death at seeing the deplorable way he was in; and fearing, from his saying they were gone, that his head was hurt—"Indeed, my dear Sir William, I have them in my own cabinet," and immediately fetched them to him. He snatched them out of my hand, and, dashing them on the floor, "Why do you bring me these damned baubles; your diamonds are gone; these are only paste."

"What do you mean?" I cried, all astonishment, "I am sure they are such as I received them from you."

"I know it very well; but I sold them when you thought them new-set; and now I am more pushed than ever."

"They were your's, Sir William," said I, stifling my resentment, as I thought he was now sufficiently punished, "you had therefore a right to dispose of them whenever you chose; and, had you made me the *confidante* of your intention, I should not have opposed it; I am only sorry you should have been so distressed as to have yielded to such a necessity, for though my confidence in you, and my ignorance in jewels, might prevent *my* knowing them to be counterfeits, yet, no doubt, every body who has seen me in them must have discovered their fallacy. How contemptible then have you made us appear!"

"oh! for God's sake, let me hear no more about them; let them all go to the devil; I have things of more consequence to attend to." At this moment a Mr. Brooksbank was announced. "By heaven," cried Sir William, "we are all undone! Brooksbank! blown to the devil! Lady Stanley, you may retire to your own room; I have some business of a private nature with this gentleman."

I obeyed, leaving my husband with this *gentleman*, whom I think the worst-looking fellow I ever saw in my life, and retired to my own apartment to give vent to the sorrow which flowed in on every side. "Oh! good God!" I cried, bursting into floods of tears, "what a change eighteen months has made! A princely fortune dissipated, and a man of honour, at least one who appeared as such, reduced to the poor subterfuge of stealing his wife's jewels, to pay gaming debts, and support kept mistresses!" These were my sad and solitary reflections. What a wretched hand has he made of it! and how deplorable is my situation! Alas! to what resource can he next fly? What is to become of us! I have no claim to any farther bounty from my own family: like the prodigal son, I have received my portion; and although I have not been the squanderer, yet it is all gone, and I may be reduced to feed on the husks of acorns; at least, I am sure I eat bitter herbs. Surely, I am visited with these calamities for the sins of my grandfather! May they soon be expiated!

That wretch Lord Biddulph has been here, and, after some conversation, he has taken Sir William out in his chariot. Thank heaven, I saw him not; but Win brought me this intelligence. I would send for Miss Finch, to afford me a little consolation; but she is confined at home by a feverish complaint. I cannot think of going out while things are in this state; so I literally seem a prisoner in my own house. Oh! that I had never, never seen it! Adieu! Adieu!

   J.S.

LETTER XLV.

TO Col. MONTAGUE.

  I acquainted you, some time since, of Stanley's affairs being quite *derangé*, and that he had practised an unsuccessful *manœuvre* on Brudenel. A pretty piece of business he has made of it, and his worship stands a fair chance of swinging for forgery, unless I contribute my assistance to extricate him, by enabling him to replace the money. As to raising any in the ordinary way, it is not in his power, as all his estates are settled on old Stanley, he (Sir William) having no children; and he is inexorable. There may be something to be said in the old fellow's favour too; he has advanced thousand after thousand, till he is tired out, for giving him money is really only throwing water into a sieve.

  In consequence of a hasty letter written by the Baronet, begging me to use all my interest with Brudenel, I thought it the better way to wait on Stanley myself, and talk the affair over with him, and, as he had promised to subscribe to any terms for my security, to make these terms most pleasing to myself. Besides, I confess, I was unwilling to meet Sir George about such a black piece of business, not chusing likewise to subject myself to the censures of that puritanic mortal, for having drawn Stanley into a love of play. I found Sir William under the greatest disorder of spirits; Brooksbank was with him; that fellow carries his conscience in his face; he is the portrait of villainy and turpitude. "For God's sake! my lord," cried Sir William (this you know being his usual exclamation), "what is to be done in this cursed affair? All my hopes are fixed on the assistance you have promised me."

  "Why, faith, Sir William," I answered, "it is, as you say, a most cursed unlucky affair. I think Brooksbank has not acted with his accustomed caution. As to what assistance I can afford you, you may firmly rely on, but I had a confounded tumble last night after you left us; by the bye, you was out of luck in absenting yourself; there was a great deal done; I lost upwards of seventeen thousand to the young *Cub* in less than an hour, and nine to the Count; so that I am a little out of elbows, which happens very unfortunate at this critical time."

  "Then I am ruined for ever!" "No, no, not so bad neither, I dare say. What say you to Lady Stanley's diamonds, they are valuable."

  "O Christ! they are gone long ago. I told her, I thought they wanted new-setting, and supplied her with paste, which she knew nothing of till this morning, that she offered them to me." (All this I knew very well, for D— the jeweller told me so, but I did not chuse to inform his worship so much.) "You have a large quantity of plate." "All melted, my lord, but one service, and that I have borrowed money on." "Well, I have something more to offer; but, if you please, we will dismiss Mr. Brooksbank. I dare say he has other business." He took the hint, and left us to ourselves.

  When we were alone, I drew my chair close to him; he was leaning his head on his hand, which rested on the table, in a most melancholy posture. "Stanley," said I, "what I am now going to say is a matter entirely between ourselves. You are no stranger to the passion I have long entertained for your wife, and from your shewing no resentment for what I termed a frolic on the night of the masquerade, I have reason to believe, you will not be mortally offended at this my open avowal of my attachment. Hear me (for he changed his position, and seemed going to speak): I adore Lady Stanley, I have repeatedly assured her of the violence of my flame, but have ever met with the utmost coldness on her side; let me, however, have your permission, I will yet insure myself success." "What, Biddulph! consent to my own dishonour! What do you take me for?" "What do I take you for?" cried I, with a smile, in which I infused a proper degree of contempt. "What will Sir George Brudenel take you for, you mean." "Curses, everlasting curses, blast me for my damned love of play! that has been my bane." "And I offer you your cure."

"The remedy is worse than the disease."

"Then submit to the disease, and sink under it. Sir William, your humble servant," cried I, rising as if to go.

"Biddulph, my dear Biddulph," cried he, catching my hand, and grasping it with dying energy, "what are you about to do? You surely will not leave me in this damned exigency? Think of my situation! I have parted with every means of raising more money, and eternal infamy will be the consequence of this last cursed subterfuge of mine transpiring. Oh, my God! how sunk am I! And will you not hold out your friendly arm?"

"I have already offered you proposals," I replied with an affected coldness, "which you do not think proper to accede to."

"Would you consign me to everlasting perdition?"

"Will you make no sacrifice to extricate yourself?"

"Yes; my life."

"What, at Tyburn?"

"Dam—n on the thought! oh! Biddulph, Biddulph, are there no other means? Reflect—the honour of my injured wife!" "Will not *that* suffer by your undergoing an ignominious death?"

"Ah! why do you thus stretch my heart-strings? Julia is virtuous, and deserves a better fate than she has met with in me. What a wretch must that man be, who will consign his wife to infamy! No; sunk, lost, and ruined as I am, I cannot yield to such baseness; I should be doubly damned."

"You know your own conscience best, and how much it will bear; I did not use to think you so scrupulous; what I offer is as much for your advantage as my own; nay, faith, for your advantage solely, as I may have a very good chance of succeeding with her bye and bye, when you can reap no benefit from it. All I ask of you is, your permission to give you an opportunity of suing for a divorce. Lay your damages as high as you please, I will agree to any thing; and, as an earnest, will raise this sum which distresses you so much; I am not tied down as you are; I can mortgage any part of my estate. What do you say? Will you sign a paper, making over all right and title to your wife in my favour? There is no time to be lost, I can assure you. Your uncle Stanley's lawyer has been with Brudenel; you know what hopes you have from that quarter; for the sooner you are out of the way, the better for the next heir."

You never saw a poor devil so distressed and agitated as Stanley was; he shook like one under a fit of the tertian-ague. I used every argument I could muster up, and conjured all the horrible ideas which were likely to terrify a man of his cast; threatened, soothed, sneered: in short, I at last gained my point, and he signed a commission for his own cuckoldom; which that I may be able to achieve soon, dear Venus grant! I took him with me to consult with our broker about raising the money. In the evening I intend my visit to the lovely Julia. Oh! that I may be endued with sufficient eloquence to soften her gentle heart, heart, and tune it to the sweetest notes of love! But she is virtuous, as Stanley says; that she is most truly: yet who knows how far resentment against her brutal husband may induce her to go? If ever woman had provocation, she certainly has. O that she may be inclined to revenge herself on him for his baseness to her! and that I may be the happy instrument of effecting it!

"Gods! what a thought is there!"

Adieu!

BIDDULPH.

LETTER XLVI.

To Miss GRENVILLE.

Oh! my Louisa, what will now become of your wretched sister? Surely the wide world contains not so forlorn a wretch, who has not been guilty of any crime! But let me not keep you in suspense. In the afternoon of the day I wrote last (I told you Miss Finch was ill)— Oh! good God! I know not what I write. I thought I would go and see her for an hour or two. I ordered the coach, and was just stepping into it, when an ill-looking man (Lord bless me! I have seen none else lately) laid hold of my arm, saying, "Madam, you must not go into that carriage."

"What do you mean?" I asked with a voice of terror, thinking he was a madman.

"Nothing, my lady," he answered, "but an execution on Sir William."

"An execution! Oh, heavens! what execution?" I was breathless, and just fainting.

"They are bailiffs, my lady," said one of our servants: "my master is arrested for debt, and these men will seize every thing in the house; but you need not be terrified, your ladyship is safe, they cannot touch you."

I ran back into the house with the utmost precipitation; all the servants seemed in commotion. I saw Preston; she was running up-stairs with a bundle in her hand. "Preston," said I, "what are you about?" "Oh! the bailiffs, the bailiffs, my lady!"

"They won't hurt you; I want you here."

"I can't come, indeed, my lady till I have disposed of these things; I must throw them out of the window, or the bailiffs will seize them."

I could not get a servant near me but my faithful Win, who hung weeping round me; as for myself, I was too much agitated to shed a tear, or appear sensible of my misfortune.

Two of these horrid men came into the room. I demanded what they wanted. To see that none of the goods were carried out of the house, they answered. I asked them, if they knew where Sir William Stanley was. "Oh! he is safe enough," said one of them; "we can't touch him; he pleads privilege, as being a member of parliament; we can only take care of his furniture for him."

"And am I not allowed the same privilege? If so, how have you dared to detain me?"

"Detain you! why I hope your ladyship will not say as how we have offered to detain you? You may go where you please, provided you take nothing away with you."

"My lady was going out," said Win, sobbing, "and you would not suffer it."

"Not in that coach, mistress, to be sure; but don't go for to say we stopped your lady. She may go when she will."

"Will one of you order me a chair or hackney coach? I have no business here." The last word melted me; and I sunk into a chair, giving way to a copious flood of tears. At that instant almost the detestable Biddulph entered the room. I started up—"Whence this intrusion, my lord?" I asked with a haughty tone. "Are you come to join your *insults* with the misfortunes you have in great measure effected?"

"I take heaven to witness," answered he, "how much I was shocked to find an extent in your house; I had not the least idea of such a circumstance happening. I, indeed, knew that Sir William was very much straitened for money."

"Accursed be those," interrupted I, "ever accursed be those whose pernicious counsels and baleful examples have brought him into these exigencies. I look on you, my lord, as one cruel cause of the ruin of our house."

"Rather, Lady Stanley, call me the prop of your sinking house. View, in me, one who would die to render you service."

"Would to heaven you had done so long—long before I had seen you!"

"How unkind is that wish! I came, Madam, with the intention of being serviceable to you. Do not then put such hard constructions on my words. I wished to consult with you on the most efficacious means to be used for Sir William's emolument. You know not what power you have!"

"Power! alas! what power have I?"

"The most unlimited," he replied, fixing his odious eyes on my face, which I returned by a look of the utmost scorn. "O Lady Stanley," he continued, "do not—do not, I intreat you, use me so hardly. Will you allow me to speak to you alone?"

"By no means."

"For God's sake do! Your servant shall remain in the next room, within your call. Let me beseech you to place some confidence in me. I have that to relate concerning Sir William, which you would not chuse a domestic should hear. Dearest Lady Stanley, be not inexorable."

"You may go into that room, Win," said I, not deigning to answer this importunate man. "My lord," addressing myself to him, "you can have nothing to tell me to which I am a stranger; I know Sir William is totally ruined. This is known to every servant in the house."

"Believe me," said he, "the execution is the least part of the evil. That event happens daily among the great people: but there is an affair of another nature, the stain of which can never be wiped off. Sir William, by his necessities, has been plunged into the utmost difficulties, and, to extricate himself, has used some unlawful means; in a word, he has committed a forgery."

"Impossible!" cried I, clasping my hands together in agony.

"It is too true; Sir George Brudenel has the forged deed now in his hands, and nothing can save him from an ignominious death, but the raising a large sum of money, which is quite out of his power. Indeed, I might with some difficulty assist him."

"And will you not step forth to save him?" I asked with precipitation.

"What would *you* do to save him?" he asked in his turn, attempting to take my hand.

"Can you ask me such a question? To save his life, what would I not do?"

"You have the means in your power."

"Oh! name them quickly, and ease my heart of this load of distraction! It is more—much more than I can bear."

"Oh my lovely angel!" cried the horrid wretch, "would you but shew some tenderness to me! would you but listen to the most faithful, most enamoured of men, much might be done. You would, by your sweet condescension, bind me for ever to your interest, might I but flatter myself I should share your affection. Would you but give me the slightest mark of it, oh! how blest I should be! Say, my adorable Julia, can I ever hope to touch your heart?"

"Wretch!" cried I, "unhand me. How dare you have the insolence to affront me again with the mention of your hateful passion? I believe all you have uttered to be a base falsehood against Sir William. You have taken an opportunity to insult his wife, at a time when you think him too much engaged to seek vengeance; otherwise your coward soul would shrink from the just resentment you ought to expect!"

"I am no coward, Madam," he replied, "but in my fears of offending the only woman on whom my soul doats, and the only one whose scorn would wound me. I am not afraid of Sir William's resentment—I act but by his consent."

"By his consent!"

"Yes, my dear creature, by his. Come, I know you to be a woman of sense; you are acquainted with your husband's hand-writing, I presume. I have not committed a *forgery*, I assure you. Look, Madam, on this paper; you will see how much I need dread the just vengeance of an injured husband, when I have his especial mandate to take possession as soon as I can gain my lovely charmer's consent; and, oh! may just revenge inspire you to reward my labours!" He held a paper towards me; I attempted to snatch it out of his hand. "Not so, my sweet angel, I cannot part with it; but you shall see the contents of it with all my heart."

Oh! Louisa, do I live to tell you what were those contents!—"I resign all right and title to my wife, Julia Stanley, to Lord Biddulph, on condition that he pays into my hands the sum of fourteen thousand six hundred pounds, which he enters into an engagement to perform. Witness my hand,

WILLIAM STANLEY."

Grief, resentment, and amazement, struck me dumb. "What say you to this, Lady Stanley? Should you not pique yourself on your fidelity to such a good husband, who takes so much care of you? You see how much he prizes his life."

"Peace, monster! peace!" cried I. "You have taken a base, most base advantage of the wretch you have undone!"

"The fault is all your's, the cruelty with which you have treated me has driven me to the only course left of obtaining you. You have it in your power to save or condemn your husband."

"What, should I barter my soul to save *one* so profligate of his? But there are other resources yet left, and we yet may triumph over thee, thou cruel, worst of wretches!"

"Perhaps you may think there are hopes from old Stanley; there can be none, as he has caused this execution. It would half ruin your family to raise this sum, as there are many more debts which they would be called upon to pay. Why then will you put it out of my power to extricate him? Let me have some influence over you! On my knees I intreat you to hear me. I swear by the great God that made me, I will marry you as soon as a divorce can be obtained. I have sworn the same to Sir William."

Think, my dearest Louisa, what a situation this was for me! I was constrained to rein-in my resentment, lest I should irritate this wretch to some act of violence—for I had but too much reason to believe I was wholly in his power. I had my senses sufficiently collected (for which I owe my thanks to heaven) to make a clear retrospect of my forlorn condition—eight or ten strange fellows in the house, who, from the nature of their profession, must be hardened against every distress, and, perhaps, ready to join with the hand of oppression in injuring the unfortunate—my servants (in none of whom I could confide) most of them employed in protecting, what they styled, their own property; and either totally regardless of me, or, what I more feared, might unite with this my chief enemy in my destruction. As to the forgery, though the bare surmise threw me into agonies, I rather thought it a proof how far the vile Biddulph would proceed to terrify me, than reality; but the fatal paper signed by Sir William—that was too evident to be disputed. This conflict of thought employed every faculty, and left me speechless—Biddulph was still on his knees, "For heaven's sake," cried he, "do not treat me with this scorn; make me not desperate! Ardent as my passion is, I would not lose sight of my respect for you."

"That you have already done," I answered, "in thus openly avowing a passion, to me so highly disagreeable. Prove your respect, my lord, by quitting so unbecoming a posture, and leave the most unfortunate of women to her destiny."

"Take care, take care, Madam," cried he, "how you drive me to despair; I have long, long adored you. My perseverance, notwithstanding your frowns, calls for some reward; and unless you assure me that in a future day you will not be thus unkind, I shall not easily forego the opportunity which now offers."

"For mercy's sake!" exclaimed I, starting up, "what do you mean? Lord Biddulph! How dare—I insist, Sir—leave me." I burst into tears, and, throwing myself again in my chair, gave free vent to all the anguish of my soul. He seemed moved. Again he knelt, and implored my pardon—"Forgive me!—Oh! forgive me, thou sweet excellence! I will not hereafter offend, if it is in nature to suppress the extreme violence of my love. You know not how extensive your sway is over my soul! Indeed you do not!"

"On the condition of your leaving me directly, I will endeavour to forgive and forget what has passed," I sobbed out, for my heart was too full of grief to articulate clearly.

"Urge me not to leave you, my angelic creature. Ah! seek not to drive the man from your presence, who doats, doats on you to distraction. Think what a villain your husband is; think into what accumulated distress he has plunged you. Behold, in me, one who will extricate you from all your difficulties; who will raise you to rank, title, and honour; one whom you may make a convert. Oh! that I had met with you before this cursed engagement, I should have been the most blest of men. No vile passion would have interfered to sever my heart from my beauteous wife; in her soft arms I should have found a balm for all the disquietudes of the world, and learnt to despise all its empty delusive joys in the solid bliss of being good and happy!" This fine harangue had no weight with me, though I thought it convenient he should think I was moved by it. "Alas! my Lord," said I, "it is now too late to indulge these ideas. I am doomed to be wretched; and my wretchedness feels increase, if I am the cause of making any earthly being so; yet, if you have the tenderness for me you express, you must participate of my deep affliction. Ask your own heart, if a breast, torn with anguish and sorrow, as mine is, can at present admit a thought of any other sentiment than the grief so melancholy a situation excites? In pity, therefore, to the woman you profess to love, leave me for this time. I said, I would forgive and forget; your compliance with my request may do more; it certainly will make me grateful."

"Dearest of all creatures," cried he, seizing my hand, and pressing it with rapture to his bosom, "Dearest, best of women! what is there that I could refuse you? Oh nothing,

nothing; my soul is devoted to you. But why leave you? Why may I not this moment reap the advantage of your yielding heart?"

"Away! away, my Lord," cried I, pushing him from me, "you promised to restrain your passion; why then is it thus boundless? Intitle yourself to my consideration, before you thus demand returns."

"I make no demands. I have done. But I flattered myself I read your soft wishes in your lovely eyes," [Detestable wretch! how my soul rose up against him! but fear restrained my tongue.] "But tell me, my adorable angel, if I tear myself from you now, when shall I be so happy as to behold you again?"

"To-morrow," I answered; "I shall be in more composed spirits to-morrow, and then I will see you here; but do not expect too much. And now leave me this moment, as I have said more than I ought."

"I obey, dearest Julia," cried the insolent creature, "I obey." And, blessed be Heaven! he left the room. I sprung to the door, and double-locked it; then called Win into the room, who had heard the whole of this conversation. The poor soul was as pale as ashes; her looks were contagious; I caught the infection; and, forgetting the distance betwixt us (but misery makes us all equal), I threw my arms round her, and shed floods of tears into her faithful bosom. When my storms of grief had a little subsided, or indeed when nature had exhausted her store, I became more calm, and had it in my power to consider what steps I should take, as you may believe I had nothing further from my intention than meeting this vile man again. I soon came to the determination to send to Miss Finch, as there was no one to whom I could apply for an asylum; I mean, for the present, as I am convinced I shall find the properest and most welcome in your's and my dear father's arms bye and bye. I rang the bell; one of the horrid bailiffs came for my orders. I desired to have Griffith called to me. I wrote a note to Miss Finch, telling her in a few words the situation of my affairs, and that my dread was so great of receiving further insult from Lord Biddulph, that I could not support the idea of passing the night surrounded by such wretches, therefore intreated her to send some one in whom she could confide, in her carriage, to convey me to her for a little time, till I could hear from my friends. In a quarter of an hour Griffith returned, with a billet containing only three lines—but oh, how much comfort. "My dearest creature, my heart bleeds for your distresses; there is no one so proper as your true friend to convey you hither. I will be with you in an instant; your's, for ever,

MARIA FINCH."

I made Win bundle up a few night-cloaths and trifles that we both might want, and in a short time I found myself pressed to the bosom of my dear Maria. She had risen from her bed, where she had lain two days, to fly to my succour. Ah! how much am I indebted to her! By Miss Finch's advice, I wrote a few words to—oh! what shall I call him?—the man, my Louisa, who tore me from the fostering bosom of my beloved father, to abandon me to the miseries and infamy of the world! I wrote thus:

"Abandoned and forsaken by him to whom I alone ought to look up for protection, I am (though, alas! unable) obliged to be the guardian of my own honour. I have left your house; happy, happy had it been for me, never to have entered it! I seek that asylum from strangers, I can no longer meet with from my husband. I have suffered too much from my fatal connexion with you, to feel disposed to consign myself to everlasting infamy (notwithstanding I have your permission), to extricate you from a trivial inconvenience. Remember, this is the first instance in which I ever disobeyed your will. May you see your error, reform, and be happy! So prays your much-injured, but still faithful wife,

JULIA STANLEY."

Miss Finch, with the goodness of an angel, took me home with her; nor would she leave me a moment to myself. She has indulged me with permission to write this account, to save me the trouble of repeating it to her. And now, my Louisa, and you, my dear honoured father, will you receive your poor wanderer? Will you heal her heart-rending sorrows, and suffer her to seek for happiness, at least a restoration of ease, in your tender bosoms? Will you hush her cares, and teach her to kiss the hand which chastises her? Oh! how I long to pour forth my soul into the breast from whence I expect to derive all my earthly comfort!

Adieu!

J.S.

LETTER XLVII.

TO Colonel MONTAGUE.

Well, Jack, we are all *entrain*. I believe we shall do in time. But old Squaretoes has stole a march on us, and took out an extent against his nephew. Did you ever hear of so unnatural a dog? It is true he has done a great deal for Sir William; and saw plainly, the more money he paid, the more extravagant his nephew grew; but still it was a damned affair too after all. I have been with my dear bewitching charmer. I have her promise to admit me as a visitor tomorrow. I was a fool not to finish the business to-night, as I could have bribed every one in the house to assist me. Your bailiffs are proper fellows for the purpose—but I love to have my adorables meet me—*almost* half way. I shall, I hope gain her at last; and my victory will be a reward for all my pains and labours.

I am interrupted. A messenger from Sir William. I must go instantly to the Thatched-house tavern. What is in the wind now, I wonder?

Great God! Montague, what a sight have I been witness to! Stanley, the ill-fated Stanley, has shot himself. The horror of the scene will never be worn from my memory. I see his mangled corse staring ghastly upon me. I tremble. Every nerve is affected. I cannot at present give you the horrid particulars. I am more shocked than it is possible to conceive. Would to Heaven I had had no connexion with him! Oh! could I have foreseen this unhappy event! but it is too, too late. The undone self-destroyed wretch is gone to answer for his crimes; and you and I are left to deplore the part we have had in corrupting his morals, and leading him on, step by step, to destruction.

My mind is a hell—I cannot reflect—I feel all despair and self-abasement. I now thank God, I have not the weight of Lady Stanley's seduction on my already overburdened conscience.

In what a different style I began this letter—with a pulse beating with anticipated evil, and my blood rioting in the idea of my fancied triumph over the virtue of the best and most injured of women. On the summons, I flew to the Thatched-house. The waiter begged me to go up stairs. "Here has a most unfortunate accident happened, my Lord. Poor Sir William Stanley has committed a rash action; I fear his life is in danger." I thought he alluded to the affair of forgery, and in that persuasion made answer, "It is an ugly affair, to be sure; but, as to his life, that will be in no danger." "Oh! my Lord, I must not flatter you; the surgeon declares he can live but a few hours." "Live! what do you say?" "He has shot himself, my Lord." I hardly know how I got up stairs; but how great was my horror at the scene which presented itself to my affrighted view! Sir George Brudenel and Mr. Stanley were supporting him. He was not quite dead, but his last moments were on the close. Oh! the occurrences of life will never for one instant obliterate from my recollection the look which he gave me. He was speechless; but his eloquent silence conveyed, in one glance of agony and despair, sentiments that sunk deep on my wounded conscience. His eyes were turned on *me*, when the hand of death sealed them forever. I had thrown myself on my knees by him, and was pressing his hand. I did not utter a word, indeed I was incapable of articulating a syllable. He had just sense remaining to know me, and I thought strove to withdraw his hand from mine. I let it go; and, seeing it fall almost lifeless, Mr. Stanley took it in his, as well as he could; the expiring man grasped his uncle's hand, and sunk into the shades of everlasting night. When we were convinced that all was over with the unhappy creature, we left the room. Neither Sir George, nor Mr. Stanley, seemed inclined to enter into conversation; and my heart ran over plentifully at my eyes. I gave myself up to my agonizing sorrow for some time. When I was a little recovered, I enquired of the people of the house, how this fatal event happened. Tom said, Sir William came there about seven o'clock, and went up stairs in the room we usually played in; that he looked very dejected, but called for coffee, and drank two dishes. He went from thence in an hour, and returned again about ten. He walked about the room in great disorder. In a short space, Sir George Brudenel and Mr. Stanley came and asked for him. On carrying up their message, Sir William desired to be excused seeing them for half an hour.

86

Within that time, a note was brought him from his own house by Griffith, Lady Stanley's servant*. [* The billet which Lady Stanley wrote, previous to her quitting her husband's house.] His countenance changed on the perusal of it. "This then decides it," he exclaimed aloud. "I am now determined." He bade the waiter leave the room, and bring him no more messages. In obedience to his commands, Tom was going down stairs. Sir William shut the door after him hastily, and locked it; and before Tom had got to the passage, he heard the report of a pistol. Alarmed at the sound, and the previous disorder of Sir William, he ran into the room where were Brudenel and Stanley, entreating them for God's sake to go up, as he feared Sir William meant to do some desperate act. They ran up with the utmost precipitation, and Brudenel burst open the door. The self-devoted victim was in an arm chair, hanging over on one side, his right cheek and ear torn almost off, and speechless. He expressed great horror, and, they think, contrition, in his looks; and once clasped his hands together, and turned up his eyes to Heaven. He knew both the gentlemen. His uncle was in the utmost agitation. "Oh! my dear Will," said he, "had you been less precipitate, we might have remedied all these evils." Poor Stanley fixed his eyes on him, and faintly shook his head. Sir George too pressed his hand, saying, "My dear Stanley, you have been deceived, if you thought me your enemy. God forgive those who have brought you to this distress!" This (with the truest remorse of conscience I say it) bears hard on my character. I did all in my power to prevent poor Stanley's meeting with Sir George and his uncle, and laboured, with the utmost celerity, to confirm him in the idea, that they were both inexorable, to further my schemes on his wife. As I found my company was not acceptable to the gentlemen, I returned home under the most violent dejection of spirits. Would to Heaven you were here! Yet, what consolation could you afford me? I rather fear you would add to the weight, instead of lightening it, as you could not speak peace to my mind, which is inconceivably hurt.

I am your's,
BIDDULPH.

LETTER XLVIII.

To Miss GRENVILLE.

Dear Madam,

A letter from Mr. Stanley* [* Mr. Stanley's letter is omitted.], which accompanies this, will inform you of the fatal catastrophe of the unfortunate Sir William Stanley. Do me the justice to believe I shall with pleasure contribute all in my power to the ease and convenience of Lady Stanley, for whom I have the tenderest friendship.

We have concealed the whole of the shocking particulars of her husband's fate from her ladyship, but her apprehensions lead her to surmize the worst. She is at present too much indisposed, to undertake a journey into Wales; but, as soon as she is able to travel, I shall do myself the honour of conveying her to the arms of relations so deservedly dear to her.

Mr. Stanley is not a man who deals in professions; he therefore may have been silent as to his intentions in favour of his niece, which I know to be very noble.

Lady Stanley tells me, she has done me the honour of mentioning my name frequently in her correspondence with you. As a sister of so amiable a woman, I feel myself attached to Miss Grenville, and beg leave to subscribe myself her obliged humble servant,

MARIA FINCH.

LETTER XLIX.

From the SYLPH.

The vicissitudes which you, my Julia, have experienced in your short life, must teach you how little dependence is to be placed in sublunary enjoyments. By an inevitable stroke, you are again cast under the protection of your first friends. If, in the vortex of folly where late you resided, my counsels preserved you from falling into any of its snares, the reflection of being so happy an instrument will shorten the dreary path of life, and smooth the pillow of death. But my task, my happy task, of superintending your footsteps is now over.

In the peaceful vale of innocence, no guide is necessary; for there all is virtuous, all beneficent, as yourself. You have passed many distressing and trying scenes. But, however, never let despair take place in your bosom. To hope to be happy in this world, may be presumptuous; to despair of being so, is certainly impious; and, though the sun may rise and see us unblest, and, setting, leave us in misery; yet, on its return, it may behold us changed, and the face which yesterday was clouded with tears may to-morrow brighten into smiles. Ignorant as we are of the events of to-morrow, let us not arrogantly suppose there will be no end to the trouble which now surrounds us; and, by murmuring, arraign the hand of Providence.

There may be, to us finite beings, many seeming contradictions of the assertion, that, *to be good is to be happy;* but an infinite Being knows it to be true in the enlarged view of things, and therefore implanted in our breasts the love of virtue. Our merit may not, indeed, meet with the reward which we seem to claim in this life; but we are morally ascertained of reaping a plentiful harvest in the next. Persevere then, my amiable pupil, in the path you were formed to tread in, and rest assured, though a slow, a lasting recompence will succeed. May you meet with all the happiness you deserve in this world! and may those most dear to you be the dispensers of it to you! Should any future occasion of your life make it necessary to consult me, you know how a letter will reach me; till then adieu!

Ever your faithful
SYLPH.

LETTER L.

TO Sir GEORGE BRUDENEL.
Woodley-vale.
My dear Sir George,

It is with the utmost pleasure, I assure you of my niece having borne her journey with less fatigue than we even could have hoped for. The pleasing expectation of meeting with her beloved relations contributed towards her support, and combated the afflictions she had tasted during her separation from them and her native place. As we approached the last stage, her conflict increased, and both Miss Finch and myself used every method to re-compose her fluttered spirits; but, just as we were driving into the inn-yard where we were to change horses for the last time, she clasped her hands together, exclaiming, "Oh, my God! my father's chaise!" and sunk back, very near fainting. I tried to laugh her out of her extreme agitation. She had hardly power to get out of the coach; and, hobbling as you know me to be with the gout, an extraordinary exertion was necessary on my part to support her, tottering as she was, into a parlour. I shall never be able to do justice to the scene which presented itself. Miss Grenville flew to meet her trembling sister. The mute expression of their features, the joy of meeting, the recollection of past sorrows, oh! it is more than my pen can paint; it was more than human nature could support; at least, it was with the utmost difficulty it could be supported till the venerable father approached to welcome his lovely daughter. She sunk on her knees before him, and looked like a dying victim at the shrine of a much-loved saint. What agonies possessed Mr. Grenville! He called for assistance; none of the party were able, from their own emotions, to afford him any. At last the dear creature recovered, and became tolerably calm; but this only lasted a few minutes. She was seated between her father and sister; she gazed fondly first on one, and then the other, and would attempt to speak; but her full heart could not find vent at her lips; her eyes were rivers, through which her sorrows flowed. I rose to retire for a little time, being overcome by the affecting view. She saw my intentions, and, rising likewise, took my hand—"Don't leave us—I will be more myself—Don't leave us, my second father!—Oh! Sir," turning to Mr. Grenville, "help me to repay this generous, best of men, a small part of what my grateful heart tells me is his due." "I receive him, my Julia," cried her father, "I receive him to my bosom as my brother." He embraced me, and Lady Stanley threw an arm over each of our shoulders. Our spirits, after some time, a little subsided, and we proceeded to this place. I was happy this meeting was over, as I all along dreaded the delicate sensibility of my niece.

Oh! Sir George! how could my unhappy nephew be blind to such inestimable qualities as Julia possesses? Blind!—I recall the word: he was not blind to them; he could

88

not, but he was misled by the cursed follies of the world, and entangled by its snares, till he lost all relish for whatever was lovely and virtuous. Ill-fated young man! how deplorable was thy end! Oh! may the mercy of Heaven be extended towards thee! May it forget its justice, *nor be extreme to mark what was done amiss!*

I find Julia was convinced he was hurried out of this life by his own desperate act, but she forbears to enquire into what she says she dreads to be informed of. She appears to me (who knew her not in her happier days) like a beautiful plant that had been chilled with a nipping frost, which congealed, but could not destroy, its loveliness; the tenderness of her parent, like the sun, has chaced away the winter, and she daily expands, and discovers fresh charms. Her sister too—indeed we should see such women now and then, to reconcile us to the trifling sex, who have laboured with the utmost celerity, and with too much success, to bring an odium on that most beautiful part of the creation. You say you are tired of the women of your world. Their caprices, their follies, to soften the expression, has caused this distaste in you. Come to Woodley-vale, and behold beauty ever attended by (what should ever attend beauty) native innocence. The lovely widow is out of the question. I am in love with her myself, that is, as much as an old fellow of sixty-four ought to be with a young girl of nineteen; but her charming sister, I must bring you acquainted with her; yet, unless I was perfectly convinced, that you possess the best of hearts, you should not even have a glance from her pretty blue eyes. Indeed, I believe I shall turn monopolizer in my dotage, and keep them all to myself. Julia is my child. Louisa has the merit with me (exclusive of her own superlative one) of being *her* sister. And my little *Finch* is a worthy girl; I adore her for her friendship to my darling. Surely your heart must be impenetrable, if so much merit, and so much beauty, does not assert their sway over you.

Do you think that infamous fellow (I am sorry to express myself thus while speaking of a peer of our realm) Lord Biddulph is sincere in his reformation? Perhaps returning health may renew in him vices which are become habitual from long practice. If he reflects at all, he has much, very much, to answer for throughout this unhappy affair. Indeed, he did not spare himself in his conversation with me. If he sees his errors in time, he ought to be thankful to Heaven, for allowing that *time* to him, which, by his pernicious counsels, he prevented the man he called *friend* from availing himself of. Adieu! my dear Sir George. May you never feel the want of *that peace which goodness bosoms ever!*

EDWARD STANLEY.

LETTER LI.

To Miss FINCH.

You are very sly, my dear Maria. Mr. Stanley assures me, you went to Lady Barton's purposely to give her nephew, Sir George, the meeting. Is it so? and am I in danger of losing my friend? Or is it only the jocularity of my uncle on the occasion? Pray be communicative on this affair. I am sure I need not urge you on that head, as you have never used any reserve to me. A mind of such integrity as your's requires no disguises. What little I saw of Sir George Brudenel shews him to be a man worthy of my Maria. What an encomium I have paid him in one word! But, joking apart (for I do not believe you entertained an idea of a *rencontre* with the young Baronet at Barton-house), Mr. Stanley says, with the utmost seriousness, that his friend Brudenel made him the *confidante* of a *penchant* for our sweet Maria, some time since, on his inviting him down hither, to pick up a wife *unhackneyed in the ways of the world.* However, don't be talked into a partiality for the swain, for none of us here have a wish to become match-makers.

And now I have done with the young man, permit me to add a word or two concerning the old one; I mean Mr. Stanley. He has, in the tenderest and most friendly manner, settled on me two thousand a year (the sum fixed on another occasion) while I continue the widow of his unfortunate nephew; and if hereafter I should be induced to enter into other engagements, I am to have fifteen thousand pounds at my own disposal. This, he says, justice prompts him to do; but adds, "I will not tell you how far my affection would carry me, because the world would perhaps call me an *old fool.*"

He leaves us next week, to make some preparation there for our reception in a short time. I am to be mistress of his house; and he has made a bargain with my father, that I shall spend half the year with him, either at Stanley-Park or Pemberton-Lodge. You may believe all the happiness of my future life is centered in the hope of contributing to the comfort of my father, and this my second parent. My views are very circumscribed; however, I am more calm than I expected to have been, considering how much I have been tossed about in the stormy ocean. It is no wonder that I am sometimes under the deepest dejection of spirits, when I sit, as I often do, and reflect on past events. But I am convinced I ought not to enquire too minutely into some fatal circumstances. May the poor deluded victim meet with mercy! I draw a veil over his frailties. Ah! what errors are they which death cannot cancel? Who shall say, *I will walk upright, my foot shall not slide or go astray?* Who knows how long he shall be upheld by the powerful hand of God? The most presumptuous of us, if left to ourselves, may be guilty of a lapse. Oh! may *my* trespasses be forgiven, as I forgive and forget *his!*

My dear Maria will excuse my proceeding; the last apostrophe will convince you of the impossibility of my continuing to use my pen.

Adieu!

JULIA STANLEY.

[The correspondence, for obvious reasons, is discontinued for some months. During the interval it appears, that an union had taken place between Sir George Brudenel and Miss Finch.—While Lady Stanley was on her accustomed visit to her uncle, she receives the following letter from Miss Grenville.]

LETTER LII.

TO Lady STANLEY. Melford-abbey,

This last week has been so much taken up, that I could not find one day to tell my beloved Julia that *she* has not been *one day* out of my thoughts, tho' you have heard from me but once since I obeyed the summons of our friend Jenny Melford, to be witness of her renunciation of that name. We are a large party here, and very brilliant.

I think I never was accounted vain; but, I assure you, I am almost induced to be so, from the attention of a very agreeable man, who is an intimate acquaintance of Mr. Wynne's; a man of fortune, and, what will have more weight with me, a man of strict principles. He has already made himself some little interest in my heart, by some very benevolent actions, which we have by accident discovered. I don't know what will come of it, but, if he should be importunate, I doubt I should not have power to refuse him. My father is prodigiously taken with him; yet men are such deceitful mortals—well, time will shew—in the mean time, adieu!

Your's, most sincerely,

LOUISA GRENVILLE.

LETTER LIII.

TO Lady STANLEY.

I cannot resist writing to you, in consequence of a piece of intelligence I received this morning from Mr. Spencer, the hero of my last letter.

At breakfast Mr. Spencer said to Mr. Wynne—"You will have an addition to your party tomorrow; I have just had a letter from my friend Harry Woodley, informing me, that he will pay his *devoir* to you and your fair bride before his journey to London." The name instantly struck me—"Harry Woodley!" I repeated.

"Why do you know Harry Woodley?" asked Mr. Spencer. "I once knew a gentleman of that name," I answered, "whose father owned that estate *my* father now possesses. I remember him a boy, when he was under the tuition of Mr. Jones, a worthy clergyman in our neighbourhood." "The very same," replied Mr. Spencer. "Harry is my most particular friend; I have long known him, and as long loved him with the tenderest affection—an affection," whispered he, "which reigned unrivalled till I saw you; he *was* the *first*, but *now* is *second* in my heart." I blushed, but felt no anger at his boldness.

I shall not finish my letter till I have seen my old acquaintance; I wish for to-morrow; I expressed my impatience to Mr. Spencer. "I should be uneasy at your earnestness," said he, "did I not know that curiosity is incident to your sex; but I will let you into a secret: Harry's heart is engaged, and has long been so; therefore, throw not away your fire upon him, but preserve it, to cherish one who lives but in your smiles."

He is arrived (Mr. Woodley, I mean); we are all charmed with him. I knew him instantly; tho' the beautiful boy is now flushed with manliness. It is five years since we saw him last—he did not meet us without the utmost emotion, which we attributed to the recollection that we now owned those lands which ought in right to have been his. He has, however, by Mr. Spencer's account, been very successful in life, and is master of a plentiful fortune. He seems to merit the favour of all the world.

Adieu!

Your's most truly,

LOUISA GRENVILLE.

LETTER LIV.

TO Lady STANLEY.

Melford-Abbey.

Mr. Spencer tells me, it is a proof I have great ascendancy over him, since he has made me the *confidante* of his friend Woodley's attachment. And who do you think is the object of it? To whom has the constant youth paid his vows in secret, and worn away a series of years in hopeless, pining love? Ah! my Julia, who can inspire so tender, so lasting, a flame as yourself? Yes! you are the saint before whose shrine the faithful Woodley has bent his knee, and sworn eternal truth.

You must remember the many instances of esteem we have repeatedly received from him. To me it was friendship; to my sister it was love—and *love* of the purest, noblest kind.

He left Woodley-vale, you recollect, about five years ago. He left all he held dear; all the soft hope which cherished life, in the flattering idea of raising himself, by some fortunate stroke, to such an eminence, that he might boldly declare how much, how fondly, he adored his Julia. In the first instance, he was not mistaken—he has acquired a noble fortune. Plumed with hope and eager expectation, he flew to Woodley-vale, and the first sound that met his ear was—that the object of his tenderest wishes was, a few weeks before his arrival, married. My Julia! will not your tender sympathizing heart feel, in some degree, the cruel anxiety that must take place in the bosom which had been, during a long journey, indulging itself in the fond hope of being happy—and just at that point of time, and at that place, where the happiness was to commence, to be dashed at once from the scene of bliss, with the account of his beloved's being married to another? What then remained for the ill-fated youth, but to fly from those scenes where he had sustained so keen a disappointment; and, without calling one glance on the plains the extravagance of his father had wrested from him, seek in the bosom of his friends an asylum?

He determined not to return till he was able to support the sight of such interesting objects with composure. He proposed leaving England: he travelled; but never one moment, in idea, wandered from the spot which contained all his soul held dear. Some months since, he became acquainted with the event which has once more left you free. His delicacy would not allow him to appear before you till the year was near expired. And now, if such unexampled constancy may plead for him, what competitor need Harry Woodley fear?

I told you my father was much pleased with Mr. Spencer, but he is more than pleased with his old acquaintance. You cannot imagine how much he interests himself in the hope that his invariable attachment to you may meet its due reward, by making, as he says, a proper impression on your heart. He will return with us to Woodley-vale. My father's partiality is so great, that, I believe, should you be inclined to favour the faithful Harry, he will be induced to make you the eldest, and settle Woodley on you, that it may be transmitted to Harry's heirs; a step, which, I give you my honour, I shall have no objection to. Besides, it will be proving the sincerity of Mr. Spencer's attachment to me—a proof I should not be averse to making; for, you know, *a burnt child dreads the fire*. These young men take up all our attention; but I will not write a word more till I have enquired after my dear old one. How does the worthy soul do? I doubt you have not sung to him lately, as the gout has returned with so much violence. You know, he said, your voice banished all pain. Pray continue singing, or any thing which indicates returning chearfulness; a blessing I so much wish you. I have had a letter from Lady Brudenel; she calls on me for my promised visit, but I begin to suspect I shall have engagements enough on my hands bye and bye. I doubt my father is tired of us both, as he is planning a scheme to get rid of us at once. But does not this seeming eagerness proceed from that motive which guides all his actions towards us—his extreme tenderness—the apprehension of leaving us unconnected, and the infirmities of life hastening with large strides on himself? Oh! my Julia! he is the best of fathers!

Adieu! I am dressed *en cavalier*, and just going to mount my horse, accompanied by my two beaux. I wish you was here, as I own I should have no objection to a *tête-à-tête* with Spencer; nor would Harry with you. But *here*—he is in the way.

Your's,
L. GRENVILLE.

LETTER LV.

TO Miss GRENVILLE.
Stanley-park.

Alas! my dearest Louisa, is it to me your last letter was addressed? to me, the sad victim of a fatal attachment? Torn as has been my heart by the strange vicissitudes of life, am I an object fit to admit the bright ray of joy? Unhappy Woodley, if thy destiny is to be decided by my voice! It is—it must be ever against thee. Talk not to me, Louisa, of love—of joy and happiness! Ever, ever, will they be strangers to my care-worn breast. A little calm (oh! how deceitful!) had taken possession of my mind, and seemed to chace away the dull melancholy which habitual griefs had planted there. Ah! seek not to rob me of the small share allotted me. Speak not—write not of Woodley; my future peace depends upon it. The name of *love* has awakened a thousand, thousand pangs, which sorrow had hushed to rest; at least, I kept them to myself. I look on the evils of my life as a punishment for having too freely indulged myself in a most reprehensible attachment. Never has my hand traced the fatal name! Never have I sighed it forth in the most retired privacy! Never then, my Louisa, oh! never mention the destructive passion to me more!

I remember the ill-fated youth—ill-fated, indeed, if cursed with so much constancy! The first predilection I felt in favour of one too dear—was a faint similitude I thought I discovered between him and Woodley. But if I entertained a partiality at first for him, because he reminded me of a former companion, too soon he made such an interest in my bosom, as left him superior there to all others. It is your fault, Louisa, that I have adverted to this painful, this forbidden subject. Why have you mentioned the pernicious theme?

Why should my father be so earnest to have me again enter into the pale of matrimony? If your prospects are flattering—indulge them, and be happy. I have tasted of the fruit—have found it bitter to the palate, and corroding to the heart. Urge me not then to run any more hazards; I have suffered sufficiently. Do not, in pity to Mr. Woodley, encourage in him a hope, that perseverance may subdue my resolves. Fate is not more inexorable. I should despise myself if I was capable, for one moment, of wishing to give pain to any mortal. He cannot complain of me—he may of *Destiny*; and, oh! what complaints have I not to make of *her!*

I have again perused your letter; I am not free, Louisa, even if my heart was not devoted to the unfortunate exile. Have I not sworn to my attendant Sylph? He, who preserved me in the day of trial? My vows are registered in heaven! I will not recede from them! I believe he knows my heart, with all its weaknesses. Oh! my Louisa, do not distress me more.

Adieu!
JULIA STANLEY.

LETTER LVI.

TO Lady STANLEY.

Where has my Julia learnt this inflexibility of mind? or what virtue so rigid as to say, she is not free to enter into other engagements? Are your affections to lie for ever buried in the grave of your unfortunate husband? Heaven, who has given us renewable affections, will not condemn us for making a transfer of them, when the continuance of that affection can be of no farther advantage to the object. But your case is different; you have attached yourself to a visionary idea! the man, whose memory you cherish, perhaps, thinks no longer of you; or would he not have sought you out before this? Are you to pass your life in mourning his absence, and not endeavour to do justice to the fidelity of one of the most amiable of men?

Surely, my Julia, these sacrifices are not required of you! You condemn my father for being so interested in the fate of his friend Woodley!—he only requests you to see him. Why not see him as an acquaintance? You cannot form the idea of my father's wishing to constrain you to accept him! All he thinks of at present is, that you would not suffer prejudices to blind your reason. Woodley seeks not to subdue you by perseverance; only give him leave to try to please you; only allow him to pay you a visit. Surely, if you are as fixed as fate, you cannot apprehend the bare sight of him will overturn your resolves! You fear more danger than there really is. Still we say—*see him*. My dearest Julia did not use to be inexorable! My father allows he has now no power over you, even if he could form the idea of using it. What then have you to dread? Surely you have a negative voice! I am called upon—but will end with the strain I began. See him, and then refuse him your esteem, nay more, your tender affection, if you can.

Adieu!

Your's most sincerely,
LOUISA GRENVILLE.

LETTER LVII.

TO Miss GRENVILLE.

Oh, my Louisa! how is the style of your letters altered! Is this change (not improvement) owing to your attachment to Mr. Spencer? Can *love* have wrought this difference? If it has, may it be a stranger to my bosom!—for it has ceased to make my Louisa amiable!—she, who was once all tenderness—all softness! who fondly soothed my distresses, *and felt for weakness which she never knew—*

"It   is   not   friendly,   'tis   not   maidenly;
Our *sex*,   as   well   as   I,   may   chide   you   for   it,
Though I alone do feel the injury—"

you, to whom I have freely exposed all the failings of my wayward heart! in whose bosom I have reposed all its tumultuous beatings!—all its anxieties!—Oh, Louisa! can you forget my *confidence* in you, which would not permit me to conceal even my errors? Why do you then join with men in scorning your friend? You say, *my father has now no power over me, even if he could form the idea of using power.* Alas! you have all too much power over me! you have the power of rendering me forever miserable, either by your persuasions to consign myself to eternal wretchedness; or by my *inexorableness*, as you call it, in flying in the face of persons so dear to me!

How cruel it is in you to arraign the conduct of one to whose character you are a *stranger*! What has the man, who, unfortunately both for himself and me, has been too much in my thoughts; what has he done, that you should so decisively pronounce him to be inconstant, and forgetful of those who seemed so dear to him? Why is the delicacy of *your favourite* to be so much commended for his forbearance till the year of mourning was near expired? And what proof that another may not be actuated by the same delicate motive?

But I will have done with these painful interrogatories; they only help to wound my bosom, even more than you have done.

My good uncle is better.—You have wrung my heart—and, harsh and unbecoming as it may seem in your eyes, I will not return to Woodley-vale, till I am assured I shall not receive any more persecutions on his account. Would he be content with my esteem, he may easily entitle himself to it by his still further *forbearance*.

My resolution is fixed—no matter what that is—there is no danger of making any one a participator of my sorrows.

Adieu!

JULIA STANLEY.

LETTER LVIII.

To Miss GRENVILLE.

Stanley-park.

Louisa! why was this scheme laid? I cannot compose my thoughts even to ask you the most simple question! Can you judge of my astonishment? the emotions with which I was seized? Oh! no, you cannot—you cannot, because you was never sunk so low in the depths of affliction as I have been; you never have experienced the extreme of joy and despair as I have done. Oh! you know nothing of what I feel!—of what I cannot find words to express! Why don't you come hither?—I doubt whether I shall retain my senses till your arrival.

Adieu!

Your's for ever,

JULIA STANLEY.

LETTER LIX.

TO Lady BRUDENEL.

Stanley-park.

Yes! my dear Maria, you shall be made acquainted with the extraordinary change in your friend! You had all the mournful particulars of my past life before you. I was convinced of your worth, nor could refuse you my confidence. But what is all this? I cannot spend my time, my precious time, in prefacing the scenes which now surround me.

You know how depressed my mind was with sorrow at the earnestness with which my father and sister espoused the cause of Mr. Woodley. I was ready to sink under the dejection their perseverance occasioned, aggravated too by my tender, long-cherished attachment to the unfortunate Baron. [This is the first time my pen has traced that word.]

I was sitting yesterday morning in an alcove in the garden, ruminating on the various scenes which I had experienced, and giving myself up to the most melancholy presages, when I perceived a paper fall at my feet. I apprehended it had dropped from my pocket in taking out my handkerchief, which a trickling tear had just before demanded. I stooped to pick it up; and, to my surprize, found it sealed, and addressed to myself. I hastily broke it open, and my wonder increased when I read these words:

"I have been witness to the perturbation of your mind. How will you atone to your Sylph, for not availing yourself of the privilege of making application to him in an emergency? If you have lost your confidence in him, he is the most wretched of beings. He flatters himself he may be instrumental to your future felicity. If you are inclined to be indebted to him for any share of it, you may have the opportunity of seeing him in five minutes. Arm yourself with resolution, most lovely, most adored of women; for he will appear under a semblance not expected by you. You will see in him the most faithful and constant of human beings."

I was seized with such a trepidation, that I could hardly support myself; but, summoning all the strength of mind I could assume, I said aloud, though in a tremulous voice, "Let me view my amiable Sylph!"—But oh! what became of me, when at my feet I beheld the most wished-for, the most dreaded, *Ton-hausen!* I clasped my hands together, and shrieked with the most frantic air, falling back half insensible on the seat. "Curse on my precipitance!" he cried, throwing his arms round me. "My angel! my Julia! look on the most forlorn of his sex, unless you pity me." "Pity you!" I exclaimed, with a faint accent—"Oh! from whence, and how came you here?"

"Did not my Julia expect me?" he asked, in the softest voice, and sweetest manner.

"I expect you! How should I? alas! what intimation could I have of your arrival?"

"From this," he replied, taking up the billet written by the Sylph. "What do you mean? For Heaven's sake! rise, and unravel this mystery. My brain will burst with the torture of suspense."

"If the loveliest of women will pardon the stratagems I have practised on her unsuspecting mind, I will rise, and rise the happiest of mortals. Yes, my beloved Julia, I am that invisible guide, that has so often led you through the wilds of life. I am that blissful being, whom you supposed something supernatural."

"It is impossible," I cried, interrupting him, "it cannot be!"

"Will not my Julia recollect this poor pledge of her former confidence?" drawing from a ribband a locket of hair I had once sent to the Sylph. "Is this, to me inestimable, gift no longer acknowledged by you? this dear part of yourself, whose enchantment gave to my wounded soul all the nourishment she drew, which supported me when exiled from all that the world had worth living for? Have you forgot the vows of lasting fidelity with which the value of the present was enhanced? Oh! sure you have not. And yet you are silent. May I not have one word, one look?"

"Alas!" cried I, hiding my face from his glances; "what can I say? What can I do? Oh! too well I remember all. The consciousness, that every secret of my heart has been laid bare to your inspection, covers me with the deepest confusion."

"Bear witness for me," cried he, "that I never made an ill use of that knowledge. Have I ever presumed upon it? Could you ever discover, by the arrogance of Ton-hausen's conduct, that he had been the happy *confidant* of your retired sentiments? Believe me, Lady Stanley, that man will ever admire you most, who knows most your worth; and oh!, who knows it more, who adores it more than I?"

"Still," said I, "I cannot compose my scattered senses. All appears a dream; but, trust me, I doat on the illusion. I would not be undeceived, if I am in an error. I would fain persuade myself, that but one man on earth is acquainted with the softness, I will not call it weakness, of my soul; and he the only man who could inspire that softness." "Oh! be persuaded, most angelic of women," said he, pressing my hand to his lips, "be persuaded of the truth of my assertion, that the Sylph and I are one. You know how you were circumstanced."

"Yes! I was married before I had the happiness of being seen by you."

"No, you was not."

"Not married, before I was seen by you?"

"Most surely not. Years, years before that event, I knew, and, knowing, loved you— loved you with all the fondness of man, while my age was that of a boy. Has Julia quite forgot her juvenile companions? Is the time worn from her memory, when Harry Woodley used to weave the fancied garland for her?"

"Protect me, Heaven!" cried I, "sure I am in the land of shadows!"

"No," cried he, clasping me in his arms, and smiling at my apostrophe, "you shall find substance and substantial joys too here."

"Thou Proteus!" said I, withdrawing myself from his embrace, "what do you mean by thus shifting characters, and each so potent?"

"To gain my charming Nymph," he answered. "But why should we thus waste our time? Let me lead you to your father."

"My father! Is my father here?"

"Yes, he brought me hither; perhaps, as Woodley, an unwelcome visitant. But will you have the cruelty to reject him?" added he, looking slyly.

"Don't presume too much," I returned with a smile. "You have convinced me, you are capable of great artifice; but I shall insist on your explaining your whole plan of operations, as an atonement for your double, nay treble dealing, for I think you are three in one. But I am impatient to behold my father, whom, the moment before I saw you, I was accusing of cruelty, in seeking to urge me in the favour of one I was determined never to see."

"But now you have seen him (it was all your sister required of you, you know), will you be inexorable to his vows?"

"I am determined to be guided by my Sylph," cried I, "in this momentous instance. That was my resolution, and still shall remain the same."

"Suppose thy Sylph had recommended you to bestow your hand on Woodley? What would have become of poor *Ton-hausen*?"

"My confidence in the Sylph was established on the conviction of his being my safest guide; as such, he would never have urged me to bestow my hand where my heart was refractory; but, admitting the possibility of the Sylph's pursuing such a measure, a negative voice would have been allowed me; and no power, human or divine, should have constrained that voice to breathe out a vow of fidelity to any other than him to whom the secrets of my heart have been so long known."

By this time we had nearly reached the house, from whence my father sprung with the utmost alacrity to meet me. As he pressed me to his venerable bosom, "Can my Julia refuse the request of her father, to receive, as the best pledge of his affection, this valuable present? And will she forgive the innocent trial we made of her fidelity to the most amiable of men?"

"Ah! I know not what to say," cried I; "here has been sad management amongst you. But I shall soon forget the heart-aches I have experienced, if they have removed from this gentleman any suspicions that I did not regard him for himself alone. He has, I think, adopted the character of Prior's Henry; and I hope he is convinced that the faithful Emma is not a fiction of the poet's brain. I know not," I continued, "by what name to call him."

"Call me *your's*," cried he, "and that will be the highest title I shall ever aspire to. But you shall know all, as indeed you have a right to do. *Your* sister, and soon, I hope, *mine*, related to you the attachment which I had formed for you in my tenderest years, which, like the incision on the infant bark, *grew with my growth, and strengthened with my strength*. She likewise told you (but oh! how faint, how inadequate to my feelings!) the extreme anguish that seized me when I found you was married. Distraction surrounded me; I cannot give words to my grief and despair. I fled from a place which had lost its only attractive power. In the first paroxysm of affliction, I knew not what resolutions I formed. I wrote to Spencer—not to give rest or ease to my over-burdened heart; for that, alas! could receive no diminution—nor to complain; for surely I could not complain of you; my form was not imprinted on your mind, though your's had worn itself so deep a trace in mine. Spencer opposed my resolution of returning to Germany, where I had formed some connexions (only friendly ones, my Julia, but, as such, infinitely tender). *He* it was that urged me to take the name of Ton-hausen, as that title belonged to an estate which devolved to me from the death of one of the most valuable men in the world, who had sunk into his grave, as the only asylum from a combination of woes. As some years had elapsed, in which I had increased in bulk and stature, joined to my having had the small-pox since I had been seen by you, he thought it more than probable you would not recollect my person. I hardly know what I proposed to myself, from closing with him in this scheme, only that I take Heaven to witness, I never meant to injure you; and I hope the whole tenor of my conduct has convinced you how sincere I was in that profession. From the great irregularity of your late husband's life, I had a *presentiment*, that you would at one time or other be free from your engagements. I revered you as one, to whom I hoped to be united; if not in this world, I might be a kindred-angel with you in the next. Your virtuous soul could not find its congenial friend in the riot and confusion in which you lived. I dared not trust myself to offer to become your guide. I knew the extreme hazard I should run; and that, with all the innocent intentions in the world, we might both be undone by our *passions* before *reason* could come to our assistance. I soon saw I had the happiness to be distinguished by you! and that distinction, while it raised my admiration of you, excited in me the desire of rendering myself still more worthy of your esteem; but even that esteem I refused myself the dear privilege of soliciting for. I acted with the utmost caution; and if, under the character of the Sylph, I dived into the recesses of your soul, and drew from thence the secret attachment you professed for the happy Baron, it was not so much to gratify the vanity of my heart, as to put you on your guard, lest some of the invidious wretches about you should propagate any reports to your prejudice; and, dear as the sacrifice cost me, I tore myself from your loved presence on a sarcasm which Lady Anne Parker threw out concerning us. I withdrew some miles from London, and left Spencer there to apprize me of any change in your circumstances. I gave you to understand I had quitted the kingdom; but that was a severity I could not impose upon myself: however, I constrained myself to take a resolution of never again appearing in your presence till I should have the liberty of indulging my passion without restraint. Nine parts of ten in the world may condemn my procedure as altogether romantic. I believe few will find it imitable; but I have nice feelings, and I could act no other than I did. I could not, you see, bear to be the rival of myself. *That* I have proved under both the characters I assumed; but had I found you had forgotten Ton-hausen, Woodley would have been deprived of one of the most delicate pleasures a refined taste can experience. And now all that remains is to intreat the forgiveness of my amiable Julia, for these *pious frauds*; and to reassure her she shall, if *the heart of man is not deceitful above all things*, never repent the confidence she placed in her faithful Sylph, the affection she honoured the happy Ton-hausen with, nor the esteem, notwithstanding his obstinate perseverance, which she charitably bestowed on that unfortunate knight-errant, Harry Woodley."

"Heaven send I never may!" said I. But really I shall be half afraid to venture the remainder of my life with such a variable being. However, my father undertakes to answer for him in future.

I assure you, my dear Maria, you are much indebted to me for this recital, for I have borrowed the time out of the night, as the whole day has been taken up in a manner you may more easily guess than I can describe.

Say every thing that is civil to Sir George on my part, as you are conscious I have no time to bestow on any other men than those by whom I am surrounded. I expect my sister and her swain tomorrow.

Adieu!
I am your's ever
JULIA STANLEY.

LETTER LX.

TO Lady BRUDENEL.

You would hardly know your old acquaintance again, he is so totally altered; you remember his pensive air, and gentle unassuming manner, which seemed to bespeak the protection of every one. Instead of all this, he is so alert, so brisk, and has such a saucy assurance in his whole deportment, as really amazes; and, I freely own, delights me, as I am happily convinced, that it is owing to myself that he is thus different from what he was. Let him be what he will, he will ever be dear to me.

I wanted him to relate to me all the particulars of his friend Frederick, the late Baron's, misfortunes. He says, the recital would fill a volume, but that I shall peruse some papers on the subject some time or other, when we are tired of being chearful, but that now we have better employment; I therefore submit for the present.

I admire my sister's choice very much; he is an agreeable man, and extremely lively: much more so naturally, notwithstanding the airs some folks give themselves, than my Proteus. Louisa too is quite alive; Mr. Stanley has forgot the gout; and my father is ready to dance at the wedding of his eldest daughter, which, I suppose, will take place soon.

Pray how do you go on? Are you near your *accouchement*? or dare you venture to travel as far as Stanley-park? for my uncle will not part with any of us yet.

Ah! I can write no longer; they threaten to snatch the pen from my hand; that I may prevent such a solecism in politeness, I will conclude, by assuring you of my tenderest wishes.

Adieu!
JULIA STANLEY.

LETTER LXI.

TO Lady STANLEY.

Upon my word, a pretty kind of a romantic adventure you have made of it, and the conclusion of the business just as it should be, and quite in the line of *poetical justice*. Virtue triumphant, and Vice dragged at her chariot-wheels,—for I heard yesterday, that Lord Biddulph was selling off all his moveables, and had moved himself out of the kingdom. Now my old friend Montague should be sent on board the Justitia, and *all's well that ends well*. As to your Proteus, with all his *aliases*, I think he must be quite a Machiavel in artifice. Heaven send he may never change again! I should be half afraid of such a Will-of-the-wisp lover. First this, then that, now the other, and always the same. But bind him, bind him, Julia, in adamantine chains; make sure of him, while he is yet in your power; and follow, with all convenient speed, the dance your sister is going to lead off. Oh! she is in a mighty hurry! Let me hear what she will say when she has been married ten months, as poor I have been! and here must be kept prisoner with all the dispositions in the world for freedom!

What an acquisition your two husbands will be! I bespeak them both for god-fathers; pray tell them so. Do you know, I wanted to persuade Sir George to take a trip, just to see how you proceed in this affair; but, I blush to tell you, he would not hear of any such thing, because he is in expectation of a little impertinent visitor, and would not be from home for the world. *Tell it not in Gath.* Thank heaven, the dissolute tribe in London know nothing of it. But, I believe, none of our set will be anxious about their sentiments. While we feel ourselves happy, we shall think it no sacrifice to give up all the nonsense and hurry of the *beau monde.*

Adieu!

MARIA BRUDENEL.